Jump, Jive, and Wail

By
Kathryn R. Biel

KATHRYN R. BIEL

JUMP, JIVE, AND WAIL

Copyright © 2015 by Kathryn R. Biel

ISBN-10: 0-9913917-5-6
ISBN-13: 978-0-9913917-5-2

Cover design by Becky Monson.
Cover image via depositphotos.com by SolominViktor.

DEDICATION

To Becky:

Thanks for taking me under your wing, imparting your wisdom, being my cheerleader, lifting me up, and offering to cut people on my behalf.

KATHRYN R. BIEL

AUTHOR'S NOTE

I was inspired to write this book while watching the ski jumpers at the 2014 Sochi Winter Olympics. Until then, I had never realized that this was the first Olympics in which women were allowed to compete in this sport . This book is a tribute to those brave women who fought for the right to represent (and represent they did!).

I took many creative liberties with the outcomes of the Sochi Olympics to serve the purpose of the story. My deep respect and admiration go to the real participants and winners.

Chapter One:
Monday, March 24, 2014
10:59 a.m.: Kaitlin

I've been told I have an anger problem. Yeah, so what. You would too if you were living my life. Once destined for greatness—for gold—now my life is crap. Complete and utter crap. So, yeah, I'm angry. Angry all the flippin' time. I also have a swearing problem. I'm working on that.

The focus of my anger at this moment is two-fold: the TSA and my brace. My stupid brace. Always that. If it weren't for the brace, I'd only be mildly annoyed at the TSA right now. I mean, don't get me wrong, I'd still be annoyed. What kind of idiot puts a bomb in his underwear or shoe? Why'd he have to go and spoil it for the rest of us? That kind of imbecile deserves to have his frank and beans blown off. Okay, so my anger here is actually three-fold and includes the eejits who attach bombs to their privates to blow up planes.

Struggling to manage my overstuffed carry-on while holding my bulky winter coat, boots, and the brace, I finally manage to get through the security gates. Careful not to let my right toes drag on the ground, I step aside, drop my load, and set about donning it—that damn brace. Kirby. That's its name. Or at least what I call it. Because having to wear a brace sucks more than an expensive vacuum cleaner. Shoving the bags off to the side and not wanting to sit down on the airport floor, I bend forward at the waist and precariously balance on my left leg while I lift my right one into the air. I'm out of the habit of squatting these days, since the plastic of my constant companion doesn't let my ankle bend that way. Sliding Kirby beneath my dropped foot, I quickly get my limp, numb, useless right leg safely encased in its flesh-colored plastic tomb. It reminds me of a coffin because my foot just lays there for all to see— dead. One nylon Velcro strap across the ankle, another around the calf and I'm good to slide my useless appendage into my Ugg. Yes, I know; it is like the worst possible choice in shoes, other than flip-flops, which I'll never be able to wear again. But I rationalize, like I do with so many other things, that my bad foot is fully supported in the brace, so the supportiveness of the shoe itself doesn't matter. (I do completely ignore the fact that I have another leg and foot that is working, for the most part.) My physical therapist doesn't buy my rationale but whatever. Let her walk—or limp—a mile in my shoes and see how she likes it.

I am getting lightheaded from being bent over, and I'm sure my ass in the air isn't the most flattering view, but a girl's gotta do what a girl's gotta do. I'm sure the underwear bomber felt the same way, but I mean, who would ever think that *that* was a good idea?

The real reason I like the Uggs is that they hide the ugliness that is Kirby. I look pretty normal wearing them. They're totally flat, which I need anyway, and they're in fashion. Don't know what I'll do when they become passé but, like so many other things in my life right now, I'll cross that bridge when I come to it.

So here I am, keister in the air, just getting ready to lift my left foot up. Balancing on my right leg is always a bit dodgy so I have to mentally psych myself up for it. The brace gives me some stability, but it is still not a skill in which I excel. The last thing I want to do is fall down in the middle of a busy airport. I open up the mouth of the boot and as quickly as I can, slide my left foot in. When I put my foot down, my weight shifts back slightly and my rear end bumps into something.

Not something, someone.

A man, to be precise. A man's crotch to be even more precise.

Before I even process what is happening, two large hands grab firmly at my hips to stabilize me. I would like to think that this is an act of kindness to prevent the poor crippled girl from falling over, but there is a teeny-tiny part of me that thinks this guy might just be some kind of pervert. After all, he is touching places my bathing suit covers.

"Hey!" I growl as I try to stand up. However, the position and grip of his hands lock my hips and I can't. He finally gets the hint and loosens his vice grip, but my jerking and attempts to break free are poorly timed with his release. Before I know it, I start to topple forward. I see the floor rising rapidly and know I'm destined for a face plant. Then, the meaty hands are back at my hips pulling me back with such a force that my rump slams into his pelvis and my body is whipped upright with my back up against his chest. I expel an involuntary 'uumph' upon contact. It is as if I forget where I am and all of the hustle and bustle of the airport freeze for just a moment. But it is a fleeting moment, because then I remember that this brute has run into me, violated my personal space, and is practically groping me.

"Sorry, sorry. Are you alright?" He has a light Canadian accent. This is not a plus in my book. Growing up in Upstate (waaaay Upstate) New York, I was never a big fan of our neighbors just over the border. Mostly, because my dumb ex-boyfriend was from there, and he gave me a stupid stuffed beaver holding a Canadian flag for our one-year anniversary. Seriously? A stuffed beaver? Ever since then, I've had a chip on my shoulder where Canucks are concerned. Immediately passing the same kind of judgment on the voice behind me, I stand there helpless as his hands move around me. He steadies me by wrapping his right arm around my waist and his left arm shoots up and around my chest to grab at the front of my right shoulder. His hands are the size of baseball mitts. I can already tell he's the type of guy to give a stuffed beaver as a gift.

"I will be as soon as you let me go and stop mauling me." Being nice never got me anywhere. In fact, it got me nowhere fast, so I left my nice girl attitude behind.

"Oh, right." He lets me go, and for a minute detachment and loneliness overwhelm me. I turn around to face him, to see this invader of my personal space with the Canadian accent.

His voice and commanding grip have not prepared me for what I see. Six foot four. Messy brown hair that betrays its styling products with escaping curls. Hazel-green eyes that crinkle as he smiles. A straight nose leading down to totally kissable lips, flanked by dimples. Dammit, he is adorable. Way more adorable than that stuffed Canadian beaver.

"Are you okay? I'm so sorry for running into you like that."

How am I supposed to answer him? I'm dumbstruck. Puppies are cute. Kittens are cute. I have no time for this in my life, but crap, this guy is cute. Shaking my head, I will the haze in my brain to clear.

"Oh shoot. Did I hurt you? Oh my God, I wasn't paying attention to where I was going. I can't believe I ran into you like that!"

"Oh, no, I'm fine." I suddenly find my voice. "I just can't believe you didn't see me with my butt in the air like that. Weren't you watching where you were going? Jeez!"

"Yeah, sorry. I was, um, a bit ..." he looks around hurriedly, "distracted. I wasn't paying attention." He keeps looking around, obviously anxious to get away from me. I understand. I wish I could get away from me as well.

I shrug. "Yeah, whatever." I turn back around and bend over to grab my bags. Hoisting my large duffle up onto my back, I lose my balance. Of course I do. I take several quick steps backwards to regain my balance but the weight of the bag on my back throws me off. My right leg can't move as quickly as the left, and it lacks the mobility it needs to catch me. I stumble backwards, expecting to go right down when—thump! I run into something. Or rather someone who prevents me from falling.

"We've got to stop meeting like this."

The weight of my bag magically lifts off my shoulder while I feel his hand steady my pelvis. What is it with this guy? This is the second time in minutes that his hands are below my waist. What the hell? Despite the weight of my bag being lifted from me, life weighs down on me, heavier than ever. I sag back into him, just for a moment. I close my eyes and wish that I were not here. That this is not my life and that the person who had been the nicest to me in the recent past is not the guy who ran into my backside. Twice.

Still leaning on him, with my eyes still closed, I finally speak, "I'm sorry. This one is all me. Thank you for catching me. Again." I pull away from him and turn around. "Can I have my bag back?"

"Can you handle it? I won't always be there to catch you, you know." He is smiling and teasing and is really, truly adorable.

"Yeah, I just got off balance. Happens a lot. I've got it now." I turn to face him.

He swings the bag around as if it weighs nothing and gently places it over my shoulder. He grasps my shoulders to steady me. "Got it?" he asks, smiling down at me. It is nearly impossible not to return his smile, but I resist.

I nod curtly. "Got it. Thanks." I shift the bag and pick up my coat, which I had dropped. "Gotta go catch my flight." Good thing I had gotten to the airport early. It had already taken me almost an hour to get checked in and get through security. Of course, I have to plan ahead and get everywhere early now. I can't walk fast anymore, let alone run through the airport. Dragging a dead leg around makes me tired and makes my back hurt. Being out of shape doesn't help the issue much either. Everything is harder for me than it used to be, including traveling. I've already forgotten what gate my flight is leaving from, so I cut left to get to the big row of monitors that span the corridor.

It takes me a few minutes to scan through the multiple monitors to find my flight. There seem to be an awful lot of flights that have the word 'delayed' in flashing red. I hope that mine isn't one of them. It had better not be. I need to get to New York City ASAP. Finally, I find it—Delta 1627 to LaGuardia. And thank God, it's on time! One small thing on this stupid day, in my stupid life that is going right. Just as I'm exhaling a sigh of relief, the monitor flickers and Flight 1627 now reads as 'delayed' like all the others. Son of a—.

******

11:02 am: Declan

"Frankie, I still can't believe you did this to me."

"I didn't do it to you; I did it for you."

"That's bull and you know it. You did it for you. You and your wallet."

"Aww, c'mon Declan baby, aren't you pleased with all the attention you've been getting? You know you love it."

My manager was right. Sort of. Kind of. Okay, halfway right. I should love it. About five years ago, I would have loved it. I would have loved the attention and the swooning ladies. I would have loved all the perks and doors that are opening for me. But right now, I'm just tired. I just want to take a long vacation. Not go on a whirlwind publicity junket before doing one last tour. I'm ready to be done. Done with all of it.

"Are you at the airport already?" she asks. She keeps a tight rein over my schedule. It's a good thing, too. I'm terrible at managing my time. Without a rigid training schedule—and with the recent introduction of this foreign concept of free time—I have no idea what to do with myself. It was terrible when I first got back. First of all, there was the time difference and jet lag throwing me off. My days and nights were messed up and it took me about two weeks to finally straighten myself out. And now I'm flying again. At least it's in the same time zone.

"Yeah. Any new report on the weather? That storm looks big."

She's quiet for a moment, but I know her well enough to know she's looking for a weather update on her phone. "You worry about the weather like some old man."

"I have to. Nat would never know what clothes to bring if I didn't keep her posted."

"Is it weird being without her at the airport?"

If anyone else asked me this question, I would lie and say yes. But Frankie was my manager and had been with me for the past eight years. Before that, she was my mom's best friend and has known me since I was in diapers. She knows me better than I know myself. She knew the truth. I didn't have to keep up the image for her. "It's nice. I can walk at my own pace."

She laughed. "You know, I always thought that was funny. You are almost a foot taller than she is, but she walks three times as fast as you do. Okay, I got the info on the storm. Yeah, it is big. Is your flight still scheduled to take off on time?"

"It was when I got here. There are a bunch of delays, and some cancellations are starting to spring up."

"I'm gonna book you a room at the hotel there. We'll cancel it if you get out, but you have it if you need it."

"Smart thinking, Frankie. What would I do without you?"

"You'd never survive, kid."

I disconnected in preparation for going through security. I kicked off my shoes and gave a disparaging glance to the guy in front of me who was wearing lace-up work boots. Like you don't know you're going to have to take them off? He obviously didn't fly often. You could tell those who did and those who didn't. I did, so within seconds I had my coat, carry-on and shoes in a bin ready to be scanned. I felt naked without my baseball hat on, like everyone was staring at me.

Ever since the issue of *People* was released, I was getting a whole lot more attention. I expected some after returning from Sochi. But I was here in the U.S., not in my home country of Canada, nor in Ireland, which I had actually represented in the Olympics. I didn't expect the Americans to make such a big deal, especially when they had their own champions to fawn over. I should be flattered and excited about the endorsement deals. If I played my cards right—meaning if Frankie did her job right—I'd be set for the next few years while I finished up school.

Passing through security, I feel like everyone is staring at me. I know, it's probably my overactive imagination, but I swear the security guard took way too much time wanding over my private parts. I know, she probably didn't even see the magazine, but in my mind every female has. I'm glad Natalya isn't here. First, I need the break from her. She drives me up a wall, not that I can let anyone know it. Frankie and my mom are the only people who know that I can't stand her. I don't even think Natalya knows herself. She always gets what she wants and is convinced that every man is in love with her. Probably like I'm convinced that every woman has seen my shirtless body in *People* magazine. I know that may seem arrogant, but at this point, it's more paranoia than anything else.

Lost in this train of thought and looking around suspiciously for possible fans, I don't see the woman stopped right in front of me. I don't see her, that is, until I'm running into her. Smack into her butt. Full-on pelvic contact. Worse than Miley Cyrus at the VMAs. Reflexively, I grab her hips and pull her into me to prevent her from falling forward. It's a very intimate position, the back of her legs against mine. With my job, it is nothing to handle a woman's body like this. Apparently, she does not share my comfort level as she yells, "Hey!" But this lady, well, she starts pulling and straining just as I start to let her go. She pitches forward, so I do the only nice thing. I grab her and pull her back toward me to counteract her forward momentum.

This causes her to rock back, and her back slams into my chest. She lets out a little groan, and for an instant I want to do the same. Yes, I handle women's bodies all the time. But they're not like this one. This one feels just right. It has curves and some softness. Natalya is skin and bones. I know she has to be, but this—this is what I want to hold onto.

I realize I've probably held onto her for a moment or two too long, so I apologize and ask her if she is all right. I don't want to let go. Her response douses me with a chill like a bucket of ice. "I will be as soon as you let me go and stop mauling me."

I let her go and she whirls around to face me. I ask her again if she is okay or if I hurt her. I apologize again. She is beautiful. In a natural, un-made-up kind of way. Full lips that I can't help but stare at. And now those full lips are yelling at me. Again, I try to apologize. I hope no one saw me barrel into this woman. "Yeah, sorry. I was, um, a bit ..." I look around to make sure no one is watching, "distracted. I wasn't paying attention."

She doesn't buy it and tries to storm off in a huff. But she's too angry and swings her overstuffed carry-on with a bit too much force, and it knocks her off balance. She stumbles back a step or two and right into me.

"We've got to stop meeting like this," I say as I lift the bag off her shoulder. She sags back into me for a moment and I have to admit, she feels damn good.

This time, she apologizes and asks for her bag back. I can't resist but say, "Can you handle it? I won't always be there to catch you, you know."

After she turns around, I gently place the bag back on her shoulder, making sure she has her balance. I smile at her and she returns my smile. The smile doesn't quite reach her eyes though. I wonder what it would take to make her really smile. She bids me thanks, picks up her coat, and walks out of my life.

Chapter Two
11:15 a.m.: Kaitlin

Just to the left of where I'm standing is this large water fountain-type thing that is more art than anything else. It looks like a flat surface until water starts shooting out of the ground in little streams. They are jetting though the air, dancing and criss-crossing each other, only to land in some pre-choreographed location. It looks interesting so I wearily trudge to the black armchairs that flank the feature. An older gentleman in a rumpled, gray suit is standing up, about to vacate, so I hurry in, anxious to plant my tuchus until I figure out what the new schedule is going to be. Of course, that is part of my problem these days—I'm always sitting. I tell myself that it is easier than dragging my dead leg around. And it is, since I've lost all of my physical fitness and muscle tone over the past two years. Who cares that it took me twenty-five years to build it up in the first place?

I dig my phone out of my coat pocket. My first instinct is to call my husband. I know calling him will be futile and useless, just like he is. He will somehow yell at me and tell me this is all my fault. Hell, he wouldn't even bring me to the airport in the first place, insisting I take a cab. Rather than deal with his guff, I go to the Delta website and angrily punch in my flight number. Looks like about a two-hour delay. Fan-freakin'-tastic. That'll get me into New York City after 4 p.m. It'll be tight to get to the 6 p.m. dinner in SoHo, especially considering my hotel is in Queens. So much for impressing my new boss. I was already on thin ice. I'm not very good at my job to begin with, thanks, in large part to my attitude.

I darken my phone screen and drop it onto my lap. The jetting water of the fountain catches my eye again. Watching the water leap in graceful arcs throughout the air captivates me. It is truly mesmerizing. The water appears to fly through the air. After watching the water briefly, sadness begins to seep in. Although the memories were growing more and more distant, when I allowed myself to think about it, I can still remember what it is like to fly through the air, arching gracefully like those streams of water. Of course, I never allowed those thoughts to pass through my mind during the day. At night, especially after drinking a bit too much, which was more common than not, I would still dream I could fly. I could feel the wind rushing my face and feel the nothing beneath my feet. Only when my eyes opened would I remember that I wasn't feeling nothing beneath my feet, but rather nothing where my foot was.

"Fancy meeting you here," said a deep voice, startling me out of my reverie. "Oh, are you okay?"

Only as I involuntarily wipe the tears from my cheeks do I even realize I was crying. "Jesus—you scared me!" I use my anger to cover up my embarrassment. Seriously though, what was with this guy? He'd run into my butt, I'd fallen into him and now he catches me crying. Was I destined to constantly make a fool out of myself in front of him?

"Are you all right?"

"Yeah, fine," I mumble as I hastily wipe the last evidence of my tears away. I can't believe I'm crying. Moreover, I can't believe that stupid water feature made me cry. I don't cry. Ever. Not when my mom left. Not when I blew out my ACL. Not when my foot died, taking all my hopes and dreams with it. And certainly not when I found out my husband was cheating on me. No sir, I did not cry.

To add insult to injury, quite literally, it appears as if the universe is once again conspiring against me, as the chair next to me became suddenly unoccupied. The giant Canadian plops himself down and starts to make small talk. With me. What in tarnation does he think he is doing?

"You delayed too?"

Glaring at him, I wish him away. In truth, I want to wish me away. Far away. Somewhere where my life is not mine, somewhere I could be the happy, motivated, lively girl I used to be. The dude is apparently blind or something—I mean, he somehow missed my butt stuck up in the air—because he's still prattling on about ... something and appears oblivious to my death glare. I'm not listening to him talk. The last person I really listened to screwed me over but good. So, I'm done listening. Permanently.

I realize he is finally not talking but looking at me expectantly. Crap. He must have asked me a question. I am totally busted. No choice but to fess up. "I'm sorry. What did you say?" Maybe if I am disinterested enough, he will leave me alone.

He just smiles at me. "I asked you where you're headed."

A fair airport question. "Oh. New York. LaGuardia."

"Me too!" His smile widens. "Are you going on business or pleasure?"

"Business." I stop there, but reconsider that I'm being too rude. Sure I want to be left alone, but this guy seems nice. Genuine. And he is very cute. A lifetime ago I would have made a play for this kind of guy—and landed him. It wouldn't hurt me to be nice to him, would it? "And you?"

"Both actually. What is your business?"

"I'm in sales." I know I'm being difficult, making him pull every answer out of me. I'm still a little pissed that he ran into me and violated my personal space. Moreover, I'm reluctant to talk to people. Being all mad and stuff generally meant that I did not make the best conversationalist. From somewhere deep within, a spark of humanity surfaces and I continue. I remember that I used to be outgoing and friendly, and suddenly I miss that about myself. "I sell medical devices, electrical stimulation units. TENS units mostly."

I expect him to ask me what a TENS unit is, so I'm totally hit off guard when he replies, "That's cool. My TENS unit is my best friend. I don't suppose you have any extra pads on you, do you?"

"Um, yeah. I mean, no. My kit is in New York already. I shipped it so I didn't have to carry it on the plane. It costs less to ship than to check the luggage." I didn't add that it was hard for me to manage all my stuff.

"Yeah, isn't it a crime what the airlines charge these days?"

"I know, and I end up flying a lot for the job. I used to fly to Europe all the time. I've gotten pretty good at cramming everything in my carry-on. On the other hand, it helps if you can then lift your own bag without falling over. I wish there was some sort of benefit program where you could earn points toward checking baggage." I don't know where that came from. I'm making witty banter. Well, at least for me, it's witty banter.

"That would be a brilliant marketing plan. What flight are you on?"

I tell him my flight number and he smiles again. Those dimples are damn engaging, if you ask me. I want to run my finger over them. "We're on the same flight. Or, we were supposed to be. I doubt if we're getting out of here tonight."

His comment rudely yanks me out of my ogling of his adorableness. "Wait—why do you say that? We're just delayed."

"Yeah, but based on the forecast, I doubt we're going to get out of here."

"What forecast?"

"There's, like, a massive winter storm moving up the East Coast. That's why there are so many delays." He whips out his phone and swipes a few times. "New York is supposed to get at least twelve inches."

"Seriously?" I look at my boots. They are boots in name only. They are really sweaters with a rubber bottom. They will be no match for snow and cold. "I'm so not prepared for winter weather."

"It's only March." He looks at me like I'm an idiot who didn't even think to check the weather of my destination. Perhaps that is just my interpretation of how he is looking at me, because that is how I feel.

"But spring started this week. It needs to start warming up soon. I can't stand winter." I protest. As if my whining is going to change the weather pattern.

"Last I checked Mother Nature doesn't take personal requests." He chided me, jokingly. "Plus, you live in Detroit. How can you not like winter? Isn't it automatically in Michiganders DNA?"

"I'm not from Michigan originally. In fact, I've only been here about six months. I don't really love it, truth be told."

"No? Where are you from then?"

"Originally, way Upstate New York, near Lake Placid. I lived in Park City, Utah, for a while as well."

"For a girl who doesn't like winter, you've lived in some pretty wintery places."

I make a face. I don't need to be reminded. "I used to love winter, but I'm over it now. I think I want to move to Florida or Arizona or someplace warm and tropical."

He leans in, obviously interested in what I have to say. I still have no idea why he is talking to me or why he finds me interesting. "What's stopping you?"

I shrug. The truth is sad. I'm lazy. Apathetic. My husband wanted to move to Michigan for his work. I moved with him because I didn't have anything better to do. I wanted to get away from my old life. I needed to. If I'd known the turn our marriage would take, I wouldn't have made the move. Back in Utah, we had our issues, but we also had a life. Here in Michigan, it was just the two of us and, frankly, we can't stand each other. Now, I was going to be stranded in a place I hated, in a life I hated. But I would stay for a while because it was the easy way out, and that was the path I was on these days. The one of least resistance.

"What about you? You're obviously not from Michigan." I deflect by turning the tables on him. Sometimes the best defense is a good offense.

"Ireland by way of Toronto, but I've been here for a while. Pontiac."

"Grosse Pointe."

"Okay she who is from Lake Placid, Park City, and Grosse Pointe, don't you think it is time you told me your name?"

"You've never asked." Holy crap, that was a little flirtatious. Where did that come from?

"Well, now I'm asking." He leans in toward me. Unless I'm mistaken, he is flirting back.

"Kaitlin."

"Kaitlin, very nice to meet you." He extends his hand and I have no choice but to take it. His hand is huge, probably double the size of mine. It's warm too, which is welcome as the airport air is chilly, especially with the breeze the water fountain creates.

"And you are?"

He looks uncomfortable for a moment. Just the briefest look betrays him. How can he be uneasy with this conversation? He's the one who wanted to exchange names.

"Declan."

"Yeah, I guess that is Irish, isn't it?"

He seems to relax. "Kaitlin is Irish too. Are you Irish?"

I shrug. "Not sure. Maybe somewhere along the line. My dad's family has been in New York for three or four generations. Most of them are French or Native American."

"You mean French Canadian? That's totally different."

"Is it? I have no idea."

He laughs. "Of course it is." He's looking at me like I'm one of those stereotypical ignorant Americans. Maybe because I am. "What about your mother?"

Wow, he hits a nerve (one of many) pretty quick. I don't like to talk about my mom, and certainly not with a stranger. "My mom left when I was four, so I don't know. She wanted nothing to do with us, so I don't care to know about her."

His grin falls and I can see the pity in his eyes. "I'm so sorry Kaitlin. I shouldn't have pried."

If there is one thing I can't stand, it is pity. I've seen the looks on too many faces too many times. All the niceness that was starting to seep in, the pleasure of having a conversation, up and disappears.

"I need to go." I say as I stand up abruptly. I put my coat on and hoist my bag up. I start walking away and give a casual, "Bye," over my shoulder.

******

11:24 a.m.: Declan

I'm not surprised to see the delay flash up on the board. I text Frankie to let her know. She'll let the people I'm supposed to be meeting up with know. I hope this doesn't affect the endorsement offer. It's not every day that I get offered this kind of deal. The best part is that I actually do use the product. Who cares that an athlete selling deodorant is cliché? I care about the paycheck. Natalya and I have one more tour—fifty-five cities in seventy days—and then I'm hanging up my skates forever. This knowledge gives me the energy that my tired and beaten up body needs. At any other point in my career, I would have been so excited to go on tour. The Olympics has drained me and I'm in desperate need of a recharge.

I head toward the shops, prepared to kill a little time. Then, I see her—the woman I ran into. She's sitting in a chair by the water feature. She looks hypnotized by it. Propelled by a desire to be near her again, I veer toward her. Her hand is in her light brown hair, absently twisting away. She's crying. That's not good. I should abort this mission and walk away. But something in her face looks so lonely and vulnerable, and I can't resist.

I sit down and start talking at her. That's my strategy whenever a woman cries. I just talk at her until I distract her from what's really bothering her. It may or may not be the reason why I haven't had a relationship in a while. Natalya is the big reason, of course, but I may be lacking in the interpersonal skills as well. I ramble on. "Sorry for running into you back there. I really am. I'm not usually very clumsy. Not at all. I don't even know why I was hurrying so much. I knew my flight was going to be delayed. Is yours delayed also?"

She's not listening, I can tell. I don't know why I'm even bothering, other than the fact that she has a look about her like a lost puppy or something. Regardless, I keep talking. That's the one thing I can do. I can talk a blue streak. It gets on Nat's nerves. Sometimes I talk just to annoy her. This girl is certainly not Nat, but I keep talking anyway. "Yeah, the last thing I want to be doing is flying right now. I'm so burnt out with traveling. I just want to stay home in my own bed. How about you? Do you like to travel? Where are you headed anyway?"

There's no response, so I'm about to get up and walk away when she actually responds. I repeat my question and am strangely pleased that we are going to the same destination. Why? What is it about her? Certainly not her personality. She's a bit abrasive. I don't need more abrasive. I've already got that in spades with Natalya.

Okay, the small talk is not quite as difficult as pulling teeth, but almost. She just looks so sad and alone. I notice that her brown eyes are a bit almond shaped and her skin is a milky white. It looks smooth and creamy and I think about how her hips felt underneath my hands. I wonder if her skin is that creamy all over.

I have to focus on what she's saying. She seems to be warming up a little bit, offering that she deals in TENS units. She seems impressed that I know what they are. I had messed up my back over the years. I was really skeptical when they told me that these electrodes connected to a device the size of a deck of playing cards would make my back feel better, but it did really work. Without my TENS—transcutaneous electrical nerve stimulation—unit, I'd probably be seriously addicted to pain killers at this point. That was one of my many reasons for retiring. My back couldn't take another four years of abuse.

I don't know why it matters, but I ask her what flight she is on. What are the odds that the one person that I literally run into in all of Detroit Metro Airport is on the same flight? Well, we're supposed to be on the same flight. I tell her my prediction that the weather is going to waylay our flight even further.

I honestly don't understand when she tells me that she has not heard there is a huge storm moving up the Eastern Seaboard. How did she know what to pack? How can she not be prepared for these things? I see her look down forlornly at her boots. They're basically just big sweaters on her feet and will be no match for the snow that's apparently already falling in the Big Apple. Maybe she's not from Michigan, so I ask her.

She tells me the places she's lived—Lake Placid, Park City, Detroit—and she hates winter? Why does she live in Meccas for winter sports? If I didn't know better, I'd think she was somehow involved in winter sports. I wonder if she is. Maybe it's just her business. There are a lot of injured athletes who could use her service. Present company included. Interesting.

Also interesting is that I'm having to work hard here. Not that I'm looking to pick up a random woman in the airport, but I usually don't have this much trouble engaging women in conversation. I'm a good-looking guy. Even *People* thinks so. I just won a bronze medal at the Olympics. Usually the only thing that keeps me from landing women is Natalya. She's a primo cock blocker. But when she's not around, it could be open season, if I wanted.

I finally get her name—Kaitlin—and she's finally engaged a bit in our conversation. She seems pleased with the fact that I'm Irish. Guess that's the luck they always talk about. Maybe she's Irish too. I ask her.

Before I know what I've even said, she's up and gone, tossing a casual but terse, "Bye," over her shoulder.

What the heck just happened?

Like I said, I usually don't have to work this hard. Maybe I'm off my game. It has been a while. Things have just been too hectic for me to focus on a woman. I try to remember the last woman I dated. I'm drawing a blank. Jesus, I'm getting old. This is just sad. Of course, the perception that Natalya and I are a couple doesn't help. Most people think that we are together. It is one of those things that we neither confirm nor deny. It is good for our image for people to think we are together. It makes us likable, and Nat needs all the help she can get in that arena.

I wish I had known when I started competing that skating wouldn't just be about skating. Every aspect of my life would be carefully handled and molded to create the perfect image and to win us favor with the judges. We can't announce our retirement until right before the tour kicks off. It's yet another strategic plan—this one to help boost ticket sales. We were lucky to even get on the tour in the first place. Winning the Bronze Medal at the Olympics has certainly opened doors for us, especially since we were not predicted to place anywhere in the top ten. Dark horse winners, that's what we are. I'll be happy when my life is not one big strategic plan after another. When my life just belongs to me and I don't have to think about how my actions will impact Natalya and Frankie and everyone else on Team McLoughlin/Koval.

Tired of sitting, I decide to walk around to kill some time. I go down to the tunnel and ride the people mover from one end to the other, enjoying the syncopated light show. It is an art form in itself. Watching the colors morph in concert with the music, I can see a program set to this. I start choreographing in my head, planning the moves to the swells and lulls in the music. I can see the costumes in a watercolor motif, representing the lights that surround the tunnel.

As I exit the tunnel, I shake those thoughts away. I don't need to choreograph anything anymore. I'm done—I'm retiring. I need to move far away from those lights and music and try to get those thoughts out of my head before I get sucked back in.

Chapter Three
12:00 p.m.: Kaitlin

Well, that was a dumb move. I'm going to be stranded in this airport for at least a couple of hours, maybe even more. It would have been nice to spend it talking to another human being. I used to like people. I used to be vivacious and lively. That was the *Before* me. This is the *After* me. I don't like *After* me. Undoubtedly, no one does. My father doesn't. My brother doesn't. My boss is growing weary of me, questioning his decision to take me on in the first place. And, well, how my husband feels about me is quite obvious.

I could have used these wasted hours in my life to talk to someone, perhaps make a friend. When our plane landed in New York, we'd have become friends on Facebook or even exchanged numbers for texting. Not that I'm looking to pick someone up. I'm not. After all, the ring is still on my finger and there has been no paperwork filed. Not yet at least.

Truth is I don't have many friends left. They were all from *Before*. It's been too hard on me to maintain my friendship with them. The closest thing I could think to compare it to would be if two women were pregnant together and one lost her baby. Expecting her to hold the other woman's child would just be too much. Oh sure, there are those stellar women who smile through the pain and take it on the chin for the sake of a good friendship. In case you had any doubts, I'm not that kind of woman.

I wander into the bookstore, looking for something that will take my mind off my latest faux pas. Perusing the books, nothing catches my eye. I don't know what I'm in the mood for. The self-help books would probably be a good buy, but I pass these over. The trashy romances will be too depressing. A diet cookbook might be something to help pass the time. I've never had to diet before. That was one of the benefits in being an athlete. I could eat pretty much whatever I wanted. Ironically, I usually ate pretty healthy foods. It was the quantity of the food that I was having an issue with now. Having to buy all new clothes in a larger size (heck, two sizes up) was a rude awakening for me.

I know I should be exercising too. I just couldn't bring myself to do it. Exercise just for exercise's sake? No, thank you. *Before*, exercise had a purpose. It was a means to an end. It was training. Now, hours on an elliptical or stationary bike because I ate too much? Ugh. But I could ugh all I wanted. This was my new reality, and one of these days I would need to come to terms with it. In the end, my guilt over being so rude to Declan wins out and I decide that it's time to turn over a new leaf and start anew. It will be the *After-After*. I purchase a healthy lifestyles cookbook and a book about mental wellness through yoga and Pilates. Feeling good about my decision, I allow myself one guilty pleasure, so I snag a copy of *People* that is right next to the register. It just happens to be the Sexiest Man edition. For once, the timing gods are on my side.

Now that I have reading material, I get a bottle of water from the convenience store and make my way to the food court. I am actually hungry, but I'm going to make myself drink the entire bottle of water first. That way, I'll be less tempted to overeat. The decadent aromas from the restaurants are not helping, but I can do this. A little hunger pain is nothing. I've overcome so much more. It is a small sacrifice to make in order to be the new me. I pull the *People* out of the bag and stuff books into a side compartment of my luggage.

The magazine is on my table, ready to be opened when I spot Declan approaching the food court. He has a baseball hat on now and is walking rather quickly. I look at him, sending him mental telepathy to look over my way. I doubt it really works, but he does glance in my direction. Waving my hand like an idiot, I grin widely, beckoning him over. It is the friendliest I've been in ages. He smiles back and veers toward me.

His grin, however, is short lived when he gets to the table. The lips that were so friendly and jovial are now hard set in a line. "Yes?" he asks.

His sudden coolness takes me aback. It makes me nervous and I falter. "I, um, well, I ..." Oh my God, what is my problem? I've turned into a bumbling idiot. "I'm sorry, Declan. I was rude before, getting up and leaving like that."

"Yes, it was rude." His tone is just shy of being rude itself. Hard to believe he's this angry with me.

"I think we're going to be here for a while, and we're on the same flight. Maybe, we, um ..." I falter a bit but pull it together, "... can get a bite to eat or something."

I notice him looking at the magazine on the table. He's staring at it. Now, he's staring at me. "Why do you want to get something to eat?" No mistaking it, his tone is hard. He's going to turn me down.

"Because I'm hungry?" It comes out like a question. Crap, this guy has really thrown me for a loop today.

"That's it?" Seriously, he could be a cross-examiner.

I glance down for a moment, trying to steel my courage. I can't believe I'm afraid of this. Me, Kaitlin Elizabeth Mackenzie Reynolds, who used to fly off the face of mountains, is scared of admitting that I'm lonely. I'm scared of everything these days.

I let go and take the plunge.

"I'm lonely. I'm sad, angry and lonely and I would like some company. Since you had the misfortune of running into my large back end, preventing me from falling over—twice I might add—and sitting down next to me to make small talk, I don't see why we can't keep each other company until our plane leaves. It seems like it's going to be a while."

"Are you being honest with me?"

Dammit, why is he giving me such a hard time? I've been so much more open with him than I have been with anyone in a long time, including myself.

"Yes, Declan I am. I just want someone to talk to for a little while."

Declan glances around. He seems very uncomfortable, which is at odds with how he presented himself earlier.

"Yes, Kaitlin, you do seem sad and lonely. I'll keep you company until we find someone more suitable for you."

"Okay. Wait—what?"

"What about him?"

I looked to see who Declan was looking toward. It was a middle-aged man who had dreadlocks that hung down his back. From the looks of it, he had last showered decades ago. "Seriously? That guy? C'mon—I wasn't that bad!"

A small smiles creeps upon his face. "I guess not. But I don't know if you're worthy of me yet."

"Wow, you think a lot of yourself, don't you?"

He smiles again. This time, it's a full smile and the dimples come out. "No, I'm just trying to see if you have a sense of humor."

"I used to, but I'm not so sure anymore."

"You know, I once saw a sign somewhere that said, 'Going through life without a sense of humor is like riding in a car without any shocks—you feel every bump in the road.'"

Considering his words, even if they were bumper sticker material, I couldn't help but agree. "Do you get all of your deep insights from bumper stickers?"

His smile widens. "Well, Kaitlin-who-may-or-may-not-still-have-a-sense-of-humor, let's get out of this food court and go find someplace that serves reputable food and drink."

******

12:15 p.m.: Declan

I feel too conspicuous sitting in the food court. After the security of the tunnel, I again have grown nervous that people are going to start recognizing me. I've put on my Tigers baseball hat, hoping that it keeps me from being noticed. But obviously, it didn't keep Kaitlin from noticing me. When I see her sitting at her table, even from far away, she still gives off an appearance of looking sad. But she wears it well and all I can think is how appealing she looks. I don't know why, but I have to talk to her again. Maybe I'm a glutton for punishment. I expect her to give me a dirty look, so I'm surprised when she smiles and waves me over. She is so natural and beautiful when she smiles.

know there's an Irish pub here, so I suggest that. It is barely noon, so hopefully it won't be too crowded yet. I'd like to get to know Kaitlin better in somewhere a little more secluded. She's taken my teasing in stride. Of course, there's still the issue of the magazine that she was reading. Although, from her candid confession, I think it may be possible that she hasn't seen my half-naked body. Right now, she appears to like me for me, and not for the fifteen minutes of fame I could possibly provide her. I need to keep it that way.

Kaitlin walks slowly. Not too slow, but certainly slower than Natalya does. Nat races through life like it is a contest. I don't know who she's competing with, other than me. I have to keep reminding myself not to compare Kaitlin to Natalya. They are two totally different people.

Natalya. What a piece of work she is. I haven't spoken to her in two weeks. It has been the best two weeks. It is going to be torture going back with her. We have five weeks of rehearsals and then almost three months on tour. I don't know how I'm going to get through it with her. She is so pissed at me for retiring. She's screamed at me on more than one occasion, calling me a selfish bastard for ruining her career.

I don't think I am, though. A bastard, I mean. I think I'm a pretty nice guy. Nat isn't really grounded in reality. I mean, she's twenty-six. She would be thirty for the next Olympics. Her body's not holding up any better than mine. If anything, hers is worse. First, her knees are shot. She's in pain all the time, which is part of the reason she's so bitchy. Then, there's the anorexia. No matter how many times we've been through it, she just can't seem to fight that demon. Plus, we hate each other. Sure, on the ice, we put on a good front. We use our hatred in our programs and people see it as passion. I have never felt less passionate for a woman who wasn't related to me than I do for Natalya. The bundled up Russian babushkas in Sochi held more appeal for me than Natalya. Oddly, Nat doesn't see any of this. She thinks she can get whatever she wants simply because she wants it. She's gone through guy after guy, and I was simply another notch on her bedpost.

It's funny. Kaitlin in some ways reminds me of Natalya. There's the anger, the bitchiness, and the mood swings. Maybe that's just a girl thing. But Kaitlin has a vulnerability that Natalya lacks. A softness that is not just in her body but her soul. She seems more like a wounded animal lashing out in defense than a predator on the prowl. Natalya is definitely the predator type.

We reach the pub and are lucky enough to get seated in the back. I take my hat off and run my fingers through my hair. I want to cut it off. It is too long and unruly, but it is part of my "look." Another reason to look forward to retirement.

We're seated and waiting for our waitress when my phone starts vibrating in my back pocket. I ignore it, but it happens continuously. I excuse myself and head to the rest room. I stop outside the door and pull my phone out of my jeans pocket.

Four text messages, all from Nat. It was like she knew I was thinking about her. Dammit.

I scroll through them, deleting them all. She's begging me to reconsider retirement. She's trying to be nice. But I know the real her and know that it is not nice. I text her back that we'll talk when I get back from New York. I hope that is enough to get her off my back for a while.

I want to be strong, but I'm afraid I'm going to let her pull me back in.

I use the rest room and head back to the table. To my dismay, Kaitlin is reading that damn *People* again. I can see she is only to the first guy in the spread. I'm on the last page of the article. I only have a half of a page, but that is more than enough for me.

"Can you please put that trash away?" I hope she doesn't hear the desperation in my voice.

When she tells me she's reading it for the articles, I want to laugh. She does have a sense of humor. I flip the magazine closed. She is only two pages away from my picture.

She doesn't know who I am. At this moment, she likes me for me. And I intend on keeping it that way.

Chapter Four
12:20 p.m.: Kaitlin

Once in the pub, we're at a table in the back, and he takes off his hat and tucks it in his carry-on. Wow, a gentleman. I can't remember the last time Tyler took his hat off when we were out to eat. I can't remember the last time we went out to eat, but that is neither here nor there at the moment. A wave of guilt washes over me. I shouldn't be here, having lunch with this incredibly good-looking, charismatic guy. I'm married. I know it doesn't mean anything to Tyler anymore, but it still does to me. I think.

After Declan heads to the bathroom, I look around for a bit. The waitress still hasn't even come over to take our drink orders, not that I know what he would want. I'm not one for drinking during the day, but that's more out of habit than anything else. I was in training for so long, treating my body like a temple. Well, at least fueling it like a temple. On the mountain, that's another story. I beat up and battered my body on the mountain. Flying off the mountain.

I start to think about this Declan character. One of the things I like about him—I like walking with Declan. He doesn't seem to notice that I walk more slowly than him and that I have a limp. I think I hide it pretty well. He doesn't hurry me, and seems okay to walk at my pace, rather than encouraging me to keep up. Tyler not only makes fun of my limp but he yells at me to keep up. If I could, I would.

I have to stop these thoughts before they spiral downward, bringing me with them, so out comes the *People* again. Flipping through, admiring the view, I don't hear Declan come back.

"Can you please put that trash away?"

"What this? I'm reading it for the articles."

He reaches over and with a swift move, flips it closed. "I don't understand why you're reading that garbage."

"Honestly?"

"Honesty is always my policy."

"I'm reading it because it is garbage. Because it is mind-numbing garbage that will not make me think. It will take no ounces of brain power, other than to enjoy the sights. Are you telling me that you never picked up a *Sports Illustrated* swimsuit issue?"

"Well, sure, in my younger years. But not now that I'm an adult."

"How old are you exactly?"

He looks taken aback. "How would you feel if I asked you that question?"

"I'm twenty-nine."

"So, Kaitlin, who is twenty-nine, what other information would you like to share with me? I don't want to ask the wrong question and piss you off again."

"I would like to share that I really need a beer right now and I'm getting pretty pissed at our waitress."

Declan looks around for a moment and flags down our waitress. She, of course, comes right over for him and we order our beers. His phone beeps and he checks it. "Looks like another delay. Now they're not anticipating take-off until after four. Departure is scheduled for four-twenty."

"Shit. That totally screws me over."

"Are you going to be missing something?"

"I'm supposed to be at a work meet-and-greet at 6 p.m. in SoHo."

"Oh, yeah, you're totally screwed."

Tell me something I don't know.

"I'd better text my boss and let him know. This is not going to go over well." I dread calling Richard. I know things have to change. I have to change. Funny, such a brief time spent with Declan and I'm more enlightened than I have been in the past twenty months. I text Richard apologetically and let him know that this is a weather-related delay, not a Kaitlin screw up. He responds with a text telling me to relax because the meet-and-greet has been cancelled due to the storm, but that he still needs me there by tomorrow afternoon.

Relief floods my body and I smile for like the fourth time today. New world record.

"That's a happy smile."

"It turns out my event has been cancelled due to the weather, so I'm not missing out. I do need to get there by tomorrow afternoon, but my boss isn't upset with me."

"Is he usually?"

"A lot of the time."

"Why is that?" Declan takes a long pull on his beer and leans in just a bit closer.

"Because I suck at my job." The truth stings a bit, admitting that out loud.

"I find that hard to believe. I think you must be quite capable."

"No, it's true. I suck because I hate my job. I don't want to be doing it, so I don't put any effort in."

"So, what you're saying is that if you put forth some effort, you could probably do a good job."

"Possibly. Probably. Oh, I don't know."

"How can you not know?"

"Declan, I don't know you and you don't know me. I've been through a lot the last two years and I've been pretty miserable as a result. I work this job because I have to, not because I want to."

"Well, what do you want to do?"

That question nearly brings tears to my eyes. "There is only one thing I want to do, and I can never do it again."

The waitress finally decides to show up, noticing our empty beers. I order a grilled chicken salad (trying that whole healthy thing, remember?) and Declan orders a big, fat, juicy burger. We get another round of beer, figuring we have at least three more hours before our flight could even possibly leave.

"So, you were telling me what you want to do but can't ever do again."

Why did he have to pick right up where we left off?

"No, Declan, let's go back. You never told me how old you are?"

"Why do you want to know?"

"Why don't you want to tell me?"

"It's personal."

"I told you how old I am."

"But you don't mind sharing. I do."

"Why would you mind sharing? Guys aren't supposed to care about age."

"In my field, increasing age isn't a good thing. It signals the beginning of the end."

"What, are you a ballet dancer or something?"

He laughs, a big, deep, throaty laugh. It seems to rumble up from his toes and I wished I could record it to have it with me always. "No, I'm not a ballet dancer."

"Well, then tell me either what you do or how old you are."

"Pushy, pushy. I can't believe you're not good in sales. Fine, I'm thirty-one."

"Oh my God, you're ancient. Have you been contacted by AARP yet?"

"What is AARP?"

"Seriously? It's the 'American Association of Retired Persons.'"

"Well, there you go. I'm not American."

"But you live here. Surely you've seen the commercials?"

"Surely you know when I'm pulling your leg."

I crumple up my napkin and throw it at him. "Jerk."

"Gullible."

Sticking my tongue out at him is childish but freeing at the same time. Dare I say it? I think I'm having fun.

******

1:52 p.m.: Declan

The beer loosens Kaitlin's tongue. It is a beautiful thing. Not only is she no longer angry, she's downright funny. I would not have expected that sense of humor based upon her earlier surliness. She's dismayed at our delay but I relish it. More time with her.

I probably shouldn't admit this, but about two to three beers in, I start thinking about hooking up with her. I don't know if it is sad that I'm thinking about having sex with a virtual stranger or sad that it took me a few beers to get to this point. She's wearing a plain ring on her left hand, but no diamond. She hasn't mentioned a husband or anything in all this time.

I should care if she's married, but I don't. I cannot stop thinking about her ass pressing into my pelvis. Dammit, I'm as horny as a teenager. Of course, I haven't gotten laid in months, so that doesn't help. It was hard to date with Natalya around. Like I said, practically a professional cock blocker.

In the back of my mind, I know that Frankie booked me a room at the Westin, right in the airport. If we get any further delayed or cancelled, I have the perfect opportunity. I slow down drinking. I want to be able to get it up when the time comes.

Kaitlin continues to slam them back. She's releasing something from deep within, I can tell. It's like she hasn't talked to another human in years. Like, really talked.

"Do you mind flying?" I ask her.

"No, not really. Before, I used to fly a lot more. My current job has me in the car more than in the air."

"Is that a good thing or a bad thing?"

She's pensive for a moment. "I guess there are plusses and minuses to both. I can't sing quite so loud when I'm on an airplane. Or at least not without being escorted off the plane."

"Have you ever seen anyone removed from a plane before?"

"Yeah, actually. I was on a flight to Poland. We had to change in Germany before the last leg. Apparently one gentleman thought he would make his own mile high club with himself."

"Ewww."

"I know. When we landed in Germany, the air marshals escorted him off quite quickly."

"I fly a lot too, but I don't think I've ever seen anyone removed."

"I haven't flown since ... before. This is my first time on a plane in almost two years. That is, if we ever get on this plane."

A few times, she has talked about "before" like it is its own event. I wonder "before" what? Best I can figure out, she had a different life back then. I wonder if maybe a marriage was the "before" that she has referred to?

There is certainly no mention of a man, other than Richard her boss. Good news for me. I turn up the flirtation. She flirts back. This is a good thing. The banter continues. It is totally superficial banter though, as she doesn't appear to know what I do. Telling a woman I'm a figure skater is always an odd thing. First thing, they assume you're gay. Even if you are having sex with them, they are still doubtful, despite being smack dab in the middle of doing it with you.

I need to tell her so I can get this elephant out of the room. I know she's going to make fun of me for it. I can just tell. I'm about to say it when our phones beep, almost simultaneously. The flight is cancelled. Her face falls and her brow furrows.

She starts babbling on, almost unable to put a sentence together. Good thing I slowed up on the drinking. One of us needs to be responsible here. What a role reversal. Natalya always assumed that I was a big dumb animal and was not capable of handling important things. Kaitlin appears to need me. That turns me on even more, as if I needed any encouragement. She excuses herself to go pee, and I watch her walk away. God bless the man who invented skin-tight leggings.

The waitress takes advantage of Kaitlin's absence to pounce. She comes up, gushing all over me. She inquires about my flight, and it doesn't take a rocket scientist to know what she's thinking. I keep looking around, waiting for Kaitlin to come back. I paste a smile on my face and pretend to listen to the waitress flirt with me. She doesn't know any better, but it is the smile I use when I'm in pain during a performance. I'm sitting on the edge of my seat, ready to hop up and get away as soon as Kaitlin comes back. I finally see her come out of the bathroom, and it is obvious that she's drunk.

She's bobbing and weaving, and I'm worried she's going to go down. Then, as if she heard my thoughts, her foot catches on the rug and she pitches forward. Already on the edge of my seat, I reach my arms out and catch her underneath her arms. I lift her up so that she's standing on her feet again. I pull her close to me and close my eyes as I smell her hair. It is not the smell of too much hair spray or perfume. It smells faintly like something floral. It is an immediate turn on.

She is just standing there, letting me smell her. I ask her if she is okay and she nods in reply. After a moment, she steps back. As much as I don't want to let her go, I'm glad she has pulled away. She hasn't noticed my hard on yet and I don't want her to. I tell her that she's got to pull herself together so we can change our flights. What I mean is that I've got to pull myself together so that I don't slam her down on the table and ravage her right here. Nothing has ever sounded so appealing.

We pick up our bags and head out of the restaurant, in search of a Delta agent to change our flights. She has her phone out and is making a call. The hard look, that angry look, is back on her face. I keep walking, giving her privacy. I can't help but wonder who she calls at a time like this. I text Frankie and tell her I'm going to be needing that room. And then I thank my lucky stars that Frankie booked it. I know I've got Kaitlin. It is mid-afternoon. By the time we get our tickets changed, we'll be able to check in. And I know what we'll be doing for the rest of the day. Oh God, now I'm that creepy guy, plotting to take advantage of a drunk girl. I wish she wasn't drunk. I need to sober her up so I know she wants this as much as I do.

I head up to the ticket agent and smile at her. I can tell from the look on her face that she knows who I am. This time, instead of being repulsed, I use it to my advantage. I look at her nametag. "Heather," I say in the smoothest voice I can manage without making myself throw up. "Here's the deal. The flight my friend and I are supposed to be on has been cancelled. I'm wondering if you can get us rescheduled."

She looks tired and scared. I bet she's been dealing with a lot of unpleasant people today. Like she had anything to do with the massive storm that has crippled the airlines.

I continue, "I know there's nothing for today, but what about the first flight out tomorrow?"

She starts typing furiously. She glances at the name on my ticket and then at me. A blush spreads over her face. She's picturing me almost naked. I know I should flirt with her to get what I want out of the flight, but it somehow seems wrong. I can at least give her a good story to tell her friends.

"You've seen the magazine, haven't you?"

Heather's blush deepens as she nods. She's typing even faster now. "I, um, it, ahh, it's a good feature."

"Thanks. I'm glad you enjoyed it. Now tell me, can you make sure to sit my friend and me together?"

Dammit, I'm bad.

Chapter Five
2:46 p.m.: Kaitlin

I'm drunk. Piss drunk. I've been drinking more lately than I ever used to, but this is a lot, even for me. Especially in the middle of the afternoon. With only a salad in my stomach. Not a good combination. Declan appears a bit on the tipsy side too. Or maybe I'm just drunk enough for the both of us. I've laughed more in the past two hours than I have in the past two years. For a day spent in the airport, it has been totally awesome.

My phone beeps the text message alert. My flight has been cancelled. Oh crap. What am I going to do? I'm totally hammered. I can't think this through right now. I still need to get to New York.

"Declan," I slur the end of his name a bit. "I need to fly morning."

"What?" He's laughing at my drunk babbling.

"I need to be flying in the morning."

"Okay, drunk girl. Let's go see the ticketing agent."

"I gotta pee first." Nothing but class here. I get up and manage to get to the bathroom without incident. I stumble a bit while in the stall. My leggings present quite the challenge to my balance and I fall against the door as I'm trying to pull them up. Luckily I locked it, so I don't go bursting out onto the floor. The water on my hands feels good as I wash them, so I splash a little on my face. I run my fingers through my mouse-brown bob, wishing it were long enough to braid again. I know the bob is a flattering look for me, but I don't want to be bothered with my hair at the moment. My brown eyes look huge right now, but that is probably because I'm having trouble focusing.

Walking out of the bathroom, I see Declan from across the pub. There is a girl who is talking to him. He's smiling politely, but it is not the smile he's given me all day. His body language is all stiff and guarded, like it was when I called him over in the food court.

I'm so focused on watching their interaction that I forget I have a foot drop and that my right leg doesn't work properly. About two feet from the table, my right toes catch on the ground and I pitch forward.

With what can only be described as superhuman quickness, Declan springs up and catches me before I face plant into the table. He's facing me and has put his arms through my arms. I'm headed toward the horizontal position, face down, so my face is buried in his chest. With a quick pull upward, he has righted me. It amazes me how he moves it around like a doll. He can manipulate my body with the flick of a wrist. I wonder what other things he could do to my body ...

Shit. I cannot be thinking about this.

It's because I'm drunk. Yeah, that's it. It is not because I'm a horrible person who is angry and lonely. It is not because my marriage is falling apart at the seams and I want to move on. Nope, it is one hundred percent the alcohol talking.

"You okay?" He murmurs into the hair I've just smoothed down. I don't care if he messes it up. It is worth it to have him whispering into my ear.

I nod, afraid of what will come out of my mouth if I try to speak. I'm afraid of the thoughts that are running through my head. I was never afraid in my life, not until the injury. Now I'm afraid all the time. I'm afraid of who I've become and what my intentions are at this moment.

I extract myself from him and stand up straight. I've got to pull it together enough to fix my flight situation. Yes, that must be my priority at the moment. Forget about the Irish-Canadian with the great smile and perfect dimples. And the rock hard ass that I may have accidentally touched when I fell into him.

He must know what I'm thinking because he says, "Kaitlin, you've got to pull yourself together so we can get our flights changed."

"Yup. Got it. Aye, aye Captain." I salute him in a mock gesture. Declan gives me a stern look but it quickly dissolves into a smile, betraying his amusement.

As we're walking toward the unlucky Delta agent, I pull out my phone and call Tyler. Not surprisingly, he doesn't answer. Lord only knows what he is up to while I'm out of town. Leaving a message will be pointless, as he never checks them. I do it anyway.

"Hey—it's me. Um, my flight was cancelled. I'm on my way to see what I can do. I'll call you back when I know more. I may need you to come and get me."

I've stopped walking while leaving the message because walking and talking is just too much for me to coordinate at this moment. Declan has already reached the agent. The young lady behind the counter looks like she's about to cry. As much as I hate my job, her job has got to suck royally right now. Declan's talking to her and she starts typing furiously. She keeps glancing up at Declan and giving him shy smiles. He must be using his mega-watt smile on her, full dimples and all. Then I see him pointing toward me and motioning for me to join them. I see the crestfallen look on her face as I approach them.

"Heather here needs your ticket." Declan instructs me. I don't feel as drunk as I had felt earlier, but the instruction is nice. I hand my ticket over to Heather behind the counter. Her blond hair is in need of a root touch up and is escaping her pony tail in little curly tendrils. She looks as tired as I suddenly feel, and once again, I thank my lucky stars that I have my job. I should probably do my best to keep it. Heather continues typing furiously until a triumphant smile spreads over her face.

"I've got you both on the last two seats on the 6 a.m. flight tomorrow morning. It was the best I could do, but I did manage to get your seats together."

"Thank you, Heather. I appreciate it." Declan grants her another magic smile and she blushes.

She drops her head, sheepishly looking up at him with her phone in her hand. "Do you mind?"

He steps behind the counter and they snap a quick selfie. Not believing my eyes, my mouth hangs agape.

He rejoins me and appears a bit embarrassed. I look at him out of the side of my eye. "That happen to you often?"

He shrugs. "Sometimes."

Huh. When I'm a bit more sober, I'm going to have to think about this one.

"So, you worked your magic and got us on the 6 a.m. flight. Thanks."

"All in a day's work, ma'am." He bends forward in a mock bow and his shoulder bag slips down. It hits the floor and tips over. The side that had been against his body lands facing up. Staring up at me are the five, brightly colored interlocking rings that have broken my heart. I can't stop looking at the embroidery on the black bag. The primary colors of the rings. Sochi 2014. It is one of the bags given to the athletes.

I can practically feel the knife piercing my heart. The old wounds, barely even scabbed over, are ripped wide open again.

"Kaitlin, are you okay? You have a weird look on your face. Kaitlin, are you all right?"

I look up but cannot meet his eyes. This time I mean it when I say, "Yeah. I gotta go."

******

3:02 p.m.: Declan

Kaitlin is gone. She turned whiter than a ghost, got a really odd look on her face, and then took off. I wonder if she is going to be sick. I wait for a few minutes. Okay, like twenty minutes. She's coming back. I tell myself that over and over. How long does it take for someone to throw up anyway? I think about the last time I threw up. It wasn't that long ago. It was while I was in Sochi. After all, we were ranked eighteenth in the world coming in and we walked away with the Bronze. It was Russia, and the vodka flowed a little too freely. I was hungover for about two days, but it was totally worth it.

I didn't think Kaitlin had had that much to drink. Maybe she had a medical condition or something. Maybe she was embarrassed. I pull out my phone and look at the time. Now I'm just worried about her. What if something happened to her?

I walk to the nearest ladies' restroom and try not to look too creepy hanging out in front of it. I pace back and forth and constantly pull my baseball hat down.

After five more minutes that feel like five hours, it dawns on me. She's not there in need of help. She ditched me. It was like she could see inside my head and knew what I was thinking. And it freaked her out.

Huh.

I'm stubborn though. I don't want to believe that she is repulsed by me. It has to be something else. Has to be.

I'm a little tired from the beer and could use a nap. I can go check into the hotel room at anytime, but I'm not ready to admit defeat just yet and leave without Kaitlin.

This isn't just about the sexual conquest. Not entirely. Outside of skating, this has been the most enjoyable afternoon I've had in, oh, I don't know how long. I was right about Kaitlin. She wasn't all prickles and abrasiveness. Underneath, when she lets her guard down, she's soft and vulnerable. Like her skin.

She's got a story and I want to know what it is. I want to listen to her talk. I want to hear her laugh. That is a magical sound—her laughter. I get the impression that she doesn't laugh much. She does this thing where she appears startled by the sound of her own laughter. I wonder what could have possibly happened to make her so sad and angry.

I wander aimlessly. I don't know where to look. I don't know why I'm looking. She obviously doesn't want anything to do with me. She's made that abundantly clear.

The airport is heinously crowded. So many people camping out, waiting for planes that aren't going to arrive to take them to their destination. I consider going to the tunnel again but know that it's not going to help. I feel unsettled. I haven't felt unsettled like this since I made my decision to retire. I spot an empty chair and snatch it up, sitting for a minute while I figure out what I'm going to do.

My phone rings again and I fish it out of my back pocket. Frankie. "Yeah, what's up?"

"How you makin' out baby? You checked in yet?"

"No, not yet." I sigh out my answer.

"What's wrong baby?"

Frankie calls me "baby." Frankie doesn't look a day over seventy, which is a shame considering she's only fifty-nine. Years of chain smoking, too much sun, and too much peroxide have not helped her appearance. She looks like a caricature. But she's a fabulous manager. She had a career in P.R. before she realized that I needed someone to keep me on the straight and narrow. She's like my mom but without the boundaries. She knows about the drunken blackout in Sochi. She knows how I feel about Natalya. She knows it all. I think it bothers my mom sometimes that I'm so close with Frankie, but she is more relieved that Frankie keeps me safe and in line.

"Oh, I just ... I don't know."

"Declan, baby, you sound so sad. Surely this is not about your flight getting cancelled?"

"No, Frankie. I'm on a flight tomorrow morning. It's ..." I sigh. How do I say I got dumped? It's Frankie—I can just come out and say it. "I met a girl when I first got to the airport. We seemed to hit it off and we've been hanging out. I kind of was thinking about asking her back to the room with me, and then she just took off."

"What do you mean took off?"

I shift the phone from one ear to the other, and then back again because it's not comfortable. "I mean, we were talking and laughing. She was a little on the drunk side, but not too bad. We got the notice that our flight was cancelled, so I worked my magic and got us rescheduled for tomorrow morning. And then she just got weird and pale and took off. I thought maybe she was getting sick or something, so I hung around. But nothing—she's just gone."

"Declan, you just met her."

"I know, Frankie. But you know me. When do I ever care about the people I meet?"

"Awww, baby, you are a very caring guy."

Even though she says it through the phone, I still blush. I don't know how to take a compliment. Off ice that is. On ice, I feel like a god. Off ice, I'm a bumbling idiot who turns beet red and looks at his shoes a whole lot. It's one of the main reasons why the magazine spread bothers me so much. I don't like the spotlight. I save that for Natalya. That's her bag.

"No, this is different."

"I can hear that it's different. I can't remember the last time you even mentioned a girl this way. I was beginning to think all those other male figure skaters had finally won you over."

I can't help but laugh at that one. I'm definitely in the minority, being a straight male figure skater. Some of my best friends are gay, and while it doesn't bother me, neither does it interest me.

"So, what's this disappearing woman's name?"

"Kaitlin." I thought for a moment. I had seen her ticket. "Kaitlin Reynolds."

"Well, since you're interested in her, keep looking. She'll be on your flight tomorrow?"

"Yeah, but what if she switches it or something?

"Do you know where she lives?"

"Yeah, Grosse Pointe."

"That's good. It's a start. If fate doesn't bring you back together tonight or tomorrow, then you can look for her when you get back."

"How am I supposed to find her?"

"Declan, you never listen to me do you? If I've said it once, I've said it a thousand times. Never underestimate my ability to find shit out."

Chapter Six
3:04 p.m.: Kaitlin

I can't believe it. What are the freakin' odds here? I must have been truly terrible in a former life to deserve the crap that keeps piling up on me. Okay, in light of all the impure thoughts I'd been having over the last few hours, maybe I did deserve some of this.

No, I didn't. I didn't deserve any of what has happened to me.

I call Tyler again. Still no answer. I leave another message. I guess I could take a taxi home. I have to be back here in twelve short hours. It will take me about an hour to get home, and at least fifty bucks. I doubt Tyler will even be around to bring me back to the airport in the morning. More like the middle of the night. Even if he did come home tonight, it's highly unlikely that he would want to bring me back for 4 a.m.

Crap. Why is this my life?

In all honesty, I have no life right now. I would have said that I'm in limbo, but it's more like hell. No longer being able to live my passion. Skiing and ski jumping had been my life since I was a small child. When my mom left, my dad didn't know what to do with us. He didn't know how to talk to us, how to relate to a four- and eight-year-old. So he took us skiing. Made sense. We lived right near Whiteface. Pretty much everyone we knew skied. It wasn't unusual to see little tiny kids out on the slopes. Kevin was a strong skier from the get go and joined the competition teams as soon as he could.

I was a natural. I couldn't get enough. The first time I went over a jump, I fell on the landing. I was probably about seven by this time. My dad was there and he raced over, concerned that I was going to be crying. I wasn't. I was mad that I had fallen. I promptly went back up the hill so I could go over the jump again. The second time, I wiped out even more spectacularly on the landing. Dad looked concerned. He didn't want me to try again. "Kaitlin, you're just a little girl. Maybe when you're bigger, you'll be able to do it. I don't want you to get hurt."

As I wander around the busy airport, I can practically feel the ire in my blood that I felt that moment over twenty years ago. No one was going to tell me what I could and couldn't do. No one was going to tell me I was too small to do something. Or that I couldn't do something because I was a girl. From that moment on, I never let anything, or anyone, stand in my way. Within weeks, I was flying. And now I'm grounded. Permanently.

I start staking out chairs, prepared to spend the night at the airport. I'm now very tired and just want to sleep. I'm going to need to charge my phone at some point as well. My luck turns slightly when I find a chair right next to an outlet. It's a small consolation in the overall crappiness that is my life right now. I plug my phone in and kick off my boots. The flesh color of my plastic brace is glaring against the black of my leggings and socks. I curl up into a ball, trying to wish my life away. Using my coat as a blanket, I cover the offensive brace and try to stop my brain from working. I only hope that sleep comes and takes me far, far away from the reality that is my life.

I'm startled out of my sleep by a deep voice. "Kaitlin, there you are! I've been looking all over for you. Why'd you take off again?"

Groggily opening my eyes, I see Declan standing over me.

"I thought maybe you went home or something. Why did you run away from me again?"

I sit up, my coat falling to the floor. The monstrosity on my right leg is now totally visible. I stare at it, wishing it away for the millionth time. No chance of hiding it anymore. Declan looks at it and then back at me. I don't want to meet his gaze. I don't want to see the horror and pity in his eyes. I'm so embarrassed.

"What you got goin' on there?" He points to my foot. His voice is so casual, so nonchalant. Like I'm not ugly and deformed.

"I have a foot drop. Nerve damage and muscle atrophy."

"Was it always like that? Do you have any sensation?" He seems not horrified but fascinated. At least he's not repulsed. I don't know how he's not repulsed. I am.

"No, I had an injury. I don't like to talk about it." Quickly I pull my Uggs back on, hoping that out of sight will mean out of mind.

"I take it you're not leaving?" He seems totally unfazed at finding out I'm a cripple.

"No, I can't get a hold of—anyone. Plus, it's such a short time anyway." I shrug. "It doesn't matter. How 'bout you?"

"Same here. Seems too short and too much of a hassle to leave and come back."

"I could use a nap though. Doubt I'll get much sleep. I think I'm a little bit hungover. And I know at some point, I'm going to need to get up, but I don't want to lose my seat." I look around and there are people sprawled everywhere. Declan and I are not the only ones pulling an overnight at Detroit Metro Airport.

Declan sits down Indian style on the floor in front of me. "Kaitlin, you never answered me. Why did you take off again? Are you okay? Were you sick or something?"

"Declan, it's hard to explain. I'm not sure I'm ready to talk about it yet."

"Well, we do have all night. But I've got to tell you, my back is too old to be sitting on the floor for long."

"Oh, that's right. I forgot that you're a senior citizen. Did you forget to take your Geritol today?"

"Aaaaand she's back."

I glance around me. "Who?" Although we're surrounded by people, no one is paying attention to us, and I feel like we're in our own private world.

"Funny Kaitlin."

I smile. "I guess Funny Kaitlin could be making a comeback. She's been gone for a long time now."

"Don't run away again, okay?"

How can I resist those pleading eyes? I want to agree. I glance down and my gaze lands on his bag. My head is pounding and I need about a gallon of water. I just want to lie in a dark room with my head on a nice soft pillow and go to sleep. I close my eyes to block out his bag and what it represents. It represents my ultimate failure. How do I tell him this? How do I tell him that, even though I know virtually nothing about him, he has everything that is missing in my life?

I've folded my body in half so that my forehead is practically resting on my knees. My arms are wrapped around each other. It's pretty much fetal position in a chair. "Declan, you've been very nice to me today. I've even had a bit of fun, which I had forgotten existed. But I can't be friends with you. I'm sorry."

"Kaitlin, I usually don't try this hard. If someone doesn't want anything to do with me, then I usually say, 'screw 'em' and move on with my life. I know I ran into you totally by accident today, but, I don't know, I just want to hang out with you."

"Why? I'm surly and bitter and temperamental. How can you enjoy being around that?"

He laughs. "Your mood swings are nothing compared to my partner's. You would have to work many years to achieve that level of bitterness and surliness."

His partner? Hmmm ... interesting. I would never have figured him as gay. He seems so manly. Everything about him just is so ... masculine. I lift my head to better look at him.

"Declan, I have so much stuff going on in my head right now. I don't know which way is even up anymore. I have a pounding headache and I just want to go to bed." I look at my watch. "Jeez, it's only 4:45. It feels like it's midnight."

"What would you do for a nice comfy bed right now?"

"I'd kill someone for it."

"What if I offered you a slightly better deal? You know, one that doesn't involve a felony conviction and a prison sentence?"

I look up skeptically, my arms still wrapped tightly around my torso. "What kind of deal?"

In this position, our faces are inches apart. This would be the moment in the movies where the couple kisses. But, as is evident as the nose on my face and the brace on my foot, my life is not like a movie. I'm married. He's gay. Not to mention the fact that my life is a train wreck and we're sitting in a crowded airport. Ugh. I can't believe I'm even entertaining these thoughts. What the heck is wrong with me? I sit back in the chair.

"I have a room in the Westin."

I raise my eyebrow and wait for him to continue.

"My, um, manager booked it when the first delay happened. She kind of had the feeling I'd be stranded here. Anyway, I'm headed up there. Why don't you come with me?"

"What's the catch?"

"No catch. Just a condition, really."

"Okay, what's the condition?" What could he possibly want from me? Obviously it won't be some kind of indecent proposal. What if he wants me to carry his baby for him and his partner? How creepy is that—picking someone up in the airport and asking them to have your baby? He seemed so normal. I can't believe he's going to spring this on me. I thought he was normal and it turns out he's some kind of weirdo freak.

"Kaitlin. Earth to Kaitlin. Come in Kaitlin."

"Oh, sorry."

"Where did you just go? You should have seen the look on your face. What were you thinking about?"

"I was thinking about what the possible conditions could be. I'm a little scared to find out."

He laughed. "Nothing ominous, I promise. I'm not some kind of psycho freak. I just want you to talk to me. About whatever is bothering you, because it's obvious that something is tearing you apart inside. I just want you to let me in and be your friend tonight."

Oh.

"You thought it was something terrible, didn't you? I can tell by the look on your face."

I feel my face growing warm in embarrassment. Looking down, I knot my hands in my lap. It was a bit unnerving how well he could read me. I had been with Tyler for nine years and he never had a clue about what was on my mind. Of course, that could be because he didn't give a shit anymore.

The lure of a bed is too strong. But then I'll have to talk about myself. I don't want to rehash the last two years with anyone, let alone Declan. I want him to like me. Crap, I shouldn't be thinking about this. Of course, there's the obvious—even though I'm totally tempted by Declan, he won't be tempted by me, so it's all good, right? Christ, why does everything in my life have to be so freakin' hard?

"Kaitlin, I'm not asking you to do long division in your head here. It's a simple question, really."

******

4:06 p.m.: Declan

After hanging up with Frankie, I'd resigned myself to a cold, lonely night. And to never seeing Kaitlin again. I had no doubt that Frankie could find her. I just wasn't sure I wanted to find her. I mean, she obviously didn't want anything to do with me. She'd made that perfectly clear.

I decide to walk down the corridor one more time. I'm scanning for Kaitlin, but have no real hopes of finding her. There are people lying everywhere, camping out for the night. A child off to the left is screaming, one of those piercing screams that is quite effective as birth control. I look over to see her harried, frazzled mother trying in vain to shush her. Turning back around, I spot her out of the corner of my eye. She's in the row of chairs that backs up to the window. She has the end seat, next to a pillar. Curled up into an impossibly small ball, she's covered up with her coat. Her boots are on the floor in front of her chair, and her bags are tucked under the seat. Her phone must be on her lap, as the telltale white cord snakes out from under her coat and into the outlet in the wall.

Before I can even stop and think, I find myself standing in front of her. "Kaitlin, there you are! I've been looking all over for you. Why'd you take off again?"

She slowly opens her eyes and looks confused. She looks angelic and I want the chance to see her wake up more than just this once. I know I should let it go, but I ask her why she ran away again. She struggles to sit up and as she gets herself upright, her coat falls to the floor.

Trying to be a gentleman (you know, the perverted, creepy, stalker kind), I start to bend over to retrieve her coat. On her right foot is a brace. It goes underneath her foot and up the back of her calf. Straps attach it to her foot at her ankle and upper shin, just below her knee. Frankie's son, Garrett, was born early and he has cerebral palsy. He's had braces somewhat like that all his life. But Kaitlin doesn't walk like Garrett does, and my curiosity wins out over my tact.

"What you got goin' on there?"

She looks down at her foot in disgust. "I have a foot drop. Nerve damage and muscle atrophy."

That's interesting. Now I have to know more. "What happened? Was it always like that? Do you have any sensation?"

She quickly shuts down any further discussion and hastily covers up her legs by donning her boots. I may be dense but even I know enough to change the subject. I ask her if she plans on staying at the airport, even though the answer is obvious.

She stops herself short when she is saying that she can't get a hold of anyone. Interesting. I bet there is someone. I look at her left hand again. It's certainly a ring. A wide band with scrolling on it. Could be a wedding band. Could be a tribal band, for all I know.

I should ask. I know I should.

My mom would want me to.

My mom isn't here, so I proceed with my plan. I'm sick of doing what everyone else wants. I want this girl and I intend to get her. She still looks pretty upset. I think I'm going to need to get her past this—whatever this is. I don't want her to take off again. I sit down on the floor in front of her. She won't look up so I get down and put myself in her eye line. She looks at me. Damn, she looks so sad. I ask her, again, why she took off.

She doesn't answer right away. I try to break the silence by making a joke about my age. I mean, she is a whopping two years younger than me. Although part of me is not joking. This hard floor really does hurt my back.

That's enough to get her out of her shell a bit as she takes the bait and continues to kid me about my advanced age.

"Aaaaand she's back."

Kaitlin looks around before I tell her that I mean her—funny Kaitlin. She gets that sad, sad smile again and tells me that funny Kaitlin has been gone for a long time. But then she gets sad and quiet again.

I don't know what I expect her to say, but when she says that she can't be friends with me, it bothers me. A lot. A lot more than it should. I bet she is married and she feels the connection between us. I mean, girls are always talking about these instant connections. Personally, until today, I thought it was a load of bull. If I were the nice guy that I'm supposed to be, I would take her answer and walk away. And leave her sitting here all night? A nice guy would give her his hotel room.

Right. That's what I'm going to do. I'm going to make sure that she's nice and comfortable for the night. *That's* the nice guy thing to do. I won't make a move on her, no matter how much I want to. I'll just be here for her, and be her friend. I'll keep my hands to myself and behave. I lay the Mr. Nice Guy routine when I say, "Kaitlin, I usually don't try this hard. If someone doesn't want anything to do with me, then I usually say, 'screw 'em' and move on with my life. I know I ran into you totally by accident today, but, I don't know, I just want to hang out with you."

She's folded up practically in half. Her head is virtually on her knees. She looks small and vulnerable. I bet she would hate knowing that she looks vulnerable. In a small voice, she tells me that I don't want to hang out with her because of her terrible moods.

Ha! If she only knew what dealing with someone who was truly surly and bitter was like. Not to mention hungry. Natalya is hungry all the time and her mood certainly reflects that. She is a bitch on a good day. Heaven help me when she was hungry. Or tired. Or hurt. Kaitlin is a kitten compared to Natalya.

I tell her this. She raises her head. She's still bent over and hugging herself. I just want to take her in my arms and hold her until she stops looking so sad and miserable. I don't know what to do next.

And then she throws me the easy pitch. She tells me that she has a headache and just wants to go to bed. That she'd kill someone for it. And I've got my in!

"What if I offered you a slightly better deal? You know, one that doesn't involve a felony conviction and a prison sentence?"

She looks at me with doubt in her eyes. Actually, it is written all over her face. Which, by the way, is just inches from mine. I so want to just grab her and kiss her. But no, I've made the decision to be the nice guy and not force her to do anything that would make her feel uncomfortable. Damn it. Nice guys do finish last.

I offer to make her a deal. She looks pained. I can almost hear the wheels turning in her brain. What the hell can she be thinking about? It is not a difficult question here—does she want the bed or not? It's apparent that she's distrustful. I wonder if it is of me or just people in general. I promise her that it is nothing bad and that I'm not a creepy guy. I wish I could live up to that promise and stop thinking about getting her into bed.

"I just want you to talk to me. About whatever is bothering you, because it's obvious that something is tearing you apart inside. I just want you to let me in and be your friend tonight."

She looks relieved. But still undecided. She's still thinking. What can she possibly be thinking about? Are her skeletons that bad? The longer she takes to decide, the more it makes me want to know her story. I've been hanging out with too many females and gay men for too long. I've turned into a busybody.

Even more than that, I'm concerned about Kaitlin's well being. She looks frail almost. Funny. I could probably snap Natalya's thin frame in half, but her constitution is so firm and stubborn that she seems invincible. But this woman in front of me, who is so much more substantial (in a good way), looks like she could just crumble at any moment. I begrudgingly push any thoughts of seduction aside as I help Kaitlin to her feet, pick up her bag, and we head to my hotel room.

Chapter Seven
4:47 p.m.: Kaitlin

I know my end of the deal is to tell him my story, but I'm going to avoid it at all costs. Of course, I don't want to hear his story either. I don't know what his sport is but hearing about any of it does not interest me.

I'm lying to myself.

I want to hear all about it. I want to know what it was like. But hearing it will crush me all over again. He's waiting for me to talk. I know he is.

Why does he care?

Why does it bother me that he cares?

Because everyone stopped caring about me a while ago. Once I stopped being the meal ticket. Once I no longer had coattails to ride, I lost my value to the people who were supposed to love me. That included myself. I was too full of self-loathing. The person I had let down most of all was me.

We're checked into the hotel room, which, thankfully has two double beds. Even though I owe nothing to Tyler at this point, I am happy that there will be no chance of me doing anything I shouldn't. Not that there will be that chance anyway.

Because there are no expectations, there is no pressure. For once in my life. I flop down backwards on the first bed, and let out what can only be described as a sigh mixed with a groan. I don't worry about impressing Declan. The bed is probably a typical hotel room bed, but it feels heavenly tonight. Today. What time is it anyway? I feel like I've been here all day. Perhaps because I have. Holy cow—it's not even five o'clock yet. What are we going to do, cooped up in this hotel room? It's too early to eat again. Too early to go to sleep.

Declan flops face down on his bed, filling the entire thing. His head is between the two pillows while his feet hang off the end. He really is a mammoth man. He moves with such grace and fluidity that you forget how big he is.

You would expect him to be a hulking presence, but he isn't. I don't know how to describe him though. Not yet.

I sit up and remove one boot, then the other. The silence in the room is sliced by the tell-tale ripping of the Velcro straps as I undo my brace. I pull my sock off and examine my foot for signs of irritation or breakdown. Because I can't stand to have one sock on and the other off, I pull off my left sock as well. Dropping them on the floor, I lie back down and curl up onto my side. My feet, trapped in toasty boots and knee socks all day are now cold in the exposed air, so I pull the side of the polyester bed cover up over them.

As I lie there, I wonder if Declan has fallen asleep. He's ominously quiet, especially for him. I mean, in the short time I've known him (has it really only been today?) he hasn't really been this quiet. I try to distill what it is I do know about him. He was in the Sochi Olympics, so he's some kind of athlete. I have no idea what though. He's very tall, so maybe hockey? I can almost picture him gliding on the ice. Obviously, with the way he ran into me earlier, I can picture him body slamming someone into the boards as well. I wonder if his teammates know that he's gay?

I'm dying of thirst and as much as I don't want to get up—I just want to lie there and think about Declan—nature is calling and she's not gonna wait. Without Kirby on, I have to pay attention to how I walk. My right foot is totally dropped, which means when I lift it, it dangles down, limp and useless. Part of its uselessness is that it doesn't push off the ground when I'm walking either. As such, I have to lift my hip and knee up when I walk, so it looks like I'm marching. Well, marching on one side. I watch my foot as I put it back on the ground to make sure that the foot is flat and not rolling one way or the other. I've sprained my ankle more than one time by rolling it out because I was trying to walk too fast without the brace on. I've learned that there is a price to pay when I try to hurry through things.

After I've gone to the bathroom, I unwrap the plastic cup from the cellophane. Not caring that it's tap water, I fill the cup and gulp it down. I repeat this about three times until I feel a bit more hydrated. I decide to bring a cup of water with me, just for good measure. Gingerly high stepping out of the bathroom, I find that Declan is indeed awake. He's still lying on the bed, but he's propped up on his side, and he's watching me. I make it around to the middle aisle between the two beds and place the cup on the nightstand. He's placed his own bottle of water on his side of the nightstand. Where did he get that? I push the pillows up against the headboard and sit down with my back against them. Extending my legs out in front of me, I cross the right ankle over the left and look over at Declan, who is watching me intently. I know he wants to know all about the leg. I just don't know that I'm ready to tell him yet.

I look at my pale feet and thank heavens that my toes are nicely painted. I got a pedicure just three days ago in preparation for this trip. It always freaked out the girls in the spa to have to work on my leg. The language barrier is too much to explain to them that my foot is fine. I can feel the bottom of it. It is just the top and outside that I can't feel. I think Kirby scares them. It scares a lot of people. This round, I chose a bright, almost neon pink for my toes. The winter had been stretching on entirely too long and I wanted something that seemed tropical.

My bright pink toes dance up and down as I wiggle them. That is, I wiggle my left toes. Try as I might, the right toes don't budge. Staring at them, I finally see a flicker of movement in my pinky toe, but that's it. Sandy, my physical therapist, had been over and over what all the muscles are, but I can't remember them all. What's the use in remembering them when they can't remember to work in the first place?

Sandy had used different electrical stimulation techniques on my foot, trying to bring it back. Trying to keep the muscles from atrophying fully. From wasting away. It was hard to tell if it was working. I didn't want to wait to find out, so I gave up. What was the point when most of the muscle was dead? According to the doctors, it was *"highly unlikely"* that my nerves and muscles would regenerate. True, there was a slim chance, but I wasn't pinning my hopes on it. Sandy told me that peripheral nerves could regenerate at some ridiculously slow rate, like one millimeter a month or something like that. It was too long to wait. Even if the nerve did regenerate, there was little viable muscle left for it to innervate. Quite literally, but the damage was already done.

"I'm going back to school in the fall," Declan volunteers out of nowhere.

I look over at him. "Really? What for?"

"I'm going to school to be a physical therapist."

I roll my eyes and groan inwardly. Okay, maybe a little outwardly too.

"What's that groan for? I take it you're familiar with physical therapy?"

"All too much. Actually, I love my PT. She's the one who convinced me to get into sales with my company. If I hadn't moved, I think Sandy and I would be hanging out frequently. I should probably call her. It's been a while since I talked to her." I remember that he said earlier he had used a TENS unit for pain control on his back. "I take it you've seen your fair share of therapy as well?"

"Yes I have."

I don't want to hear his details because it will be like old soldiers trading war stories. I don't want to reveal my recollections from the foxhole just yet. Well, I never do, but I certainly don't want to tell Declan. Changing direction, I ask, "Where are you going to go to school? Michigan I presume?"

"Yeah, I've been taking classes there forever. I've gotten all the prereq courses out of the way."

"Wait—you're thirty-one? Have you been in school since you were eighteen? That's, like, forever." I knew I was treading dangerous water, asking about the past. But the thought of being in school for all those years was just unfathomable.

"No, yes, not really."

"Well, that's about as clear as mud." I hesitated for a moment and then continue. "This is going to sound odd, but you know that I'm odd by this point. I don't want to hear about the main thing that you do."

"The main thing—you mean the—"

I cut him off before he could finish. "Yes, that main thing that has interrupted your schooling. I don't want to talk about it."

"Why?" I could hear the puzzlement in his voice. He continues quietly, "That's what everyone wants to hear about."

"I'm not everyone, in case you hadn't noticed. Please just—I have my reasons for not wanting to hear about it." I look away and rest my head against the headboard, staring at the ceiling. I think that was the longest I had maintained eye contact with anyone in forever. It made me uneasy, like I might start caring about something again. I keep talking, prattling on. "I started community college in New York after I finished high school. But then I moved to Utah and took a few years off. I tried taking a few classes at BYU but it was too long of a commute. Plus, I kept getting hit on by all these Mormon missionaries who wanted me to convert. So I stopped taking classes."

"Because you were getting hit on?"

"No, because they were trying to convert me. I wanted no part of it."

"Are you otherwise religious?" He reaches over and unscrews his water bottle. Out of my periphery, I see him start to take a drink.

"No, not really. I just didn't want to give up booze, coffee, and sex. I enjoy them all far too much."

Apparently that statement is just too much for Declan as he spits his water across the room, sputtering and choking. I look over at him and see the shocked look on his face. "What?" I ask. Not ask, challenge.

A grin—a sinful one—spreads over his face as he wipes his mouth. "Nothing, just not what I expected to hear."

"You said you only do honesty. That was me being honest."

******

5:36 p.m.: Declan

Holy crap, she did not just say that? My immediate impulse is to order her a shit load of booze and see what happens. Of course, I've just spit my water all over myself, so I doubt that will count in my favor. I look over at her to see what her face is telling me.

"You said you only do honesty. That was me being honest." She has a shit-eating grin on her face. Damn, I think I love this woman.

Well, not love. Lust. I lust this woman.

She continues. "I like to swear a lot too, but I've been trying to give that up."

"Why the fuck would you do something like that?"

She grins at me. It is a wicked, evil grin. I haven't seen her this relaxed, not even when she was toasted earlier today. Holy cow, was that really just a few hours ago?

"Because Richard—my boss—told me it was *unprofessional* to swear while talking to customers." She makes little air quotes when she says unprofessional.

"I had no idea that could be considered unprofessional." I make the same air quotes back at her.

"Yeah, just reason five-hundred and sixty-seven of why I suck at my job."

"You don't really suck, do you?" As soon as I say it, I realize how it could be interpreted. Hey, maybe it will give her an idea or two.

"Yes, no. I don't know."

Obviously she missed the double-entendre. Good. Or not.

"Why did you take the job in the first place?"

She's quiet for a moment. "Sandy thought I'd be good at it. Having personal experience and all. And I needed to do something. I had no idea what I wanted to do." She shrugs. "I guess I still don't."

"So this was an unplanned career change?"

"You could say that. This is what I call my *After* life. Not as in Heaven, but as in my life *After*." She emphasizes the word after with unmistakable bitterness.

"After what?"

"As opposed to *Before*."

She's talking in circles again. She had talked like this before too. I wish she would just explain the before and after stuff. I wait for a minute, taking another drink. I doubt any raunchy or revealing comments are about to come out of her mouth. She sits quietly for a minute and then scrambles to stand up on the bed.

I swing my feet onto the floor and am now facing her. She's standing on her bed, looking at me. Then, she folds her body into an impossibly low crouch. I have no idea what she is doing or why.

"What are you doing?"

"What does it look like?"

"If I knew, I wouldn't be asking you."

Adjusting her stance, testing out her balance on the bed she says, "Imitation jumps."

"I guess the question should be what are imitation jumps and why are you doing them?"

I watch her. She's still folded in half. Her right leg looks like it is working overtime just to keep her balance. "So are you just going to hang there like that?"

"No, but I need to mentally prepare myself. I wonder if I can still do it."

"Okay." This chick does have a lot of mood swings. Shit.

"I was starting to feel bad again, thinking about the *Before* and *After*. But then I started trying to remember the last time I felt good. And it was when I was jumping. This is not the same. It is nowhere near the same."

"What are you, some kind of crazy adrenaline junky or something?"

"You could say that. I used to be fearless."

"Used to be?"

She doesn't answer, but tells me to bend over and touch my toes. I give her a skeptical look but do it anyway. The stretch feels surprisingly good on my back.

"Okay, Declan, whatever you do, don't move."

What the hell could she be doing?

I feel a large thud as she lands, belly first on the bed next to me.

"Why'd I have to bend over?" I say as I sit up.

A little bit breathless, she replies, "I didn't want you to see me jump."

"You're a bit weird, you know that?"

She flips over and is lying on her back. Her legs hang off the bed, next to mine. "I've been told that, although not recently."

"Why not recently?"

"Because I've been too bitter and miserable to talk to anyone recently. People just think I'm a bitch." She stands up and does a few squats. She assumes her crouch position, pauses for a moment, and then she bounds across back to her bed.

"Didn't your mother ever tell you not to jump on the bed?"

"Nope. Keep up! I told you—my mom left us when I was four. Said she was going out for groceries and never came back. I missed out on a lot of that informative mom stuff."

"Who's us? You didn't tell me that."

"My dad and my older brother, Kevin. Dad did the best he could but missed a lot of the finer points."

"So, that's why you got upset and walked away. When I asked about your mom?"

She's lying on her bed, facing the ceiling. Her legs are hanging off the side of the bed. I stare at her pink toes. Looking at her feet in this relaxed position, I can't tell that one of them doesn't work right.

"Yeah, probably. I don't know why it bothered me today. I mean, she's been gone for twenty-five years. She didn't want to be a mom. We were probably better off without her. Dad did a good job with Kev and me. I mean, maybe if she'd been around I would be a little more girly. I wish I could be more feminine."

To me, she's plenty feminine. She's soft and curvy. Her hair frames her face in a natural way. She plays with her hair all the time. I bet she doesn't even know she does it.

"What do you mean by that?"

"You know, like makeup and stuff like that. I'm a tomboy."

"You think makeup makes a girl?" Now this is an area where I actually know something. Occupational hazard.

"Yeah. I mean, I wear some, but I don't know how to make myself up all fancy and stuff."

"Fancy isn't always better. A lot of time, fancy is just used to mask what is underneath. If you've nothing to hide, you don't need to cover it up. And you, my dear, have nothing to hide."

She blushes. I can tell she's not used to compliments. Who the hell has she been hanging around with who doesn't compliment her? She stands up and starts to test out her crouch again. I think this might be a diversionary tactic. When she doesn't want to talk, she starts jumping again. This time, I want to get more out of her.

I stand up so I can reach out to her and stop her from moving. However, as I've reached full standing, she launches herself over toward my bed again. This time, I'm standing in the way and she plows right into me. Reflexively, I grab onto her, my arms encircling her mid section. Her momentum is too much, however, and we fall backwards onto the bed.

She lets out a little bit of an "oomph" when we land. She's lying right on top of me, her body pressed into mine. My hands are still around her waist and her arms are reaching around my shoulders, clinging to me.

Dear Jesus, thank you.

Chapter Eight
5:48 p.m.: Kaitlin

I know this talk is going to make me feel bad. I can already feel the darkness closing in on my heart. I've never told anyone about *Before* and *After*. I can't even believe I've said those words aloud. Why did I have to go there? Why couldn't I have just told Declan about the swear jar that Richard made me start? Why did I have to start babbling about this? He's going to think I'm nuts. I have to do something. I need to get up and move or I'll scream.

Before I even know what I'm doing, I'm standing and getting into my crouched, in-run position. I've assumed this position a thousand times, standing on a block, readying myself to jump up onto my coach's arms to practice my take off. Imitation jumps. The off slope training used to involve jumping over and over, camera rolling so we could analyze my form before I got on the jump. All I can think is how I miss it. That moment of taking off. How much I miss soaring through the air, skis pointed out in a V, body leaning forward. The wind rushing past, the feeling of flying.

This is nothing like that, and I'm not even sure I can do it anymore. My ankles feel tight and the backs of my calves are screaming, just getting into this position. I've lost so much range of motion. Of course, I can barely squat when I'm wearing my brace. I'd never be able to get into this position.

Declan, of course, thinks I've lost it. He asks me what I'm doing. I give him a snarky response. He continues to question me about why I'm standing on the bed, tucked in half.

I want to be honest. So I tell him I want to see if I can still do it. He's trying to digest that when I continue. "I was starting to feel bad again, thinking about the *Before* and *After*. But then I started trying to remember the last time I felt good. And it was when I was jumping. This is not the same. It is nowhere near the same."

He asks me if I'm an adrenaline junky. The answer is yes. I was addicted to the high I got when my skis left the jump, and there was nothing beneath my feet, when I was defying gravity. That rush when you let go of the bar and there is nothing to stop you. Now I'm an addict without a drug to fuel the addiction. I don't want to think of myself that way. I'd rather think of myself as someone who used to be fearless.

"Used to be?" he questions.

How do I tell him that without the rush I get from soaring through the air, I have nothing? I want to try and jump across to his bed, but I'm afraid I won't get enough push off. My quads are not what they used to be, my glutes and core are flabby, and, well, we all know the right foot is useless.

"Bend over and touch your toes." I instruct him. He complies. I contemplate trying to jump over him but figure I'll never make it. Once upon a time, I could have made that jump, no sweat.

"Okay, Declan, whatever you do, don't move," I say as I launch myself over to his bed.

When I land, he sits up and looks at me. He tells me I'm weird. For some reason, it doesn't bother me. I roll over and let my feet dangle off the bed next to his.

It does, however, bother me to admit that I don't talk to anyone anymore because of my attitude. I'm a poor excuse for a human being. I want him to think better of me. Not to see that I'm broken goods, both physically and emotionally.

"Didn't your mother ever tell you not to jump on the bed?"

This time, it doesn't bother me when he brings up my mother. Only when I'm really down does talking about her bother me. I came to terms with it a long time ago. She left us. It was because she was defective, not us. Not me. Although, sometimes, when I'm really blue, I forget that. Declan caught me in a vulnerable moment this morning. I jump back to my bed to distract myself. And to move myself away from him. Being near him is tempting. Too tempting. I just want to reach out and touch him.

I know the jumping is weird. But in a very odd way, it is making me feel good. Like I'm still the person I used to be. The Kaitlin I liked.

I hear myself telling Declan that I wished my mom was around so I wasn't such a tomboy and so plain. I wished I knew how to curl my hair or put false eyelashes on. I've never told anyone that before.

"Fancy isn't always better. A lot of time, fancy is just used to mask and hide what is underneath. If you've nothing to hide, you don't need to cover it up. And you, my dear, have nothing to hide."

When he says this, I feel my face growing warm. It is the nicest thing anyone has said to me in a very, very long time. I don't know how to take it, so I cope by getting up and getting ready to jump again. I bounce a few times before lowering myself into my crouch. Now I'm ready to launch myself back to his bed. I don't realize he's standing up until I'm in mid-air, crashing into him.

He catches me, latching his arms around me. For like the fourth time today. My forward momentum is too much and we topple over onto his bed, me planted squarely on top of him. My hands have come over his shoulders to break the fall on the bed. He is holding tightly onto me. His body feels so good pressed into mine.

I look up to meet his gaze, those hazel eyes now only inches from mine. Our noses are practically touching. I can't breathe. I want nothing more than to close the small gap between our mouths. I'm panting slightly. Partly because the jumping has me winded. Mostly because I'm lying on top of Declan.

"I think you got a sixth-tenths deduction on that landing from the Russian judge." His smile grows wide. His eyes crinkle.

Without thinking, I reply, "No, not the Russian judge. It was always the Austrian judge who marked me down on style points. Heartless bitch."

He laughs. "The Germans hated us." Then his eyes grow serious and darken. If I didn't know better, I would think it was with lust. Somehow, his hands have crept underneath my sweater and shirt and are on my bare back.

His touch has me on fire. I can barely think as he gently caresses my skin.

"Why?"

I can feel him shrug underneath me. "I don't know exactly. I mean it's not like Germany is known for its figure skating. Of course, Ireland has never been a threat before either."

"You're a figure skater?" I don't know why this is a surprise to me. I mean, I already know he's gay. He lives in Pontiac, which is a big hub for training. Even so, he just seems too masculine to be a figure skater.

He meets my gaze again. "Is that a problem?"

"Nope, not at all. Just not what I, ah, expected." I guess that was not lust in his eyes. Dammit. He's so, ugh— I'm so turned on right now. If he's a figure skater, then he's definitely gay. I struggle to get up, but he's still holding on tightly to me.

"Kaitlin, just stay there for a minute, okay?"

I rest my head down on his chest. It is firm, and I can hear his heart beating. Every time I inhale, my breasts press into him, turning me on even more.

I know this is wrong. First, I've just met him. Second, he's gay so I shouldn't throw myself at him. And thirdly (and this is the biggie), I'm still married.

He strokes my back as we lie in silence. Finally, I can't stand it anymore.

"Why do you want me to stay here?" I had to be crushing him. I was not a lightweight wisp of a girl. I slide off to the side.

He shifts me slightly and I can feel his mouth against my hair, just above my ear. "Because you need someone to hold you and tonight that's going to be me."

******

6:02 p.m.: Declan

I can't help it. I have to touch her skin. I have to find out if it is as soft as it looks. She doesn't flinch as my hands move under her shirt. Jesus—how many layers does she have on here? Oh, no, this is a mistake, touching her. I'm not going to be able to stop.

I say something and she replies. I have no idea what I just said. I can't even focus on what she's saying back to me. I'm simply staring at those full lips. I can barely even process that they're forming words. I just want to taste them. To bite them. To suck on them. Somehow, one part of my brain is still functioning the way it should and is managing to carry on my end of the conversation. She's breathing heavy. Is it possible that she wants this as much as I do?

I look at her. She looks like she's holding back. All I need to do is tighten my grip and the millimeters of space between our lips will disappear. She licks her lips but pulls back slightly. A mixed message if ever I saw one. I shift her to the side slightly. I'm growing hard again and I don't want her to find out. The expression on her face obviously shows some kind of conflict. She's just opening up to me, and I don't want her to shut down again.

She puts her head down on my chest and snuggles in. I tell her that I intend on holding her all night. She's got to figure out whatever it is she's working on. I'm too invested in her to literally screw her over right now. No matter how much I might want to.

I don't know what to do next. I want to flip her over, get on top and tear off her shirt. She's unusually quiet though. I wonder if the moment has passed for her.

At that moment, my stomach lets out a rather loud and altogether unattractive growl.

"Was that you?" she asks, propping herself up on her elbow. She's totally on the side of me now, except for her right leg, with is draped casually over my legs.

I smile. "Apparently, it's feeding time at the zoo."

She sits up and I do as well. I try to adjust myself on the way up. She's running her fingers through her hair again, trying to pull it back into a ponytail. It's not long enough and falls back down around her face. After years (and years) of being around women who shellacked every strand of hair into place, I find the movement in a woman's hair beautiful.

She stands up and takes the three steps back to her bed. I can see her foot drop now when she walks. She bends over and retrieves her socks and brace from the floor.

I can't help but watch her, in fascination, as she sets about donning her brace.

She looks up at me and sees me watching her. "What?" The bitterness is back in her voice and is unmistakable.

"Just watching you." I pause. I know whatever I say is going to come out wrong. It's a gift I have. "It's interesting."

"No, it's not. It's grotesque."

I can't believe she thinks of herself that way. "You wanna see grotesque? You should see backstage at the ice arena. There's make-up flying, enough hair spray to choke a horse, and sequins and feathers everywhere. And that's just the men's dressing room."

She laughs. Mission accomplished. She's quickly pulled on her boots and I notice that as soon as her brace is covered up, her mood improves. Ben, my psychologist, would have a field day with this one. I wonder how Kaitlin would take it if I gave her Ben's number. Ben's a sports psychologist, so I doubt if he would even be able to take Kaitlin on as a client.

And at that moment, it occurs to me—I need to find out what happened to Kaitlin.

"Is there a restaurant downstairs?" she asks, disrupting my thoughts.

"Yeah, I think." I get up and start looking in the drawers and finally find what I'm looking for on the desk. I pick up the room phone and call down to the restaurant, to get a table. They have one at seven-thirty. I look at the clock. It is twenty after six now. The polite young man on the phone suggests the lounge to get a drink while we wait for our table.

I hang up and relay this information to Kaitlin. She looks down at her clothes.

"I'm not dressed appropriately."

The brochure tells me what I need to know. "Dress is casual."

She shakes her head. "Can I have a few minutes to freshen up and change?"

I shrug. "Sure. Table won't be ready until seven-thirty."

She picks up her bag and heads into the bathroom. After she closes the door, I look down at what I'm wearing. Faded jeans, thermal Henley. I decide I can use a freshening up as well and pull a blue button down shirt out of my bag. I shake it out and put it on. I trade my faded jeans for a dark pair and adjust myself in my boxer briefs again. Damn this girl has me all sorts of twisted up.

I get out my travel bag, which is an old-fashioned leather shaving kit that I inherited from my father. His initials, which don't match my own, are embossed in the faded brown leather. It drives Natalya crazy that the monogram is wrong. She has bought me no less than two others and can't understand why I don't use them. I dig out my hair gel and run a little through my hair. Another coat of deodorant won't hurt, so I use that too.

She steps out of the bathroom. The transformation is incredible. But she's the same too. She has on a shirt-sweater thing that is the green of the Irish flag. It is big, but clings in all the right places. One of her shoulders is bare in a sexy-Flashdance sort of way. She still has the leggings and boots on. Her face is glowing.

For once in my life, I'm speechless.

Chapter Nine
6:33 p.m.: Kaitlin

I close the toilet lid and sit down, trying to process what just happened. When I was lying in Declan's arms, I felt more content than I had in forever. He gives me a sense of warmth and security that I had forgotten even existed. When I'm with him, it's like we're in our own private world and none of the outside stuff matters.

Sometimes he chatters on, but when we were on the bed, he was quiet. I wish I knew what he was thinking about. Probably counting the moments until I'd get off of him. I hope he didn't mind too much because I loved it.

I wish I knew what he was thinking.

I wish he wasn't gay.

I wish I wasn't married.

I need to stop wishing the time away and get ready to go down to dinner. I rifle through my bag and pull out my green tunic sweater. I won't need to change my pants and boots to go with it. It's clingy in the right places, but forgiving in those others that need a little help. The best part is it shows a little shoulder, which to me is sexy. I touch up my make-up as best I can, which for me is a little powder, a little blush, some mascara and lip-gloss. I comb my hair, wishing again that I hadn't cut it in this short bob. I want to be able to braid it again and get it off my face. I'm pleased with the results, though. I always used to be pretty confident in how I looked. I've lost that over the past two years. But right now, I feel pretty good about myself. At least for the moment.

I walk out of the bathroom and he stops me in my tracks. He's changed too. His hair is slicked down in an unbelievably sexy way. He's wearing a fitted blue button-down shirt that makes his hazel eyes seem almost green. His black jeans hit his hips in a way that makes me think all sorts of impure thoughts. God, it's not fair. He's got an adorable personality, but he's great looking at the same time. After lying on top of him, I can tell he's made of muscle, and that shirt certainly confirms it. He's warm and caring, and funny to top it all off.

And gay. I have to keep telling myself that.

He just stands there looking at me for a minute. I thought I looked good, but now I'm rethinking the outfit. I always had an athletic build, but the softening of my muscle (in other words, turning to fat) gave me a curvy appearance that I wasn't used to. I was still learning how to dress my body. Apparently, this was not the right way to go.

"Ready?" he finally speaks.

Dropping my head, I mumble affirmatively. I grab my wallet out of my purse and tuck my room key into it. I pick up my cell from the desk and head toward the door. Declan has reached the door before me and holds it open so that I may walk through. It is a chivalrous gesture, one to which I'm not accustomed.

If only he weren't him and I weren't me, this would be perfect.

"Are you okay?" he asks as we're headed to the elevator.

"Yeah, sure. Fine. Why?"

"I dunno. You've got this look and you're all quiet now."

"I'm fine."

"You say that a lot, don't you? You tell everybody that you're fine all the time. They believe it, and most of the time, so do you."

We're in the elevator and the doors close, leaving us encased with his words hanging in the air. I feel trapped. Trapped by the doors. Trapped by his words. Trapped by my own inability to deal with my life. I'm finding it hard to catch my breath.

He continues. "You wanna run right now, don't you? Admit it: If you weren't trapped in this elevator, you'd have taken off by now."

Dammit. How does he know me so well already? I nod, hoping he won't continue. But he does. We're standing side by side. I cannot look at him right now. I clench my hand into a tight fist. The wallet and phone are in my other hand. I clench those too.

"And everybody just lets you run away. No one tries to stop you, do they? They just let you go."

Finally, I find my voice. With a bit of indignation, I stick my chin out. I say, "It's what I want them to do. I don't want anyone to stop me."

"Really?" He grabs me by the shoulders, turning me to face him and looks down at me. I can't maintain his eye contact so I drop my head. "No, Kaitlin, look at me. Let me look at you. I don't think you want to run away. I think you want someone to stop you. I think you want someone to care." He shakes me slightly so I have to look at him.

The elevator doors open, and I use the distraction to break free of his grasp. I head toward the restaurant and wait for Declan to check in. I look around. I still can't look at him. We walk in silence over to the lounge and find two seats at the bar that are just being vacated. I slide into my seat, still refusing to look at him.

"Why do you care?" I finally say after the bartender has taken our orders. Blue Moon for me, Grey Goose and tonic for him.

He smiles as the attractive bartender with the big boobs slides our drinks in front of us. She fawns over him like every other female does. He's friendly with her, just as he was with the ticketing agent. Just as he is with me. I'm nothing special to him. I'm nothing.

After he's generously tipped the boobs, guaranteeing us prompt service as long as we're sitting here, he swivels his chair to face me. His knees are touching my legs. I continue staring straight ahead.

"I don't know why I care Kaitlin. Certainly not because you've been so warm and forthcoming. I never know what to say because you're so edgy. So, I don't know why I care ... but I do. And that should be enough."

In a small voice that I'm not even sure he'll be able to hear over the din of the lounge I say, "No one cares. That's the problem. No one cares."

Apparently, he could hear me because he slams his hand down on the bar, making me jump. "Enough!"

I look at him, a little shocked. "Enough what?"

"Enough of this wallowing in self-pity. Whatever it is, you need to work through it. Talk about it, get it out of your system. You need to stop ruminating about it. Move on."

I take a drink of my beer. Holding the frosty glass in my hands, I stare at it for a moment. Finally, it occurs to me. "You're right." I turn my head to look at him. "I need help. I know I do. It's, ah, I've ..." I break off, not sure of what to say next. Taking a deep breath, I continue. "I don't even know where to start. Would it make sense to say that I'm totally lost?"

He smiles and leans in, putting his head—no, his lips—on my bare shoulder. After a moment, he lifts his head slightly and says, "I think you feel that way certainly. Maybe it's true; maybe it's just your perception of the situation. But what is true is that you're never going to be anything but miserable if you don't deal with it."

My shoulder feels cold where his lips have been. It wasn't a kiss, not really. Why does he keep doing this to me? Doesn't he know he's making my situation worse? Because, on top of it all, the last thing I need to add to my pile is falling for someone who can never love me back.

I swivel my chair, my knees facing his. One hand remains on the bar, holding tight to my beer. The other is in my lap, fidgeting with the hem of my sweater. "You're right. I know you're right. It's just ... I've been, um, so shut down for so long that I don't even know where to start." He reaches over and takes my hand.

"You said that already. Instead of hemming and hawing about where to start, just start. It doesn't matter if it's the beginning. Just start."

I take another drink of my beer while he holds tightly onto my right hand. I hope I can do this. I have to.

******

6:47 p.m.: Declan

The silence in the elevator is more than awkward—it's downright uncomfortable. I want to take this beautiful, damaged woman in my arms right now, but I know I can't. This whole thing—being with her—is a bad idea. It is going to end badly. I know it is, but I can't help myself. And I've never been one to deny myself either. That's why I pay Frankie the big bucks to keep me in line.

Taking her by the shoulders, I just want to shake some sense into her. She's on the verge of running away. It occurs to me that she is not that dissimilar to Natalya. They both throw tantrums. Kaitlin runs away, and Nat literally throws things. Usually at me. It's one of the reasons why Nat and I broke up. I couldn't handle her temper. I implore Kaitlin to face her demons.

"No, Kaitlin, look at me. Let me look at you. I don't think you want to run away. I think you want someone to stop you. I think you want someone to care." I do end up shaking her, but gently. I don't want to hurt her.

The elevator doors open, pulling my focus from her. She uses the diversion to break free. I expect her to run away, but she heads toward the restaurant. She doesn't look at me. Frankly, she is working overtime looking around at the restaurant.

But she follows me into the lounge. Two businessmen get up from their seats at the bar, and without hesitation she slides into hers. Within moments, the bartender has zeroed in on me. Does she not see the woman that I am with? Does she think I'm going to abandon Kaitlin for a romp in the back room or something? Kaitlin orders a beer and I get a drink.

Finally Kaitlin speaks. In a quiet voice I hear her say, "Why do you care?"

I don't answer right away because the bartender has come back. I smile politely at the bartender as she places our drinks in front of us and tip her generously. Frankie has taught me well.

I turn to face Kaitlin but she is stubbornly staring straight ahead. I'm honest with her when I tell her I don't know why I care. I don't know. I just know she's gotten under my skin. And then when she starts spouting about how no one cares, it pushes me over the edge. I slam my hand down on the bar.

"Enough!"

She starts babbling about how she doesn't know where to start, still staring straight ahead. Her shoulder is bare. That damn sweater. I smile at her, but I can't focus on what she's saying. Again. Before I can stop myself, I realize I'm leaning in to that delicious shoulder. Just as my lips touch her shoulder, I stop myself. She stills. I expect her to back-hand me but she doesn't.

Again, I have no idea what I say to her. But whatever it is, it works because she turns toward me. Her left hand is still holding onto her beer while her right hand is in her lap. She's playing with the bottom of her sweater, a sure sign of nervousness. I place my hand on top of hers, unable to resist touching her in some way, giving her the encouragement she needs to start. And then she finally does.

I wish I had kept my big mouth shut.

"I guess the least of my problems, but a big one nonetheless, is that my marriage is in the toilet."

Boom. There it is. She's married. Damn it all. I can't help myself from saying, "Oh, you're married?" I want to pull my hand back, but I don't. It's not that I don't want to be holding her hand, 'cause I do. It's that I shouldn't be doing it. "Why do you think your marriage is in trouble?

"Well, let's start with the fact that my husband doesn't love me. I'm no longer useful to him in his life aspirations."

"How does one become no longer useful?" I take this chance to remove my hand from hers and pick up my glass. I take a slow, thoughtful sip. I don't want her to feel deserted.

"He had hitched himself firmly to my coattails. But, of course, I didn't realize this until I no longer had coattails left for him to ride. Thus, I've outlasted my usefulness."

"Does this have to do with your, uh ..." I glance down toward her legs, "... injury?"

"It has everything to do with my injury." She takes a long drink. I do as well.

"Oh, and then there's the fact that he's screwing everything that walks by."

I choke on my drink as she says this. Unexpectedly, she laughs. "That's twice I've made you spit your drink out."

"I didn't expect you to say that. You often don't say what I expect you to."

At that moment, the hostess comes up and tells us our table is ready. Kaitlin picks up her beer, finishes it, and leaves the glass on the bar. I take my drink with me. I need to keep my wits about me now that I know she's off limits.

We're seated at a small table next to a granite pool. The restaurant is set in the middle of the lobby, with the rooms looking down on it as if it were a courtyard. We situate ourselves and are quiet for a moment while we peruse the menu.

When she sets her menu down, I expect her to continue, but she doesn't. She seems a million miles away. The waitress appears and Kaitlin orders a water. I follow suit. Alcohol will only make this night more difficult. Plus, I'm too old to get drunk twice in one day.

Chapter Ten
7:32 p.m.: Kaitlin

Did I see a look of repulsion on his face when I said I was married? No, I'm just being paranoid. I'm projecting my own feelings of disgust at my behavior. I shouldn't be disgusted by my behavior. I was totally justified. Tyler is a louse and a lying, cheating louse at that. And somewhere, way deep down, I blame him for my leg.

I laugh as Declan chokes on his drink for the second time tonight. Is it me, or does he have an issue whenever I mention sex? That was probably the most depressing thing about my failing marriage. We never had sex anymore. Well, not since I found out what he was doing. We hadn't been too intimate since my injury. Depression does that.

The hostess tells us that our table is ready. While it gets me off the hook for a few moments, I'm afraid I'm going to lose my courage in the meantime. I drain my beer and put the glass back on the bar. I notice that Declan still has his drink. Perhaps I should take a cue from him and slow down. I don't need to be drunk twice today.

Our table is a cozy little two-top positioned next to a serene granite pool. The whole restaurant is really cool, modern and romantic all at the same time. Sleek granite softened with relaxing bamboo. The hotel rooms circle around above, looking down on the diners. It is fabulous.

The silence has indeed made me lose my nerve. I look over the menu. The grilled chicken salad from lunch seems so long ago. I decide on the seared Michigan walleye entree. I switch to water when the waitress asks and Declan follows suit. Yep, my nerve is gone, so I switch the topic.

"So, Declan, tell me about your partner."

He's taken aback by my question, or at least it seems that way. I do admit that it's a bit out of left field, but like I've said, the best defense is a good offense.

"Um, that's not something I really like to talk about."

Wow, his hackles are up and quickly. Of course, I can't let it go. I have to push. "Why? What's the story?"

"Um," he shifts in his seat. "We're, ah, announcing our split soon."

Interesting. I wonder who he's making this announcement to—family, friends? Do they have any kids together? I ask him that.

"What—kids? No, definitely not." He looks disgusted.

"Sorry, jeez. Didn't mean to get your knickers in a knot there."

"I guess I've never gotten that question before. What made you ask it?"

"I was wondered why you have to announce your split? Why can't you just split up?" I pause for a minute. Then, quietly, I say, "I guess I should ask myself that same question. I wonder why I haven't left Tyler."

He looks at me, waiting for me to continue. Finally, I say, "Okay, so let me pick your brain about splitting up. How did you decide that you're going to do it?"

"It was inevitable. I'm retiring and going to school. There's nothing left to be done otherwise."

I immediately felt bad for Declan that his partner doesn't support him as he leaves his competition days behind him. It occurs to me that maybe Declan and I have a lot more in common than it would appear. Yes, he's a figure skater who is retiring of his own free will, whereas I was forced out by injury. But it appears that his partner is no longer interested in him, as Tyler is no longer interested in me.

"If you weren't retiring?"

He's thoughtful again. Then he says, "I don't know. It would be easy to continue because we've been together for so long. There's that familiarity. That comfort. But in all honesty, we don't get along and haven't in a very long time. It is hard to stay with someone you don't like or respect. Especially when you don't even have the physical part anymore. I mean it's been years since any of that happened."

Years? Holy crap. Poor guy. "So you can empathize with what I'm going through then, I guess. Tyler doesn't like or respect me, that's for sure. He could never treat me the way he does if he had any kind of respect for me."

"And what about you? You've mentioned that your husband doesn't love you and he doesn't respect you. How do you feel about him?"

This question makes me pause. It shouldn't, but it does. In all of my ruminating and stewing and festering, I've never really stopped to think about how I feel about Tyler. I tell Declan that.

"And why do you think that is?"

I know what that answer is. I don't want to say it aloud though. I haven't stopped to think about Tyler because I haven't stopped to think. I've just been stuck in an endless cycle of anger. Once again, I am saved by the impeccable timing of the restaurant staff as our meal is served.

The food is richly delicious and much nicer than anything I've had in a long while. We eat in companionable silence. I don't know what Declan is thinking about, but I'm thinking about how my life will be different after this day. First things first, I'm going to divorce Tyler. Second, I'm actually going to put forth effort in my job and try not to suck. As we're scraping our plates, I tell Declan what I've decided.

He smiles in encouragement. "Good. I think that's a step in the right direction."

The bill arrives and there is that awkward moment. I snatch it out of Declan's hands. He begins to protest, but I reach across the table and put one finger over his lips to shush him. "Stop. I've got this. You've been nothing but kind to me all day, even when—especially when I didn't deserve it. This is a trivial thing, but let me do it."

Declan concedes, but it is apparent that he's not happy about it. Grumbling, he says, "Where I come from, women don't pick up the bill for the men."

We're up from the table and walking out of the restaurant. "And where exactly was that—the stone age?" I elbow him playfully in the ribs. My arm then brushes against his, and with an impulse I can't control, I take his hand in mine. It is a bold move I know, but it's not like it means anything to him. God, I wish it meant something to him.

We hold hands back to the elevator and until we get to our room. Suddenly, the silence is awkward as the preparations for bed begin. We've got to be up at an un-Godly hour, so turning in now is totally acceptable. I'm beat from the day I've had. I again go to the bathroom, this time changing into my flannel pajama pants and oversized t-shirt. My teeth are brushed and my contacts are out. The brace is off for the night, so I continue my high-stepping around the room.

He goes into the bathroom next, while I flip through the channels, trying to find something to watch on TV. Nothing appeals to me, so I pull out my *People*. The dog-eared page tells me where I left off. I flip to the next page. And then I see why Declan was so hell bent against me reading this magazine.

Staring back at me is a mostly-naked Declan. My mouth instantly waters at the sight, and I feel a tingling sensation that I haven't felt in a long time. Dear God, this man is a thing of beauty. Broad shoulders, abs that look chiseled out of granite, all leading down into that deep V that is so appealing on a man. He has an Olympic medal around his neck and not much else on. I read the blurb, although it is generic and does nothing to tell how special this man really is.

Well, that explains all the attention from the female staff. The baseball hat and the selfies with the Delta clerk.

I lick my lips, staring at the picture, when suddenly the bathroom door opens. Holy shit, I'd forgotten he was right there! Startled, I throw the magazine across the room.

"What was that?" He looks over in the corner, where it had bounced off the wall and landed down by the desk.

He's wearing gym shorts and a t-shirt. All I can see is his naked chest. I swallow hard. I close my eyes and remind myself that he has no interest in me. He's made his way over to the corner and picks up the magazine.

He picks it up distastefully and with disappointment in his voice says, "You saw, didn't you?"

******

7:47 p.m.: Declan

Why is she asking about Natalya? I thought we were talking about her. She was opening up about her marriage. This, I was interested to hear. I mean, if her marriage is over, then ... then what? What does that mean for me? But now, here she is, changing the topic, putting the focus on me. I tell her the truth, that Natalya and I are splitting up. It will be public knowledge soon enough. Frankie is counting on heartbroken fans to gobble up the tickets for our tour. Frankly, I hope they do as well. The financial payout is the only thing that makes staying with Natalya worthwhile.

It's difficult to describe what's between Natalya and me. I can't stand her—I really can't. She's irritated me from day one. But, on the other hand, she has a fire and tenacity that can be enticing and appealing. She's definitely been my motivating factor. On the ice together, we just fit. Frankly, we fit in the bedroom too. It was just all that in between stuff that got too hard for me to deal with.

And then she asks me if we have kids together? Where the hell did that come from? Natalya and I haven't been a couple in that kind of way in about five years. We broke up before the Vancouver Olympics, which most likely was one of the major reasons we tanked there. Our coach, who was also Natalya's uncle, screamed and berated us until we moved past the romantic break up. We both screwed enough faceless, nameless people during those first two years apart. Always in competition, she had to bring home someone every time I did. Yes, it was wrong, and I am ashamed of my behavior during that time. But good God, kids with Natalya? It would be like mating with a rabid pit bull.

I don't understand why Kaitlin is confused about our split. Since we're no longer a couple, there's no need for us to stay together after I retire. Kaitlin looks across the table with a sadness in her eyes. I hope she doesn't start carrying on about how she loves to watch us skate and how she wishes I wouldn't retire. Then I realize it—Kaitlin never talks about my skating. She talks to me as me, not as an Olympic medalist. She doesn't want the gory details. I can't remember the last person who didn't want the gory details. Maybe that's why she's so appealing to me.

Now she's looking at me with what I can only say is pity in her eyes when I talk about retiring. I guess no one but another athlete can understand why I would want to retire. Why I'm just so tired. Why I'm done with abusing my body. Why I need to move on. Why I need a break from Natalya. Why I need a break from the limelight and all the attention.

Trying to turn the attention back on her, I ask her how she feels about her husband. She's been clear that he does not love her but has never indicated what her feelings are. She escapes answering my probing questions when our dinners are served. I try not to stare as I watch her eat her meal. Every time she brings her fork to her lips, all I can think about is tasting those same lips. I know that it is clichéd, but now that I know she is unavailable, I want her even more.

The food is good, I guess, I think. I'm focusing on her, not what I'm eating. I'm a bit surprised when she tells me that she's decided to end her marriage. I guess that answers that question about her feelings toward her husband. When the check comes, her hand shoots out with lightning quick speed, snatching it from my grasp. I start to protest when she silences me with a single finger. Her finger is on my lips. What would she do if I started sucking on it? Jesus, I needed to get a grip.

I don't like that she's paying for dinner. Ironically, in the past I seemed to have no objection to women wining and dining me. And then I took them to bed without a feeling of guilt that they spent their money to woo me. I gave that all up a few years ago and haven't looked back. I know she's not trying to wine and dine me to woo me. I know she's doing it because she's thankful for what I've done for her today. God, if she only knew what I was thinking about, she'd go running, screaming into downtown Detroit.

"Where I come from, women don't pick up the bill for the men."

She elbows me in the side and makes fun of my age again. Then quietly, quickly, her hand slips into mine, and she holds it warmly as we walk out of the restaurant and toward the bank of elevators. We remain holding hands while in the elevator riding up to our floor. This trip in the elevator is much more pleasant. However, I can almost cut the sexual tension in the air with a knife. Good lord, it's going to be a long evening.

We get to the room and she finally pulls her hand from mine. I just want to grab her again. To hold her all night long.

It's a bit uncomfortable in the room now. I wonder if she knows what I'm thinking. God, I'm an awful person. I've slept with I don't even know how many women, and that never bothered me. But I always drew the line at a married woman. If I knew she was married, she was off limits. I mean, hell, my parents were married for thirty-five years before my dad passed away. They taught me that even when they fought, even when they didn't actually like each other, marriage was a sacred bond that you didn't break. If I hadn't known she was married, I don't know, maybe I could have, hell I know I would have gone for it. But I know that she's married, and I don't think I can ask her to break her vows, even though her husband apparently has. Maybe that's something she needs to work out.

I'm lying on my bed, mulling this all over while she's in the bathroom changing. I try not to think too closely about what she's doing in there, because I only have so much restraint left. She comes out of the bathroom wearing men's flannel pajamas and a faded, worn oversized t-shirt from the 1980 Lake Placid Olympics. I find it humorous that she's wearing an Olympic t-shirt. I mean, what are the odds of that? She's got glasses on, and they give her a different look. She looks scholarly, wise. Certainly wise beyond her years. Like she's been around and seen a lot.

I go into the bathroom and change my own clothes, brush my teeth, and splash some cold water on my face. I think about taking a cold shower because I think it may be what I need to get through the night. Leaving the bathroom, I see her lying on her bed reading that goddamned magazine. She's so engrossed in it that my coming out of the bathroom startles her. She jumps erect and throws the magazine across the room. I walk over and pick it up, and I can tell by the look on her face that she's finally seen me in the magazine.

"You saw, didn't you?" I ask, accusingly.

She looks guilty for a minute and then says, "So I guess this is why you don't want me reading this sort of— what did you call it? Trash?" Her voice is husky and thick. "You know, I wouldn't be all that proud. I mean, you were the last one in the article. It's not like you're hot stuff or anything." She smiles at me, teasing me as my heart melts a little more.

"Oh, c'mon. You know you enjoyed it. I saw you, having a good eyeful."

"Yes, all the other eligible bachelors. I'm plotting who is going to be my next man after I can get my divorce finalized. This seems like a good place to start." She pauses for a moment before continuing. "Of course, it says they're all eligible. I only wish that were true." She sounds wistful.

I wonder what she means by that.

Then, the look on her faces changes. Quietly she says, "So ... you won a medal?" She chokes on the words that come out. They seem difficult for her to even say.

"Um, yeah. The bronze." I pause. "Did you watch?" I sort of stumble over the words, a bit incredulous that she didn't watch the Olympics. I mean, who doesn't watch the Olympics? The whole world watches the Olympics.

She's sitting Indian style on her bed, her hands knit tightly in her lap. She's staring intently at her hands. "No, I didn't watch. I couldn't watch. I didn't follow any coverage about it at all."

"Really? None? None at all? You didn't follow the—"

She cuts me off. "NO. None of it. I didn't want to hear about it." After a moment, she says in a voice so low that I have to walk over to her bed and sit right in front of her to hear, "But ... but you got to stand on the podium?" Another pause. "How was it?"

And I think back to that moment when the officials placed the medals around Natalya's and my necks and gave us the flowers, us waving at the crowd. The deafening roar of the crowd. So what if it wasn't the Irish national anthem playing. I didn't care. We had been eighteenth in the world and not expected to make it as far as we did, let alone to come in third. No, it wasn't the gold, but it was a great note to go out on, and I was pretty happy with it.

"Standing on the podium was like something I'd never dreamed of. It was unbelievable. The weight of the medal around my neck. The smell of the flowers. The roar of the crowd. The—" I stumble on my words, overcome by the emotion of that moment that has resurfaced. "It was one of the best nights of my life."

And then I look over and I see her tears falling into her lap. "Kaitlin, what's wrong? Why are you crying?"

She angrily wipes the tears away. "This is why I didn't want to talk to you about it. I don't want to hear about it. I can't hear about it. It kills me to hear about it."

"What do you mean it kills you to hear about it? How can this—I don't understand." I'm truly lost. I have no idea what she is talking about.

"Your dream was my dream. And it's gone."

"You were a figure skater?" I ask.

She laughs through the tears. "No, not figure skating. I don't skate that well at all. But I had a dream, and it was ripped from me. I got bad guidance, I listened to the wrong people, and I let my own stubbornness take it away from me. And now my dream is gone, and I have nothing left."

She's crying and won't tell me why. I don't know what to do for her. God, I hate it when girls cry. I feel so helpless.

Kaitlin's furiously wiping the tears away. "I'm so sorry I'm crying."

"You don't have to apologize. It happens." I say with a shrug.

"Not to me it doesn't. I don't cry."

I try teasing her a bit to lighten her mood. "Well, I find that hard to believe. This is the second time today I've seen you cry."

She looks up at me, giving me a watery smile. "Maybe it's you. I haven't cried in several years."

"Really?"

"No. I dunno. Maybe I'm broken or something. Hell, I know I'm broken. But nope, I don't cry. I don't know why I did today." She looks at me again, and I swear she can see right through me. "Maybe it's you."

Chapter Eleven
8:46 p.m.: Kaitlin

Oh my God. I can't believe I just said that. Why? Why would I ask him about the Olympics? I know I can't talk about it. And then, he starts telling me what it was like—the podium, the medal, the flowers, the crowd. And all the wounds that I've been trying to ignore—the ones that didn't heal, the inside ones—are ripped wide open again. I can't help it. I'm crying, for the second time today.

I try to play it off, but I just get madder at myself for crying. The anger consumes me and it makes me feel better. Because when I'm angry at people, and I'm angry at myself, I don't hurt. I use it to cover up the pain inside of me. The feeling of loss. The grief that I've never dealt with.

Deflecting yet again, I tell Declan that maybe he's the reason I'm crying. And in a way, he is, but it has nothing to do with him and everything to do with me. He sits down on the bed next to me and takes me into his arms, giving me a nice friendly hug. It is so comforting, so warm, and I want to stay here forever. Wrapped in the protection of his arms, I feel safe and like nothing can hurt me ever again.

But I'm not used to being comforted, so I don't know what to do. After my surgery, Tyler wasn't there to comfort me. Once he found out my career was over, he was busy seeking his own brand of comfort. My dad and brother were there, and they tried, but I pushed them away. I wouldn't let myself be comforted, and before I knew it, there were no more offers of comfort left.

The comfort of Declan's arms doesn't feel so bad. In fact, it feels downright good. And so, even though he represents everything that I've lost, I ask him to stay.

"I know it's an odd proposition, and I understand if you don't feel comfortable. I could just use a friend right now. Will you stay in my bed with me?"

He looks reluctant for a moment, and then consents. "But I get the remote."

My lips curl up involuntarily. "I can live with that." I stand up and he pulls back the coverlet. I set the alarm clock for the middle of the night when we have to get up, and I lie back. I feel a bit awkward being in bed with a different man. I mean, Tyler and I've been together for nine years, married for five. I never pictured myself as a cheater. Now I know, this doesn't actually constitute cheating. Not really. On the other hand, if I found Tyler in bed with a woman, no matter that nothing had happened, I'd consider it cheating.

I mean, I know Tyler actually has cheated, but does this mean that I have as well?

It doesn't matter. It should, but Declan just feels so good next to me that I don't care. I also know that if he weren't gay, I would cheat on Tyler in a heartbeat. Declan's shown me more care and compassion in the last twelve hours than Tyler has in years. I should be unsettled that I'm so willing to throw away my marriage. On the other hand, it's pretty apparent that I don't really have a marriage left. If I could be real with myself, I could admit that my foot was not the only thing paralyzed. My whole life was. Somehow, lying here next to Declan, it didn't seem so hard to admit.

As he's flipping through the channels, I snuggle in closer and within moments, the day has caught up with me, dragging me into a deep sleep.

Next thing I know, the unfamiliar alarm is blaring in my ear. I disentangle myself from a lightly snoring Declan (so he does have a flaw) and silence the menacing noise. Sitting up on the edge of the bed, I roll my shoulders a bit. I have not slept that soundly in a very long time. On the downside, I'm a bit stiff and feel older than my twenty-nine years. I guess all those years of abusing my body have finally caught up to me.

I stand up and make my way to the bathroom, grabbing my bag on the way in. I take a quick shower and dress in the same traveling clothes I wore yesterday— leggings, stretchy turtleneck, oversized cardigan. My hair is dried quickly with the hotel wall hair dryer and I wish, not for the first time, that I had not cut my hair off impulsively. After years of plaiting my hair to fit under helmets, in a fit of rage one day, I cut it all off. It was growing back and didn't look that bad, but I missed being able to braid it again. Someday, I'd have my hair and my life back. The life would be different. The hair would be the same.

To give my eyes, still heavy with fatigue, a break, I forgo the contacts. Glasses will do today. Coming out of the bathroom, I sit on the foot of the bed to don my brace. Declan is sitting up and has a serious case of bed head. I begin to wonder if this is what his hair would look like after a roll in the hay. His brown curls have taken on a life of their own and he looks like a little boy, especially when he smiles at me.

"Just need a few minutes. We can grab coffee once we're by our gate. In my experience, the stuff in the room is usually terrible."

With that, he's off into the bathroom. I want to quip at him some comment about staying in hotel rooms with women he's just met, but I figure it would be in poor taste. As it is, I'm still trying to figure out how I feel about it. I know that in all honesty, I've done nothing wrong. So why do I feel guilty?

While Declan is in the bathroom (and I'm trying not to focus on the thought that he's naked in the shower in there), I decide that I finally get why women have gay best friends. Declan's been nothing but great to me. Even though I've just met him, I feel very close to him. Maybe it's because I'm finally feeling again. Although I know with the good feelings will come the bad—the pain, the loss. I look down at my right foot, now hidden in my boot once again. It's time to move on.

Declan emerges from the bathroom dressed, hair wet and curling around his ears. He's wearing jeans and a Henley again. This one is green, which makes his eyes look more green than hazel. I should probably not be noticing these types of things. They are only going to lead to heartbreak for me.

Within a few minutes, we have all our stuff packed up. It's just after four o'clock in the morning, which is simply too early to be up and at 'em. It's too early to be up, let alone to engage in conversation.

We're checked out and heading through security again. There should be some law against having to go through airport security twice within twenty-four hours. Normally, I would be supremely annoyed by this. Declan seems to have a positive calming effect on me and I don't mind taking Kirby off. I pile my stuff in the bin on the conveyor belt and make it through with ease. Declan is just behind me. This time, he holds my elbow and steadies me as I put Kirby and my boots back on. I smile, remembering how he ran into my posterior. I can't believe I felt violated and accosted by him. He's smiling back at me, and I bet he's thinking of the same thing.

"Coffee?" he asks.

We've been up for over an hour now, and the time doesn't seem so obnoxious anymore. But I need coffee. Desperately.

I nod and we start to walk. The airport has an eerie stillness to it. There are people milling about, but many of the stores are still dark. It is not yet five a.m. The fountain seems noisy compared to the stillness of the terminal. We set off, trying to find someplace open to get a cup of coffee. But then I stop suddenly, my eyes playing tricks on me. I squint, staring through my lenses that obviously need to be updated. Declan keeps walking for a few steps until he realizes I'm not matching his pace. I take my glasses off and clean the lenses on my shirt hem. Putting them back on, I realize that my glasses are just fine and my eyes are not playing tricks on me.

Un-freakin'-believable.

"Hey, you okay?" Declan has a worried look on his face. He should. This is going to get ugly.

Already in my head, I'm cursing a blue streak. I pull my wallet out and whip out a twenty. Declan looks at me. "Kaitlin, you got dinner last night. I'll get the coffee. Provided we can find some place that's open. I hope we do though. I really need some coffee."

I shake my head. "No, that's not for coffee. That's an advance on my swear jar. I want to make sure I have enough to cover what I'm about to say."

******

10:03 p.m.: Declan

Fall asleep. It's time to fall asleep now. We've got to get up freakishly early. I need to sleep. How the hell am I supposed to fall asleep? Kaitlin has finally rolled over off of me, but she's still right here, next to me. I should have told her that I couldn't sleep with her.

I'm trying to be a good guy here. I'm trying to do the right thing.

Thankfully, she fell asleep right away. I watched hockey and then *Sportscenter*, hoping the dullness of it all would take my mind off the girl lying next to me. Every so often, she lets out a little sigh or mewing noise. Damn, I could watch her sleep all night.

I turn my focus back to the TV, willing sleep to come. I don't know why the fact that she's married bothers me so. I mean, it's pretty apparent that her marriage is over. And, it's her business, not mine. But I can almost hear my dad in my head, expressing his disappointment. My arm, which has been wandering over toward her, pulls back to my side.

Finally, eventually, well after midnight, sleep comes.

Next thing I know, she's banging on the alarm to make it stop that awful bleating. I feel the bed shift as she gets up. I'm in and out, still dozing, when I hear the blow dryer. I know it means she'll be out of the bathroom soon and that I need to get up. I'm not much of a morning person, and this is still the middle of the night, for cryin' out loud.

I take my turn in the bathroom, taking a quick shower and getting dressed. I really need a cup of coffee. I'm too old for this. This was supposed to be one of the benefits of retiring. No more early mornings. I'd had too many years of being at the rink by five a.m. You would think I'd be used to it by now.

When I come out of the bathroom, I see Kaitlin's again sitting on the bed, looking at me with lust in her eyes. At least I think she's lusting after me—it's either that or she has indigestion. She licks her lips, although again, I doubt she even knows she's doing it. I will not do anything. I will not do anything. I keep repeating it to myself. I will not do anything, unless she makes the first move.

I know that if she initiates something, I'm not going to hold back.

We're ready, so we head on down to the lobby. We turn our keys in to a sleepy looking clerk and head back toward the terminal. We have to go through security again. Kaitlin's in front of me. I'm amazed with her speed and agility in taking off her brace. She piles it all in a bin on the conveyor belt and steps through. I watch how she walks without the brace, seeing her gait change. I admit, I'm interested in it. I guess that's a good thing. I'll be analyzing people's gaits for the rest of my life once I become a physical therapist. I'll get paid to people watch.

After I'm scanned, I retrieve my belongings and follow Kaitlin to where she has stepped off to the side. I see her bent over and can't help but smile. I wish I'd taken the time yesterday to appreciate her ass while it was pressed against me. I hold onto her elbow and let her lean on me while she's putting herself back together. I can't believe I didn't see her in front of me doing all this yesterday. On the other hand, I'm glad I didn't.

I don't want her to catch me staring at her and think I'm some sort of creep. "Coffee?" I ask. It's a good distraction, and I could really use some.

She nods and we head on toward the gates, hoping to find a place open at this early hour. There are not many people here, but more than normal at this time due to the flight delays yesterday on the Eastern Seaboard. God, I need coffee. I'm thinking about that and then I realize that Kaitlin's not next to me anymore. I turn and see her standing still, staring off in the distance. She takes her glasses off and cleans them on the bottom of her shirt.

She doesn't look right. "Hey, are you okay?" I ask her. Her face is doing this weird thing and she doesn't look okay. Something is definitely up. She starts digging around in her purse and pulls out her wallet. Okay. Maybe she can't go one further step without coffee. She pulls out a twenty. I refuse it, and tell her that the coffee this morning is on me, as soon as we can find an open vendor.

She gets an eerie smile on her face as she shakes her head. "No, that's not for coffee. That's an advance on my swear jar. I want to make sure I have enough to cover what I'm about to say."

Kaitlin puts the twenty in my hand, rolls her shoulders back, lifts her head, and walks over to a couple that has just come through security. They're that annoying type of lovey-dovey, hands-all-over-each-other type of couple. I mean, get a room, man.

When the guy sees Kaitlin, he freezes. There is some heavy staring for a moment. I wish I could see what her face is doing. I've gotta see this. I walk over closer to where they are. Not so much that I'm invading Kaitlin's space, but close enough to be here if she needs me. Oh, and so I can hear what's going on as well.

"Seriously?" I hear Kaitlin accuse.

The guy, who looks like a total dweeb, lamely shrugs. His face looks almost bored. The girl standing with him looks scared. Her hair is dyed an unnatural shade of red, entering into the magenta family. Her skin is overly tanned, which, being Michigan at the end of winter, just adds to her unnatural look. Her tight sweater reveals another asset that, if I had to guess, is just as real as her hair and skin.

Kaitlin lights into this guy with a litany of curses. Damn that girl can swear! I'm impressed. If she were on TV right now, it would sound like a string of bleeps with the occasional word thrown in. He shifts and tilts his head in a cocky manner.

"Is that all you've got?" he baits her.

"Did you even listen to your messages? Or did you just ignore me like you always do?"

He lifts his shoulders and lets them fall nonchalantly. "I saw that you called."

"I will speak slowly so your peanut brain can understand. Did you or did you not know that I was stranded here in the airport? 'Cause if you knew, and just continued on with your latest whore, I swear I'm gonna—"

"Gonna what? What can you do to me? I can just run away. Your fat crippled ass can't catch me anymore."

Kaitlin is spluttering and spitting. Hell, I don't know who this guy is, but no one talks to another human being like that. Especially not Kaitlin.

"Is that the best you can come up with?" She turns to the red head who is standing there, mouth open, catching flies. "He's yours now. And, in case you don't know, he has a very tiny dick and doesn't know the first thing about how to give a woman an orgasm."

The guy, who is apparently better at slinging insults that receiving them, grows beet red, which pretty much confirms the penis size comment. "It never seemed to bother you. Of course, you're such a whore that I doubt you even realized who was screwing you most of the time anyway. I took pity on you."

Kaitlin cocks her arm back and I step in, grabbing her arm just in time. She is turned to face me and her eyes are wild. "Ma'am, I just happened to be walking by and heard the altercation between you and this scuzz bucket. Um, he's not worth it. Don't hit him, because he's not worth it."

I try to communicate with her to calm down, and she must get my non-verbal message. She nods ever so slightly. She turns back to the guy who is now talking feverishly to his companion. Kaitlin breaks her right arm free from my grasp and tugs anxiously at the ring on her left hand. She throws it at the guy, beaning him right in the head.

"There you go, you piece of shit. Expect to hear from my lawyers. As far as I'm concerned, we're no longer married."

She picks up her bag from where she dropped it and storms off. I don't even look back to see what her husband's reaction is, and I take off after Kaitlin. I catch up with her in an alcove by a bank of payphones. Who knew there were still payphones in existence?

She's sitting on the ground, her knees pulled up to her chest. She's quiet. She's not crying, just staring off into space. After seeing her cry yesterday, I would expect her to be crying now. Most women would be a puddle after that confrontation. Then I remember her saying she never cries. Wow. I guess she's right.

Finally, unable to stand the silence any more I say, "So, I have some good news and some bad news."

She continues staring ahead, arms folded around her legs, chin resting on her knees, saying nothing.

"What do you want to hear first?"

After a moment she says quietly, "The good."

I sit down next to her, my legs stretched out in front of me. Although I'm fairly flexible, I'm still over six feet tall and can't turn myself into a little ball like she is. "The good news is that I am completely and utterly impressed with your ability to swear. I mean, like a truck driver mated with a red-neck, trailer-park sailor from New Jersey, with no disrespect to any of those classes."

Still barely above a whisper, but with a hint of a smile, she says, "And the bad?"

"You owe the swear jar another twenty."

Remaining in her little ball, she leans into me and knocks me a bit. I knock her back with my shoulder.

"So, that was my husband."

"Yeah, I gathered. He's, um, a ..." I don't know how to even finish that sentence.

"Yup, that's him."

"Does he really have a tiny dick?"

She bursts out laughing and rests her head on my shoulders. "Well, not tiny, but certainly nothing to write home about. His moves, however, are decidedly lacking."

"How do you even handle that? He was pretty harsh."

"Yeah, well, I deserved some of it."

I stand up and pull her to her feet. "Kaitlin, how can you say that? No woman, hell, no person deserves to be talked to the way he talked to you."

"No, I know that. But I've been pretty hard to live with for the past two years. Like miserable. Twenty-four, seven. Do I deserve to be cheated on? No. Am I a fat-assed cripple? Yes, absolutely."

Chapter Twelve
5:10 a.m.: Kaitlin

Yeah, that could have gone better. I mean, it's not like I didn't know that Tyler was cheating on me. I mean, why else would he need to buy (repeatedly, I might add) condoms when I have an IUD?

Even though I knew he was cheating, I still can't believe I caught him going away with some plastic bimbo. Not only that, but I was stranded at the airport all night. Or at least he should have thought I was. That shit head didn't even listen to his messages to find out that his wife was stuck overnight in the airport. Oh no, he was too busy planning his get away to God-knows-where with his latest tramp. Damn, she was all sorts of ugly too.

I totally do not feel guilty about having impure thoughts about Declan anymore. I don't even feel badly about sharing a bed with him. For all intents and purposes, my marriage is done.

I'm in an alcove, curled up as small as possible. If I weren't in public, I would start rocking. Movement has always made me feel better. But, I don't want to look like more of a freak than I already do.

Now I need to figure out what to do next. How do I disentangle myself from that loser without going bankrupt? My job pays very well. I've made more money in the last year than I had in the previous ten combined. Well, I don't have the expensive habit of ski jumping anymore either, so saving is a little easier.

Absorbed in my thoughts, I barely notice Declan sliding down beside me. His long legs extend most of the way across the alcove, and he rolls his legs in and out so that his feet tap together.

I'm still curled up in my fetal position. I seem to be assuming this posture quite frequently these days.

"So, I have some good news and some bad news."

I don't answer him. I wish the floor would swallow me up whole. To know that he witnessed that whole terrible encounter, that he heard all those atrocious things Tyler said to me, makes me want to crawl into a hole and die.

"What do you want to hear first?"

I don't think I can handle any more bad news right now. "The good," I whisper.

Apparently, the good news is that he's impressed with my swearing ability. Most men don't find it attractive. They want a whore in the bedroom and a lady everywhere else. Swearing isn't exactly ladylike. I guess it comes from growing up without a feminine influence and being surrounded by men. I mean, I was competitive in a sport that was not only male dominated but didn't even have women's divisions in the Olympics until recently. Until Sochi. But that's a whole other topic for another time when I want to be even more depressed.

Not sure I can handle it, I test fate. "And the bad?"

When he tells me I owe the swear jar more money, I have to break out into a little smile. I lean over and nudge him, and he nudges me back. In case there was any doubt, I tell Declan the confrontation was indeed with my husband. He can't even form a coherent sentence. I know the feeling.

Of course, Declan focuses in on the penis size comment. I know that was childish and immature of me. Tyler had slung all sorts of insults at me, so I feel like I was totally justified.

Declan, being sweet, sensitive Declan, asks if I'm okay. I do fess up that I've been terrible to live with for the past two years. I've been a raging bitch to everyone around me, but especially to Tyler. I can't argue with the assertion that I am, in fact, a fat-assed cripple.

By this time, Declan's pulled me to my feet and there's that moment where I just want to lean in and kiss him. Damn, this is hard. I never knew I could be so attracted to somebody who wasn't attracted to me. I mean, not since David Fischer in eight grade has a guy not returned my advances. Being one of the few females in a male-dominated sport did have some advantages. As a female athlete, I had a healthy sexual appetite and thrived on challenge and adrenaline, which made for an interesting love life, to say the very least. I can't remember the last time

Tyler and I had sex. This has got to be the longest dry spell since I started, which was at the age of sixteen.

I break the moment and start to walk toward the gate. We should be boarding in about twenty minutes. Jesus, it feels like I've already put in a full day.

"Hey Kaitlin. You still want that cup of coffee?"

"Do you think it's too early for them to put some whiskey in it?"

Declan smiles at me as we get at the end of the queue for the coffee cart. "Perhaps, just a tad."

I'm still quiet, and he is too. I like that he respects my need not to talk and rehash what just happened. Although I don't know Declan that well, I do know him well enough to know that he's dying to ask me about Tyler. It's funny—he's more like a girl and I'm more like a guy when it comes to talking and the whole relationship thing. I guess we are meant to be friends after all.

We get to the front of the line and place our orders. As we step off to the side to add our cream and sugar, I can tell he's waiting for me to say something.

"So, what are you up to once you hit the City?"

"Really, Kaitlin? That's what you got?"

"Yes, Declan, that's all I got. What am I supposed to say? I'm a horrible woman, married to a horrible man. I got what I deserve."

"That's bull."

"How is that bull? That's the truth."

"No. It's not. I refuse to accept it."

"You don't have to accept anything Declan. It's my shitty life. Dammit, now I owe the swear jar even more."

We've reached our gate and find two seats by the window. Our plane is there, so we'll be boarding in a few minutes.

"No, Kaitlin. You're telling yourself and everyone else that you're horrible and you deserve this. You know you aren't and you don't."

Not quite convinced by his words, I speak the words I usually don't let surface. "If I'm not horrible, and I don't deserve this, then why does all this bad stuff keep happening to me?"

Declan's answer is interrupted by the announcements and the call for first class and business class passengers. He stands up and picks up his bag. Looking down on me he says, "You coming?"

"Yeah. Did they call us? I thought I just heard first and business class travelers."

"Um, look at your ticket. We're business class."

"No way." I pull my ticket out of the end pocket. I have to put my coffee down, otherwise I'd end up wearing it. Sure enough, we're in business class.

"Way."

"How the heck did you manage this one?" I think back to yesterday. I was a bit inebriated when we switched our tickets, but I do vaguely recall Declan taking a selfie with the enamored agent. Picking up my coffee and standing up I say, "You used your sex symbol status to get us this, didn't you?"

Blushing, Declan looks down.

"Holy cow, are you blushing?" This is amusing. "You really don't like all the attention from this, do you?"

He doesn't answer and won't raise his head to meet my eyes. I follow him and walk through the line, presenting our tickets and walking down the gangway without talking. We reach our seats, and Declan swiftly puts both our bags in the overhead compartments with ease. I would have struggled with that, especially considering I'm still holding my coffee. Of course, I'm holding Declan's as well, so at least I'm not totally useless.

******

6:02 a.m.: Declan

I can't believe Kaitlin called me out on not liking the attention that I'm getting now. I mean, what man doesn't want women falling at his feet, giving favors and special privileges? Luckily, it's time to board the plane, so I'm spared from having to talk about it anymore. Of course, if Kaitlin is impressed that I was able to pull strings, then who am I to complain?

I hand her my coffee so I can stow the bags. She offers me the window seat, but I pass, in favor of the aisle. I like to be able to stretch out my legs. Easing into the seat, I buckle my seatbelt and then take back my coffee. I finish the last few sips and steal a glance at Kaitlin. She's holding her coffee in her left hand, balanced on the armrest. Her head is back and her eyes are closed. If not for her right hand, clenched in a fist, I would have thought she was totally relaxed and maybe even sleeping.

"Does anyone ever call you Katie?"

"Not if they want to live."

She says this without batting an eye. Hell, without even opening an eye.

"I think you look like a Katie, so that's what I'm going to call you from now on."

She turns to look at me and says, "Did you not just hear what I said?"

I can't help grinning. She can be such an easy target sometimes. Taking stock of my face, she swats at me with her left hand. Unfortunately for me, she's still holding her cup, which has a little bit of coffee left in it. It splashes onto my jeans.

Mortified, she says, "Oh my gosh. Declan, I am so sorry."

Immediately, she reaches across and begins dabbing at it. I don't want her rubbing my thigh. It will be much too long a plane ride if she starts doing that. After all, I highly doubt she wants to join the mile high club right now. I reach down and grab her hand, lifting it slightly off my lap. It's awkward, me holding her right hand, pulling it across her body, forcing her to twist toward me. But she rotates a bit more and rests her head on my shoulder. Her legs are drawn up into the seat. I'm amazed at how she can curl herself up into such a small package. I can feel her sigh.

"So this is a something, isn't it?" I ask.

"I'll say. I feel like my life is changing. I mean, obviously it is. I guess when I come back, I won't have a husband anymore."

"It seems like you didn't have much of one to begin with."

After a moment she says, "No, not since this." She waggles her right foot.

"Are you going to tell me what happened?"

"I had anterior compartment syndrome. It's when the muscles in the front of my shin swelled up, which cut off blood flow and caused the nerves and muscles to die off."

"Actually, I do know what it is. I've known a few figure skaters who started to develop it. But they were treated and were fine after."

"I should have been, but I got bad medical advice."

"Did you sue?"

I can feel her shaking her head against my shoulder. "There was no point. It was a big convoluted mess. I doubt I would have been able to prove anything. Long story short, it all happened so quickly. Muscles can only tolerate ischemia—losing their blood supply—for about four hours. After six, the damage is irreversible. So, waiting eight hours was probably a mistake."

"And there's nothing that can be done?"

"No, the nerve is dead. The muscles have atrophied away. I mean, you saw what it looks like, all puny and deformed. They did a fasciotomy, but it was too late. This is what's left."

The airline attendant comes through and collects our cups. Kaitlin sits up and looks out the window.

"One more thing and then I'll let you be."

Without turning to look at me, she says, "Why do I highly doubt that?" I don't need to see her face to know there is a small smile on it.

"Will you be okay? On this trip?"

"Yeah, I'll be fine. I'm going to be really busy, so that will be good. Plus, remember, I decided not to suck at my job anymore? Putting effort in should be good for me and keep me nice and distracted."

"What's on your agenda this week?"

She sits back in her seat, still not looking at me, as the plane starts its take off. I can't imagine what is so exciting on the back of the seat in front of her, but she is engrossed. Finally, when we've reached cruising altitude she says, "Today, I drop my stuff at the hotel and meet up with Richard. We're doing an in-service at Hospital for Special Surgery, but at two different locations. Tomorrow, there's a medical trade show at Javits Center. I think that's two days. Then, on Friday, I think we're at Presbyterian in the morning and Burke in White Plains in the afternoon. We head back into the City and then I'll fly home Saturday morning. I won't be able to call a lawyer until Monday, but I can have all his stuff in a pile on the lawn well before that."

"That's a busy week."

"No kidding. What about you? It's got to be just as hectic."

"Um, sort of. I'm meeting up with some friends tonight. Tomorrow, I have a meeting with some corporate types for an endorsement deal. I think then there will be a photo shoot as well. I'm doing *Good Morning America* on Friday. I'm spending the weekend with my brother and friends and then I go back on Monday."

"An endorsement deal? Seriously? For what?"

"Deodorant."

She leans in and sniffs me. "I guess you don't smell, so it could work."

"Um, thanks for the vote of confidence. I think."

"An endorsement deal is pretty cool, actually."

"I mean, it's no Wheaties box but it's nice compensation. Will definitely help while I'm in school for the next few years."

"Oh yeah, that's right. You're getting out of the business. I forgot." She pauses. "What I don't understand is how you can just give it all up and walk away."

I shrug. "I dunno. I guess, I'm just ready. I'm tired. Like my body is tired. It's not fun anymore. I can't remember why I wanted to do it in the first place. So it's time to move on."

"Will you still skate? You know for fun or coach or something?"

"I think I'll be pretty busy in school. I'm not the smartest guy out there, so I think it's going to be kind of hard." I hadn't thought about this before. I don't know why this never occurred to me. "You know, I pictured myself hanging up the blades and never looking back, but I've skated almost every day since I was six."

"So that's a super long time considering how old you are."

I had to smile at her jab. She did have a good sense of humor. It's too bad that she's been so miserable that she forgot about it.

"Ha ha. You're hysterical." I nudge her with my shoulders—any excuse to touch her really—and continue. "Youth is wasted on the young."

"But you think you can just walk away and do something totally different?" Her voice becomes pensive. "Are you going to work with skaters once you're a PT?"

"Yeah, probably. Hadn't really thought that far ahead. Now that you mention it, I can't see myself working with little old ladies with back pain or hammer toes."

"Eeeew. Old people feet." She shudders, repulsed by the thought.

"I know, right? Yeah, I'll probably stick to athletes. Mostly skaters, since I understand what they have to do."

"So, then, don't you think being around all those people in the business will make you miss it? Yearn for it?"

I know she's making a valid point, but hearing her say the word 'yearn' makes me think of other things I'm yearning for at this moment. Casually shrugging my shoulders, trying to remain aloof, I reply, "Maybe. I never thought about it before. I figured I'm done and I'm moving on."

"How is it that men can do that? How can you just move on from something that is your whole life? From someone who is supposed to be your whole life?"

"Whoa, Nellie. Slow down there. Don't go lumping me in with your jerk wad of a husband."

The plane hits a jolt of turbulence and Kaitlin grips the armrests. It seems to be an isolated event, and she finally relaxes her hold.

"You're right, Declan. I was lumping you in with him. But in a way it's the same thing. I don't get how you can just move on."

"Does that mean you still love him?"

She's quiet as the attendant announces our descent, asking us to return our tray tables and seatbacks to their full and upright positions. That was the quickest hour-and-a-half plane ride I've ever been on. While she's still confined next to me, I grab her iPhone out of the seat pocket in front of her and quickly enter my number in it.

"What are you doing?"

"Giving you my number. Before we go our separate ways. You call me, text me, whatever. Anytime."

She nods.

"No Kaitlin, I mean it. Anytime. If you need anything at all. Even if you just want to hang out. I can beat people up too. Oh and don't forget you owe me some electrodes."

"What do you mean, I owe you electrodes?"

"You promised, when we first met. And I'm going to make you live up to that promise."

Chapter Thirteen
8:10 a.m.: Kaitlin

As he grabs my phone, I wonder what the hell he's doing. He's giving me his phone number. He's reaching out. We're going to be friends after this. I'm going to have a friend. And boy, I sure could use one.

My head is whirling with the events of this morning. Waking up in the same bed as Declan. Seeing Tyler and the confrontation. Declan had asked me if I still have feelings for Tyler. If I'm honest with myself, I'm hurt. Not because I still want Tyler—I don't. My pride has taken a beating. I'm hurt, licking my wounds. Not only doesn't he want me, but he has so little respect for me that he's blatantly out screwing around. And not even attempting to go behind my back. That hurts more. The fact that he was unapologetic that he left me stranded at the airport to go on a trip with his girlfriend and couldn't care less that I caught him. Bastard.

Declan gets my bag down and we walk up the gangplank, side by side. We look like a couple. I wish we were. Declan would never treat me like Tyler does. Of course, Tyler was always the bad boy. It's what I was drawn to in the first place. I was a young, stupid, arrogant twenty-year-old. I've mellowed and want someone nice this time around. I know it won't be Declan, but I can look for someone like him.

"Where are you headed?" he asks.

"I'm staying at the Holiday Inn out here, so I've got to find the shuttle."

"Oh, I'm staying in mid-town by Penn Station."

"How you gonna get there?"

"I'm gonna grab a cab."

"That's gonna cost a fortune!"

He laughs. "Yeah, but the company that is keeping me smelling so fresh is also footing the bill, so I don't care."

"Must be nice to live the life of a celebrity."

We're at ground transportation. I don't want to leave Declan. I want to stay with him. Uncharacteristic for me, I throw my arms around him. Clinging tightly so he can't see my tears, I bury my head in his shoulder.

His face is tucked into the side of my neck. "I'm so glad I ran into your ass."

"It's the best accosting I've ever had."

"I mean it, keep in touch. You're driving here. It's in your hands."

I have to tear myself away, or I won't be able to leave him. "I don't know what I'm going to do for the next few days without you. But you'll hear from me, definitely." Pulling back, I give him a quick peck on the cheek. "Now I see what's so great about having a gay best friend."

I step back and walk toward my shuttle. I look over my shoulder and see Declan still standing there. I wonder if I'll ever see him again. I want to. I know that without a doubt. And at this point in my life, there is not much I am sure of. I have no idea who I am anymore. That's the result of having been involved in an all-encompassing activity.

I need to approach my life like I approached the adversity I'd faced while jumping. Back then, it didn't matter to me that I entered a male-only sport. Sure, there were female ski jumpers, but we were certainly the minority. Especially here in the U.S. I wasn't going to let something as stupid as that stop me. I kept training and pushing myself. I campaigned and lobbied to get women's ski jumping into the Vancouver Olympics, all while training so I could be in top form when the time came. I was twenty-one when women's ski jumping hit the world circuit. Twenty-five when Vancouver came and went without us competing. Twenty-six when I competed my best in Worlds. Twenty-seven when I blew out my right ACL.

And now I'm twenty-nine and that life is gone. All of it is gone. Tyler was probably the last holdout, and now he's gone too. Good riddance I can say to that one.

As I carefully descend the steps and retrieve my bag from the underside of the shuttle, I realize that the last twenty-four hours have changed my life. I had totally forgotten who I used to be. Once I could no longer jump, I lost all sense of who and what I was.

That ends today. I'm ready to get my jive back. Today, as corny as this sounds, is the first day of the rest of my life. Crap. I'm now quoting cheesy bumper stickers as my mantra. But it's true. I was making myself miserable. It is up to me to make myself happy. I check into my room and a feeling of aloneness washes over me. I don't want to be alone anymore.

Of course, I want to be with Declan, but I know that's not a possibility. It's time to put on my suit pants, violet turtleneck and suit coat so I can face my day with my new perspective. Donning my Mary Janes, which are the least orthopedic, orthopedic shoes I own, I examine myself in the mirror. Not great, but it could be worse.

Time to get going with the new me.

******

8:26 a.m.: Declan

We're at ground transportation, so I know we'll be parting any moment. I don't want her to leave me. I don't want to leave her. I can't explain it. Usually, even if I am attracted to someone, I have no problem leaving. She's different.

She's hurting. She's vulnerable. She's natural. She's throwing her arms around me. Her head is on my shoulder, so I bend my head down toward hers. I'm going to kiss her when she looks up. That'll guarantee that she calls me. Her head is still buried up against me. I smell her neck, trying to resist the urge to put my lips on her. Instead I say, "I'm so glad I ran into your ass." Of course, that brings directly to mind what her supple hind end felt like pressed into me.

She replies and I say something back, not even sure what is coming out of my mouth. I'm urging her to call me. Finally, she pulls back, looking up at me. This is it. I start to lean in but she meets me first, placing her lips on my cheek. She starts to step away and, as she does, says, "Now I see what's so great about having a gay best friend."

What? A what? Gay—best—friend? Holy shit, she just called me gay.

Too stunned to speak, I just stand there as she walks away. I see her look back over her shoulder a few times, and she waves as she approaches her shuttle.

She thinks I'm gay.

Why the hell would she think that? She couldn't be so narrow minded as to think that all male figure skaters are gay. Or could she?

How the hell did I get myself into this one?

It's not the first time that someone assumed that I had to be gay because I'm a figure skater. Most people, men especially, live under that assumption. I try to figure out what I could have possibly said to give Kaitlin that impression but come up with zilch. Maybe it's because I didn't make a move on her. Of course, her jerkwad husband has done such a number on her self-esteem that she probably wouldn't think that someone would even hit on her in the first place. I start to call after her but my phone buzzes in my pocket. It's Frankie. "What's shakin' baby?"

A cab pulls up and I hop in. I've given the driver the address and sink back into the seat. I can't believe Kaitlin thinks I'm gay. This is going to eat at me. I have to set her straight. No pun intended. But I can't with Frankie yammering on in my ear.

With a sigh I try to cover my frustration. "Not much. I'm here. In a cab trying to get to my hotel."

"Declan, what's wrong? Are you sick or something?"

"Nah. It's just—aww, it's nothing."

"It's not nothing. You're the happiest guy I know and you sound miserable. Is it Natalya?"

"No, not Natalya. She's been trying to get in touch though. I told her we'd talk after I got back from this trip. Hopefully that buys me some peace and quiet."

"If not Natalya, then who? That girl you met? What did you say her name was?"

"Kaitlin. Kaitlin Reynolds."

"Did you sleep with her?"

"Frankie, you know I don't want to talk with you about stuff like that. It's gross. But no, I didn't. She's married."

"Oh. Yeah, your mom would have your hide if she found out about you going after a married woman."

"Yeah I know. And I know you'd tell her too. But her marriage is pretty much done. She saw her husband at the airport leaving on a trip with some bimbo."

"Ouch. And you still couldn't seal the deal? You're off your game."

"No, well, we only saw him this morning. But ..." I trailed off. The next part was embarrassing.

"But what?"

"Apparently, she thinks I'm gay."

I have to pause while I hear Frankie on the other line, choking and sputtering on her coffee. Serves her right, the old wind bag. Still laughing she says, "Oh Declan, baby, that just made my morning." Finally she notices my silence and says, "I take it you are not amused?"

"No, not really. I'm so glad I'm getting out. I won't have to be pigeon-holed by dumb stereotypes anymore."

This time, Frankie's laugh is a little more bitter. "That's right. Because the one time you get stereotyped, you are all offended. Try being a woman some time."

I can see where this is headed and I don't want to fight with her. "I'm sorry, Frankie. I didn't get much sleep last night."

"All right baby. You close your eyes and get some rest. I'll be in touch and see how the shoot went."

Disconnecting, I drop my phone in my lap. I need to think about something else besides Kaitlin. I close my eyes, and the next thing I know, the cab driver is telling me we've reached our destination. Giving him my credit card, he swipes, gives me the receipt and I'm out of the cab. The concierge opens the door for me and I'm into the hotel.

Once up in my room, I look around. There is one king bed. Before I can get all maudlin and depressed, my phone starts lighting up. My friend from childhood, Vic Nguyen, has an epic night planned for us. His nights are always epic. Maybe not the best idea considering I have a meeting with the deodorant people tomorrow, but just what I need to stop mooning over a married woman. Who thinks I'm gay.

Chapter Fourteen
Thursday, July 24, 2014
5:45 a.m.: Kaitlin

The music from the club reverberates through my chest, pounding like a second heart beat. Pushing through, I need to find Declan. There are people everywhere and no one looks like him. Surely his tall frame should stick out, but between the throngs of people pressed together and the fog created by the smoke machines, I can barely see my hand in front of my face. Pulling out my phone, I text him again. "Im here. Cant see u. Where r u?"

I wait impatiently for my phone to light up. I keep swiping the screen, as if refreshing it will make Declan text me back. I can't believe I'm doing this, meeting up with him like this. Will he look as good in person as he has in my imagination for the past few months? Sliding into an opening at the bar, I order a shot of vodka. I'm not one for liquor but am in desperate need of liquid fortification at the moment. The alcohol slides down smoothly and I return to my search. I feel like a cat on the prowl. Maybe because I am.

I'm almost at the back of the club. Before I can even process what is happening, Declan is in front of me. He grabs me by the waist and swings me around. I know I shouldn't be surprised at his strength, but I'm not one of those waifs he throws about the ice.

My smile is so wide that it threatens to break my face. Just seeing him again makes me feel good inside. I can't believe it's been four months since I last saw him. I can't believe it took me this long to get in touch with him. With his arm still around my waist, he guides me over to a group standing around a high top table. The amount of used glassware on the table indicates that the party has been here for a while and is probably feeling no pain. Introductions are tossed around, but I really can't hear any of what Declan is saying. The only time I can hear him is when he is talking directly into my ear. Of course, then I can't really concentrate of what he's actually saying since I'm so aware of *him*.

A waitress circles around and delivers another round of drinks. I'm not sure how it worked out but there was a shot for me, and everyone else seemed to have one as well. After the ritual clinking of the glasses, I toss back my second shot. I've never been one for doing shots, so I'm surprised this one goes down so easily, without even threatening to turn around like it normally would.

Wiping my mouth with the side of my hand, I can't help but watch Declan lick his own lips and wish I could do it for him. Perhaps me plus alcohol plus Declan isn't the best equation. One more round of shots appears and I find myself unable to resist Declan when he starts pulling me out to the dance floor.

Shouting into his ear, I tell him, "I don't dance."

"Tonight you do."

He has me out on the floor before I can protest again, and our bodies are moving in rhythm with each other. I don't want to be touching him. Oh, who am I kidding? I want nothing more than to touch him. I'm trying to be good but all those shots are making it difficult. Actually, Declan's making it difficult. His body is pressed into mine and his hands are pulling my body into his. He leans in and says, "I thought you said you don't dance."

"Normally I can't."

"It's because you've never had the right partner before."

"Is that so?" We're talking into each other's ears to be heard and it is so intimate. His breath is hot against my neck. I want so much to kiss him. I need to kiss him. And, as if he can read my thoughts, he leans in and plants his mouth on mine. It is hard and urgent. My hands are in his hair, frantically pulling him into me. If he breaks contact with me at this moment, I think I'll die. I'm so engrossed in this fantastic first kiss that I barely notice Declan's moved us off the dance floor. Our hands are groping each other and I can't pull myself off of him. Apparently he feels the same way as his hands are on my face, pulling me into him.

I keep stepping backwards as Declan moves forward. It's a wonder we haven't run into anything. Just as I think that, my back slams into a wall. Barely able to focus, I see that we're in a hallway. I hadn't even noticed this hall before and I am really disoriented. Declan grins the most sinful grin at me and dives in toward me. His hands travel down around my ass and he grips me tightly. His left hand starts to travel down my right thigh, and I lift my leg, allowing him to move in even closer. I'm so thankful I chose to wear my short black skirt tonight so that I can feel his warm hands stroking my thigh.

Groaning, I tilt my head back, giving Declan full access to the front of my neck. He kisses down, making his way to my breasts, which he has somehow managed to expose by unbuttoning the top several buttons on my crisp white blouse. I can't believe this is happening. I can't believe I'm kissing Declan. And that Declan is kissing me. We're in a club, and I could have sex with him right here, right now. And I just might. My right leg bends up, giving him any access he could possibly want. His hand moves up under my skirt and then down my right leg. He caresses my calf, his hand gliding over my silk stockings. As I feel his hand on my calf, my head whips forward and I look down, watching his hand. He is still kissing the side of my neck and doesn't seem to notice that I've stopped. I can't stop staring at my leg. Full and healthy, with a foot clad in a stiletto heel.

This time, when my eyes fly open, I'm in my dark bedroom alone. I am sweaty and hot and bothered to say the least. I roll over and look at the clock. Dammit, I could have slept for fifteen more minutes.

I can't believe I had such a vivid sex dream about Declan. Again.

******

6:26 a.m.: Declan

I know what the pounding on my door is. I'm late for training. Again. I just don't want to get up. We're only ten days into the tour and I want to quit. Forty-five more days, I tell myself. Forty-five more days. Because of our travel schedule today, we need to get a quick workout in this morning (supposedly at six a.m.) before the bus drives us from Columbus back to Detroit. Tonight, I'll get to sleep in my own bed, after I meet up with my brother. The pounding begins again. Sighing, I throw back the covers and fling the door open before Natalya wakes the entire floor of the hotel.

She's dressed and ready to go to the hotel gym, of course. "Did I wake you, Sleeping Beauty?" She tries to be funny but she's not. Everything she says or does grates on my nerves at this point. The only time I don't hate her is when we're on the ice. Something about those few minutes transports us to a different place. I can feel passion, I can feel love. I can not want to wring her neck.

"Give me a minute." I head to the bathroom, do what I have to do, and brush my teeth. I'm dressed in gym shorts already, so I simply pull on a t-shirt and put my socks and sneakers on. We're just doing light cardio since we're on the ice tonight.

I expect Natalya to be pacing around my room like a caged wolf when I come out of the bathroom. I don't expect to see her curled up in a little ball on my bed. This is not normal.

"You okay?"

She doesn't answer.

"Nat, are you okay?"

"Why do you care?" Her voice is muffled, her face still hidden.

How to answer this question? I'm not heartless. We've been together for sixteen years. I was fifteen when I started training with Natalya, who was only ten. I hadn't started figure skating until I was eleven, so I was still a relative newcomer at that time. Nat was born with skates on. Her parents, also skaters, had emigrated from Russia when Nat was about three. When they learned I was still an Irish citizen, they applied for citizenship there, rather than in Canada. We were romantically involved with each other for about five years, breaking up almost five years ago. Yes, I know, a twenty-one-year-old getting involved with a sixteen-year-old is a bad idea. But at the time, I was young and stupid. Now I'm just stupid. Our relationship is so twisted. We've been together so long and have such a complex history. Hell, for my entire career, we've been known by our last names together—McLoughlin-Koval. Sometimes I don't know where I end and Natalya begins.

Still not answering her, I grab my key and head toward the door. "You comin'?"

She heaves herself off the bed. Her loose tank top shows her skeletal arms, covered by small, tight muscles. I hate looking at her body. I hate touching it. I know she's killing herself. It's gotten even worse since Sochi. I don't know what else to do. I've begged and pleaded, screamed and threatened. Natalya needs help and I'm not the one who can give it to her. I don't know who is.

We head down to the hotel gym and start our workout. Compared to off-ice days, this is an easy one. Merely the treadmill, elliptical and bike, fifteen minutes on each. We don't talk while working out. There's nothing left to talk about. Instead, I listen to a podcast on my iPod. I don't know what Natalya's listening to. We finish and head up to the restaurant for the breakfast that's included with our room. Typical hotel breakfast. Rubber scrambled eggs, overcooked pancakes, greasy bacon. No wonder Natalya doesn't eat. As I pile eggs and home fries on my plate, I ignore Natalya's scornful look. I head to a table and put my plate down. I go back up to get some coffee and juice. Nat is holding a plate that has yogurt and a banana on it. She's standing in front of a basket of muffins, and I see her hand quiver, reaching toward one.

This is interesting. She's going to eat a muffin. Then I really watch her. Her hand is moving forward and back in tiny incremental movements. Now, it becomes painful to see. She is literally wrestling with herself about whether or not to take that tiny muffin. Why can't she just grab it and put it on her plate? I don't understand. What could possibly be so hard about putting a muffin on your plate? Unable to watch anymore, I walk over to her, grab the muffin and plop it down on her plate. Without waiting for a reaction, I turn back around and sit down.

I'm pretty intent on shoveling food in my face for a few minutes. This is why I don't get her not eating. I'm starving all the time. All the time. I eat pretty much what I want as well. I mean, it's a protein heavy diet, and I don't eat much junk, but I don't deny myself either.

When I look up, Nat's staring at me. The banana peel is empty, along with the yogurt cup. The muffin is sitting alone on her plate.

I don't want to fight about this. Not again. Either she's going to eat it or not. Most likely not. I can't control what she does. I can only control me. I'm about to stand up and storm off when it starts to dawn on me.

As I rest back in my seat, I look at her. She is looking at me, her blue eyes icy. She folds her arms over her chest. Typical defensive posture. She's waiting for me to tell her to eat or to make some snide comment about the muffin. Instead, I say, "Is it about control?"

"Is what about control?" Her voice is cold and hard. Her defenses are up. This isn't going to end well. I'm ready to give up before I even start. She's worn me down over the years and I just don't have the energy to fight with her anymore. Standing up and clearing my place, I give it one last half-assed effort.

"I think you should talk to Ben. Really."

Never breaking eye contact with me, Nat says with her Cheshire Cat grin, "I don't think so. He's not really ... objective anymore."

Shaking my head in disgust, I know I should walk away without taking her bait but I can't. "Seriously Nat? He's married."

"Yeah, but I always get what I want and I wanted him."

"Natalya, you're twenty-six years old. It's time you learn that you can't always get what you want." Another prime reason why we didn't work out. I got tired of giving in to her demands.

"You're the king of teaching me that, aren't you?"

"What was your plan? Screw him so you don't have to talk about your issues? So you don't have to admit your faults? So you don't have to admit where you've f'd up?"

"You're my biggest fuck up, Declan. Always have been and always will be."

Glancing around the breakfast area, I'm thankful that there are very few people and no one seems to be paying attention to us. I'm still standing over the table, tightly gripping my disposable plate and coffee cup.

"I don't wanna rehash this again, Nat. I'm not your biggest screw up. I'm just the one who finally said 'no' to you. We don't work. We shouldn't have gotten involved in the first place."

She stands up with a huff. "I know that Declan. I'm not stupid. I know we shouldn't have gotten involved. I know we don't work. But it doesn't stop me from wishing we did."

And with that bombshell, she storms out of the room. My feet are planted, not able to move. What did she mean by that? Does she want to get back together? I can't even believe she's thinking about that. We were terrible together. Her revelation has left me standing there like an idiot. After a moment, I start to walk away. I throw my trash out and turn back to clean up Natalya's mess. Left alone there on her plate, untouched, is the muffin.

Chapter Fifteen
5:15 p.m.: Kaitlin

Staring at the envelope in my hand, I'm paralyzed. With fear. With excitement. With indecision. With desire. What do I do?

"Whatcha got there?" Trina says as she walks by. Her headset is still on as she bustles through to her desk. Trina handles the paperwork and insurance for salespeople across three states; we'd be lost without her expert organizational skills. Over the past couple of months, since I've actually committed to doing a good job, I'd say we've started to become friends. Okay, maybe not friends yet, but I'm making headway.

"Um, did you see where this came from?"

"No, I think it was in the mail. Sometime in the last few days. Maybe Monday?"

I've been out of the office and just stopped in for the afternoon to wade through an enormous stack of paper. I almost missed the envelope. Examining it for answers only leads to more questions. A plain white envelope, addressed to me, care of the company. My name is printed in neat, block handwriting. Nothing gives me a clue about whom it's from, except for the contents. I study that too. One ticket.

Trina leans in over my arm. She's too short to look over anyone's shoulder. "An ice skating show? Oh, that's tonight."

"Yeah, I know." I take a closer look and turn the ticket over. Nope, nothing.

"Why did someone send you one ticket?"

"I would guess they want me to come to the show."

Trina gets all excited. I mean, she actually starts jumping up and down. "Are you dating? Is this a blind date or something? Are you on the internet yet?"

"No, I'm not internet dating. Tyler's only finally been gone a few weeks. I have no desire to get involved with anyone right now." That is a total lie because the person I want to be involved with would not want to be involved with me. On the other hand, in my hand, is this ticket. He had to have sent it. There's no other plausible explanation. "On the other hand, in my hand, is this ticket to the ice show at the Joe Louis Arena."

"Are you gonna go?"

Trying to play it casual, as Trina could hear my racing heart, I shrug. "I dunno. The show is at 7:30. By the time I go home and change and get down to the Joe, and you know what parking's like and ..."

"Stop it. You have to go. You've been working like a dog for the past few weeks. And with the Tyler thing—"

"Oh please, I'm better off without that louse."

"I know you are. You seem better off without him. It's like he was poisoning your aura or something. Ever since you got back from that New York trip with Richard and kicked Tyler out, you've been in a much better frame of—" She stops and looks at me.

"You and Richard didn't ... you know. Did you?"

It takes me a minute to realize what she was insinuating. "Oh God, no. That's just ... no."

Trina looks visibly relieved. "Oh that's good. I mean, you've been in a great mood so I didn't, well, I, um, I'll just shut up now."

Whereas before her stammering and conclusion jumping would have irritated me, I found amusement in her blushing embarrassment. I couldn't help but laugh. I like Trina and want to be friends with her. Amazing how being less negative and opening myself up brought good things. Declan taught me that. My heart leapt at the thought of seeing him again. Even if it was from the stands, I could see him again. Tonight.

"Well, I guess if I'm gonna make it to this show, I'd better get going." I drop the rest of the mail on my desk and pull my large bag out from under the desk. As I pull the door open, Trina calls out, "Good luck. Maybe you'll run into the man of your dreams there."

From her lips to God's ears.

Driving back to my condo, I mentally inventory my clothing options for the night. I don't know why it matters.

I'm going to be one of the nameless, faceless people in the arena. It's not like Declan will even know that I'm there. And on the long shot that I do see him, what do I say? Sorry for never calling you? I can't stop thinking about you? Ugh. I'm an idiot. I shouldn't even go to this thing. It is only going to set me up for heartbreak. More heartbreak, that is.

It will be tight timing to make this happen. It is a good thirty minutes back to my condo, barring no accidents on 94. I don't even bother pulling my car all the way into the garage. Running into the house and up to my room, I yank open my closet door and stand there, lost. What does one wear to this sort of thing? How did I turn in to this girl who is worrying about what to wear?

I grab my favorite pair of nice jeans and a flash of white in the closet catches my eye. It is my white button down blouse, like I was wearing in my dream. With my eyes closed for a moment, I relive those delicious images and can almost feel his hands on my body. Buttoning up the shirt, I pivot and twist, looking at myself in the mirror, pleased with the definition the gathering and ruching gives me. Even though it is July, I know the ice will make the arena chilly. I throw a hazel green jacket on over it and am pleased with the result. The jacket is the color of Declan's eyes, but that is totally coincidental.

Grabbing a protein bar and a bottle of water, I'm back in the car in under thirty minutes. Not bad. My car is heading down East Jefferson toward the city; I hope that the flow of traffic will be going the other way. Letting my mind wander, I think about what I would tell Declan if I saw him again. About how I finally kicked Tyler out and divorced his sorry ass. About how I am doing well in my job and finally feeling successful with it. About how, for the first time since I stopped jumping, I don't feel terrible all the time. And that it is all because of him.

Realizing how pitiful my thought process is, I bang my head on my steering wheel while stopped at a light. Just when I think I'm putting my life back together, I'm stuck, mooning over yet another impossible, unreachable goal. I am such an idiot.

******

7:15 p.m.: Declan

Backstage, Natalya and I are running through some last-minute elements of our programs. While one of our programs is an old one we could do in our sleep, we have a new number that still isn't as fluid as I'd want, in addition to the two full-cast numbers that we had to learn. We weren't going to add a new number but Nat insisted after hearing this song. She begged me to choreograph something. We'd let our choreographer go after Sochi but I had a knack for it, if I do say so myself. I would never admit it to Nat, but she has an ear for music and what works for us. She was right to push me to do this one last number. We were lucky that the show choreographers let us put it in.

The muffin incident of this morning is forgotten as we get into our zone. It is a bit harder to focus tonight, being in front of the local crowd. There are people from our rink here. Friends and colleagues. Frankie is here, as well as my brother Ronan. He really hates figure skating but I promised him this is the last time he has to watch me. Natalya's parents are here, which is making her more tense than usual.

After she messes up the run-through again, I stop her. "Nat, you've got to relax. You're thinking too much. Stop thinking."

"Don't you think if I could stop thinking I would?" she snaps back.

"What has got you wound up so tight?"

"Are you that much of an idiot? Can you really not see?"

Apparently I am, because I have no idea what she is talking about. "See what?"

"Declan, I don't want this to end."

Sighing, I sit down. Even the thought of having this discussion again drains my energy. "Nat, we've been through this. I'm too tired to keep going. Your knees are shot, and you're even younger than I am. You know we don't have another four years left in us. This way, we're going out on a good note."

She sits down next to me. Sitting is a bad idea, seeing as how we have to get warmed up before getting on the ice. Her thigh is pressed into mine and she leans her head on my shoulder. Our bodies are so used to being intertwined with each other that sometimes she feels like an extension of me. "No, not about skating, about us."

Her words are quiet but powerful. Suddenly, things come into focus for me. Her song choice for us to skate to, that she was so insistent on. "Stay with Me" by Sam Smith. Her anger toward me, toward my retirement. The escalation of her anorexia as a result of her loss of control. She's not upset to be finished with skating. She doesn't want to lose me.

As I stand up, I swallow hard. I start jogging in place, trying to get warm again. She stands as well and does the same, but won't meet my eyes. I need to give her some answer. I need to say something to her. But what? Finally, she looks up at me with those sad eyes, all traces of steel gone. I pull her into me and hold her tight. We used to have passion for each other. Now I only feel that passion when I'm out on the ice. But when we no longer have that outlet, then what? She's not what I want, but maybe she's what I need.

I rest my chin on the top of her head. I would kiss it, but then I'd get a mouthful of hairspray. "We'd better get our costumes on."

Getting dressed, I try to find a moment of peace before it's time to skate. I don't know why, but this curveball Natalya has thrown at me has really shaken me. Maybe she's right. Maybe we do belong with each other. To each other. It would be easy to be complacent but not easy to be with Natalya. The thought of complacency in a relationship brings my mind back to Kaitlin.

Damn Kaitlin. I can't believe she never contacted me after leaving me at the airport. Perhaps I should take Frankie up on her offer to find her. And do what? Say what? "Um, hey, not gay here and I want you?" Ugh, that sounds bad, even to me. No, that ship has sailed and I need to focus on the one that's in front of me. Natalya. It might be like hopping aboard the Titanic though. Shit.

I hear my name being called and it is almost time for me and Natalya to go out on the ice. We're skating our old routine first, with the new one right before the all-cast finale. My head is so not in this right now. I'm going to make an ass out of myself in front of my friends and family. Ronan would never let me live that down. I need to focus before that happens.

Chapter Sixteen
7:22 p.m.: Kaitlin

Now I know why I was hesitant to come to this show. By the time I get back into Detroit, pay an arm and a leg to park my car in the garage, and walk to the arena, I'm ready for bed. I have a pass to park in the handicapped spots so I don't have to walk as far, but I'm too proud to use it. There are hordes of screaming children everywhere. Okay, maybe not hordes but it is definitely a family friendly show. Please God, don't let me be sitting next to a bunch of little kids for this. I make my way through the crowds, dodging little people here and there. I stop and get a beer. I think I'm going to need it to get through tonight, especially when I see the souvenir stands selling t-shirts with Declan's face on them. They are truly hideous, and I consider buying one just to mock him. But then I can see me, in my desperate lonely state, making out with it or something pathetic like that, so I resist the urge.

I look at my ticket. I'm in the first row, right in the center of the arena. Best seats in the house. I wonder if Declan will see me. He obviously will look for me since he sent me the ticket. I'm going to have to text him after this. How do I tell him why I never got in touch with him in the first place? How clichéd is it for the lonely, sad girl to fall for the unavailable, gay friend? I make myself want to puke.

Making my way down the steps one at a time, I finally reach my seat just as the lights start to dim. I'm toward the middle of the row and have to climb over a few people. It's always uncomfortable to do this while holding a drink and a large shoulder bag and not stick your rear end in people's faces. I get to my open seat and plop down. The strobe lights are flashing in a seizure-inducing fashion, and I relax into the anonymity of the arena. As the first few skaters come out, I sit back and sip on my beer. I see an older woman who—even in the darkness of the arena, appears to have a fake tan—glances at me. I wonder if drinking beer at this sort of thing is frowned upon. If they don't want me drinking it, they shouldn't sell it.

As I watch the skaters zip about the ice, my breath is taken away by their athleticism and strength. I glance about me and see most of the people in the audience have a look of wonder and pleasure on their faces. Apparently I am the only one who is fighting off crushing depression and anxiety watching them skate. Over the last four months, I thought I had made progress in dealing with my issues. I guess not. I probably should go see someone about them.

A voice next to me whispers, "Why do you look so serious? This is supposed to be enjoyable. You look like you're about to get a root canal without anesthesia."

Turning my head slightly, I see a profile that reminds me of Declan. Damn, I've got to get him out of my head. "I don't look that bad, do I?"

He turns and looks at me. "You don't look bad, but you look uncomfortable. Obviously, you need to drink more."

A smile spreads on my face as I say, "I got some dirty looks carrying this in. Why would they sell it if they didn't want me drinking it?"

"They have to sell it; otherwise, men would never come. There's a lot of dads and boyfriends who are forced to come here and need this to make it palatable. If there were no beer, it'd be a deal breaker."

"I didn't realize there would be beer, but it makes the evening automatically better."

"Beer makes everything better."

"You got that right. Where's yours?"

He leans forward and lifts his mostly empty cup up off the floor. "Gotta pace myself."

"Because you'd have to go to the bathroom too much?"

"That too. Because I'd fall asleep and it would get me in trouble."

I look around. He's sitting next to the super tan woman. I see no wife or kids in tow. "With who? Your mom?" I nod at the woman next to him.

He laughs. "Nah, that's not my mom. Although it is my mom's best friend, so she's worse."

"Doing your good deed for the day bringing her?"

"Something like that. What about you? You don't seem thrilled to be here."

"I, um, ahh, I was given the ticket. This isn't normally my thing."

"What is your thing?" I can tell he's flirting with me. I even consider flirting back. But then, out on center ice, there's Declan. God, he looks even better than in my dreams.

Out on the ice, he's different than he was with me. Gone is the laid-back, funny Declan. He's commanding and forceful. Powerful in his push offs. Tight black pants betray overdeveloped quads. And his ass. A girl could thank God for something so beautiful. With him is this impossibly small girl. She's about the size of my wrist bone. What gets me is how they move in perfect synchronicity. Like they are two halves of a whole. There is none of the klutzy, awkward, bumping into each other that seemed to keep recurring during our day together. As I watch him, my mouth goes dry and waters all at the same time. This was a mistake. I shouldn't be here, watching him.

I don't even realize that I'm on the edge of my seat and that every muscle in my body is tense. As Declan and his partner hit their final pose, I finally exhale, releasing the breath I don't know I'm holding. I sink back into my seat, drained of energy as if I had just skated the performance with them.

I can't do this. I can't be here watching him. Other skaters come on and I try to watch, but I just can't. I glance at the guy next to me and his eyes are closed. I elbow him slightly. "Wake up. It's rude to sleep through the show."

Without opening his eyes, he says, "I cannot tell you how many times I have had to sit through one of these things."

"And I take it you're not a fan?"

"Unless there's a puck and they're all carrying sticks, not really."

"I used to be more of a hockey girl myself."

"Used to be?"

"I haven't followed sports in a few years. It was kind of a self-imposed ban." The next thing I say surprises me. "I miss watching and going to sports."

"Well, it is the middle of July so we're out of luck for tonight. Maybe next season?"

Is this dude asking me out?

I peek at him, not wanting him to see my mouth agape in shock. He's scrolling on his phone. "Actually, the Tigers are playing the Angels tonight. It's a late game from California. Wanna hit Cobo Joe's after and watch the game? Ease back into sports by watching some?"

"Sure, why not? I'm Kaitlin by the way."

"Ronan. I'm supposed to hang with my brother after this. You don't mind if he joins us, do you?"

Okay, so maybe this guy is not hitting on me after all. The ink is now dry on the divorce papers, so maybe easing back into both sports and dating isn't such a bad idea.

******

9:15 p.m.: Declan

The show is almost over. Natalya and I have our one last number, the new one, and then the group finale. This is my last time professionally performing in Detroit. I'm supposed to go out with Ronan after this. That'll be good. Keep me from getting too emotional and rethinking my retirement. I've changed into my costume and Nat comes out, adjusting hers. As she turns, I see one layer of her skirt is caught up. Motioning for her to come over, I free the trapped layer and smooth her skirt down over her bottom. She looks at me expectantly.

"I don't want this to be over. I don't want us to be over."

"Natalya, we were over years ago."

"No, we've never been over. We can't stay away from each other. You know it as well as I do. You're just too much of a blockhead to realize it."

"Nice way to try to convince me to love you."

"You do love me Declan, even though you don't know it. You think you hate me but you don't. You still feel every ounce of passion for me that you used to. I can see it when you skate. I can feel it when you hold me."

Jesus, maybe she's onto something. We've been together for so long. It would easy to be with her. Hell, who am I kidding? Being with Natalya is never easy. She's demanding and stubborn and spoiled. Not to mention the whole unhealthy thing. But if I were with her, maybe that's all she'd need to get better. Crap. I can't believe she's throwing this at me. I can't believe I'm considering it.

"I'm going out with Ronan after the show. Why don't you come out with us? Hang out and we'll see how things are."

"What do you mean by that? See how things are?" Uh-oh. She sounds pissed again.

"Nat, I don't know what I want. I agree that we have a certain chemistry on the ice. We wouldn't have lasted if we didn't. But I don't know if I can do a relationship right now. If I *want* to do a relationship right now. So, for tonight, I just want to hang out with my brother and friends and relax. Can you do that? Can you fit in and be a part of my life that way? 'Cause if you can't then there is no way, no how that things will work out between us."

She's pissed, that's for sure. But she doesn't have time to fire back. We're out on the ice again. I have to say, I'm happy to be skating this number last. I think it could be my favorite of all the ones we've ever done. Since it is for a show, I worked with the crew on a lighting component that was inspired by the airport tunnel show. This being my last tour, they humored me. And the song is emotional and raw and needy. Just like Natalya and me.

I've mentioned love but Natalya never has. She just says she wants me and she needs me. Maybe it's like that Meatloaf song, "Two Outta Three Ain't Bad." I don't think about love often. I don't know the last time I was in love. It was probably with Nat, but those feelings are gone. I think.

I have to focus on the routine. I carry the weight of our conversations with me as we move about the ice, separating and then colliding, all in perfect timing. The words of the song for the first time permeate me, and I understand why she felt so connected to this song, as Sam Smith's soulful voice laments that he knows the relationship won't work, but begs his lover to stay regardless.

I look at Natalya, holding her body in front of mine. Her legs are wrapped around my torso and she's arched backward. As she lifts her head, our eyes meet. In that moment I want to love her. But then she's down and away from my body. The moment is gone and I focus on the toss throw over my head. Throwing her away from me. Is it metaphoric? Jesus, Declan, get your head in the program before you drop Natalya on the side star lift.

But as we get to the end of the program, I feel the emotion wash over me again. We finish on our knees, sliding into each other, wrapped in each other's arms. I hold her a moment longer than I need to and a bit tighter than I should. Without breaking hold, I lean back so I can look into her face. I rest my forehead on hers while the crowd claps thunderously. We stand, hands linked and take our bows, pivoting to face each side of the arena.

As I stand back up, I see Ronan and Frankie standing, clapping wildly. Frankie's crying. It makes me start to tear up a bit too. I'm going to miss this. This feeling, in this moment. I blow a kiss to Frankie and give a little air-fist bump to Ronan. As I'm turning to leave the ice, something catches my eye.

The woman sitting next to Ronan looks just like Kaitlin.

Skating off the ice, there is no time to be thinking about this. To be thinking about her. How she never called. We've got to get our costumes changed, stripping down just off the ice, with production assistants ripping our clothes off and shoving new ones on. Someone's hand gets a little too close to my junk (this happens a lot) and I think about how I will not miss this part. Especially the ugly-ass, spandex, salmon and red costume monstrosity I'm forced to wear for this.

Natalya and I are back on the ice, skating with the group and keeping up with the fast-paced finale. It's a lot to do after the previous, but nothing we can't handle. A few more lifts, one more throw-triple Salchow during our solos. Natalya doubles it but who cares? The crowd is on its feet, stomping and clapping. No matter how tired I might be by the end of the show, I am always invigorated during the finale. I have only so many left.

Before I know it, the finale is done and we're bowing again. I search out Ronan. The seat next to him is empty. Man, I hate when people leave early. Don't they know we're skating our hearts out until the end? The least they can do is stay. All because they want to beat the crowd out to the parking garage.

Ronan gives me a thumbs up and signals for me to call him. I nod back and spin Natalya around again for our final bow. We head off the ice in the Joe Louis Arena for the very last time.

Chapter Seventeen
9:20 p.m.: Kaitlin

I'm watching Declan have sex. No, he's not having sex. This is making love. That's what he and his partner are doing out on the ice in front of twenty thousand people. This number is so full of want and need and hunger and angst. Oh God, and the way he looks at her! I would die— die—if he ever looked at me like that. He must be a better actor than I ever imagined. You can practically cut the sexual tension between him and his partner with a knife. Of course, it is not helping my current situation of lusting strongly after him.

I want to get out of here. I need to get out of here. I can't sit through this anymore. The number finally ends and Declan and his partner are wrapped up in each other on the ice. His forehead is resting on hers. It wouldn't surprise me if they started tearing off each other's clothes any second. The look in his eyes is unmistakable lust and hunger.

They stand and are bowing. Ronan and the woman next to him are on their feet, clapping and cheering. Declan blows a kiss in our direction and I notice the woman next to Ronan is crying. Wow. She really gets into this.

There is a moment or two of quiet before the finale starts. Ronan leans in. "I was serious about going to watch the game after. You in?"

I look at him. He's definitely cute and definitely flirting with me. Why the hell not? I'm not married anymore. I still have a healthy sexual appetite. Why not take a bite? "Sure. Sounds fun."

The finale starts and the cast comes out in these hideous, coordinating costumes. They are a terrible salmon color with red sequins all over. If I were still in contact with Declan, I would so make fun of him for having to wear it. The only thing that could make it worse would be feathers. Or gloves. Or gloves covered in feathers. This thought puts a smile on my face.

Watching the finale, I'm amazed by the performers. They've been out here for two hours. I admire their stamina. I've been exercising more these days but have nowhere near the endurance I once had. However, as entertaining as the skaters are, I can no longer ignore the fact that I desperately have to go to the bathroom. Urgently. I lean over to Ronan. "I've got to use the bathroom before we go, and I want to avoid the lines. How 'bout I meet you at the main entrance?"

He smiles and nods, and then turns his body to let me pass. It is hard to get out, and I hear more than one set of grumbles as I climb over people. I make it up the stairs and luckily there is a bathroom just to the left. I head in and nearly want to groan in relief when I finally empty my bladder. I finish up and wash my hands. Looking in the mirror, I see that I still look pretty good. I add a little lip gloss and head out. The crowds are starting to leave now and before I know it, I'm pressed in on all sides by the mass exodus.

I get to the main entrance, and I hear Ronan calling my name. I wave and he finally makes it over to me.

"I thought I'd never get through. I was body checked by this little blond with pigtails."

"You should have run the zone D."

He puts his arm around me. "You ready to get out of here?"

I glance around and see the t-shirt with Declan's face on it. "Yeah, I'm ready to go somewhere new."

We walk the few blocks to Cobo Joe's. The bar is crowded but not obnoxiously so. Not like it would be after a Red Wings game lets out. I guess not many of the figure skating set are sports bar people as well. We don't manage to get seats but are able to claim a high-top table to lean on. The first round of beer goes down quite easily. As does the second and the third. Ronan is funny and flirty. Just what I need to get over Declan. But damn, he does remind me of Declan. I need to drink more until that thought goes away. Ronan's been on his phone throughout the night, texting. Finally, as the liquid courage kicks in I say, "Who is so important that you're ignoring me to text? You lining somethin' up for later?"

He smiles. "I thought I took care of that already."

"Oh, you're bad." I smack him. My hand stays on his arm maybe a moment or two longer than it should. "But you still have to tell me who you're texting."

"My brother. He's going to meet up with us."

Our fourth (or fifth?) round of beer has arrived by this point and I put a good dent in mine with one long drink. Wiping my mouth with the back of my hand I say, "Your brother? I'm not that kind of girl. Well, maybe I am."

Please tell me I did not just say that.

Ronan smiles at me. "I think my brother is bringing a girl with him tonight, so I think it will be just us later, if it's all the same to you."

The distance between our bodies is diminishing. I lick my lips. "I'm pretty sure that is perfectly fine with me."

"Damn, Kaitlin. I wish we could get out of here already."

I lean in, closing the gap between our mouths. "Why don't we?" As I close my eyes, the bar spins around me. I grab on tightly to Ronan's arms to keep from falling over. His mouth is on mine, hot and wet. Dear lord, I am making out with a virtual stranger in a bar. Oh, and I may be a little hammered as well. It is nothing like my dream and I do my damndest to push all thoughts of Declan out of my head. Tonight, it will only be Ronan.

******

11:15 p.m.: Declan

We've showered, changed and gotten a bite to eat. Natalya and I beg off from the cast dinner and head over to meet up with Ronan. Apparently, he picked up some chick and is not planning to be there long. Typical Ronan. He's a player with a capital P. He is everything I don't want in life. Oh sure, I used to be like him. A little bit. And it's not like I don't get offers, because I do. But I'm tired of that lifestyle. I wonder why he isn't.

I don't know that bringing Nat out with me is a good idea. I still don't know what I want from her. If anything. But she needs to go out and have fun just as much as I do.

Maybe even more. And if anything, a night out with Ronan is guaranteed to be a night no one forgets.

We get there and the bar is packed. Die hard Tiger fans, watching the game from the West Coast. My height gives me an advantage and I use it to look over the crowds. I see Ronan toward the back. He's standing at a high top, his hand holding a mostly empty glass on the table. And he's making out with some girl. I can see her arm clutching his tightly and even still, she's swaying. His hand leaves the bar glass and cups her face, pulling her closer into his body.

I lean down to Natalya. "Looks like Ronan has made a friend," I say, nodding in their general direction.

"When hasn't he made a friend? He's pretty much a male slut."

"Nat, stop."

"Why? He screws everything that walks. He'd probably screw things that didn't as well."

Suddenly, it is perfectly clear to me why I do not want a relationship with Natalya.

Ronan is facing us, still making out with his new friend. His eyes are open and he is looking around. He spies us and waves a little bit, signaling us to come over.

"Ugh, he's so disgusting. He can't even stop sucking face with that tramp for five seconds. You know they're just going to be all over each other and will probably go have sex in the bathroom."

I stop in my tracks. It takes Natalya a few seconds to realize I'm no longer by her side. She comes back, her impatience apparent. "What?"

"Really?"

"Yes, really Declan. What the hell has your panties in a bunch?"

"He's my brother Natalya. He's my best friend."

"He's a disgusting slime bag."

"One could have said the same thing about the both of us after we broke up. I don't remember either of us being too choosy or discreet back then."

"Yeah, but that was because we were hurting. It was a phase and we moved past it. This is his way of life."

"Did you ever think that he's hurting? That he has some reason for acting like this?"

"Yeah. He's a whore."

I sigh and shake my head. She just doesn't get it. And never will. I can't be with her. I don't know what I was thinking. Natalya is not the girl for me. She's poison, her negativity seeping into everything. I step back and look at her. She's wearing skin-tight black pants that look like they could be leather. Her back is bare, showing every bone in her spine. Her black hair cascades down over her shoulders. I know for a fact that is has so much crap in it that you could not run your fingers through it. Her makeup and jewelry are heavy, as if she doesn't know the difference between performance and casual attire. Her look repulses me.

Finally, we've made it to Ronan and his friend. Just as we get there, Nat turns to me. "Declan, I am parched. Get me something to drink, okay?"

Dejected, I turn back toward the bar. This is my life. This is going to be my life if I stay with Natalya. It is not what I want. I want a woman who ... well, who's not a huge bitch.

I wish I could just walk out of the bar and leave her behind. But I can't. The bus leaves in the morning and we'll both be on it. Forty-five more days with her. I can do it. I order a shot and down it quickly. I'm going to need it to get through tonight.

I feel like an ass ordering Natalya's fruity drink in a sports bar, but I do it anyway. Reason number one thousand and one why we don't belong together. She wants top-shelf, fancy drinks and I'm excited that they have Pabst Blue Ribbon on tap.

Taking our drinks, I elbow my way back to Natalya and Ronan. Natalya stands slightly away from the table as if she's too good to touch anything and shakes her head in that haughty way she does. I wish this night were over already. I'm gonna have this one drink and then go home. I will have plenty of time to spend with Ronan once I retire, so cutting this night short will be no big deal.

As I get closer, I hear Natalya say, "Well, get used to it Ronan. We're back together, so I'm going to be around a lot more in the future."

"He's not going to have time for you once he's in school. You know that."

"Ronan, stop being an ass. He loves me, always has and always will. Deal with it."

I slam Natalya's drink down on the table with a little more force than intended, pink liquid splashing all over my hand.

"Jesus, Declan, look what you did! Now you have to go get me another one!"

It takes every ounce of restraint I have not to dump the whole thing on her head. "Drink this first, and then we'll get you another one."

I turn to face Ronan, ashamed to look him in the eye. He may be a male whore, but I'm the one who lets Natalya lead me around like a ball-less wonder. I know he's going to give me endless shit for this. I don't know what I'm going to do, how I'm going to make it through the rest of the tour with Natalya without her thinking we're together. 'Cause we are so not.

Just when I think this evening cannot possibly get any worse, I see the girl who is Ronan's flavor of the night. Damn it, it was her in the arena!

Kaitlin.

Chapter Eighteen
11:25 p.m.: Kaitlin

The voice is so icy that I feel like I was just doused with a bucket of cold water. I break apart from Ronan to see who is interrupting us.

"May I help you?" I can be icy too. I've had a lot of practice.

"I asked *Ronan* if he would be coming up for air anytime soon." It is clear this bitch is judging me. Little does she know that no one judges me. Also, I'm pretty drunk so my combative nature is that much more present. I turn around so I can face this person who has interrupted my make out session. I wipe my mouth and take another drink of my beer. Okay, so Ronan is a bit of a sloppy kisser. But then again, maybe it's just me because I'm a sloppy drunk. I miss what Ronan says to the evil one, but then she replies, "He's at the bar, getting my drink."

I would never have pegged Ronan to be rude, so I'm a bit shocked when he says, "Trying to escape you already?"

She stiffens. She's wearing black leather pants that are painted on. She has a royal blue halter top that not only shows her back but lets everyone know that she's not wearing a bra. The blue brings out her eyes, especially in contrast with her mass of dark hair. She's impossibly skinny and looks like she could break in half any moment, but she also has an air of toughness that makes me think she could kick my ass. She looks familiar but I can't tell why. Maybe it's because everything is a little fuzzy.

"Ronan, you need to check your attitude at the door and get used to me. I'm going to be around for a long time to come."

"Natalya, I bet he has a countdown going until the second he's rid of you. Hell, I can't wait until I don't have to deal with you."

Okay. Ronan continues to glare at the skinny bitch. It's pretty obvious he doesn't like her. Based on first impressions, I don't either.

Ronan continues lighting into her. "Well, get used to it Ronan. We're back together, so I'm going to be around a lot more in the future."

"He's not going to have time for you once he's in school. You know that."

"Ronan, stop being an ass. He loves me, always has and always will. Deal with it."

Ronan's brother has apparently heard his darling girlfriend as he slams her drink down on the table beside her. Predictably, she is more upset about the spilled drink than about fighting with her boyfriend's brother.

I'm leaning into Ronan, mostly because I can't feel my legs so good right now. I mean the good leg, obviously. His arm is around my waist and his hand occasionally runs over my bottom. I look up at Ronan and then follow his gaze to his brother.

Declan.

I think I'm going to throw up. Holy hell. Well, no wonder Ronan reminded me of Declan. Declan is staring at me. That woman he's with is winding herself around him. His arm is around her waist, looking like it naturally belongs there.

Okay, wait. I'm thoroughly confused. Declan's gay. How is he with this woman? He told me about his partner. Partner. Oh snap. She's his partner. Like on the ice. And apparently off as well. Are you kidding me?

Good thing I gave up swearing, otherwise I'd be cursing a blue streak right now.

Ronan's introducing me. "Kaitlin, this is my brother Declan and his—" He stops, almost choking on the words, "Natalya."

What do I do? Do I pretend that I don't know him? Do I apologize for never calling him? Do I yell at him for misleading me about being gay? Do I just grab him and kiss him? Kiss ... oh no. I just kissed his brother. I'm about to have sex with his brother.

"Katie is it?" Declan's got a wicked smile on his face. Okay, so that's how he wants to play it.

"Kaitlin. And you're ... Deacon?"

The horrid woman chimes in. "Don't you *know* who we are? We're the Olympic bronze medalists. We were just in a sold-out show at Joe Louis."

"Oh, you were there too? Didn't you just love the Russian couple? Oh, they're just divine to watch." I know I'm baiting her, but frankly, I don't care. She's a nasty person. It's apparent. I can't believe Declan is with her. Well, first, I can't believe he's not gay. Second, I can't believe that he would choose to be with someone as awful as this person.

A slow smile spreads over Declan's face and he knows what I'm doing. He has to respond by baiting me. "Surely you must have heard of us. After all, you did buy a ticket for the show."

Ronan's just watching us with an amused expression on his face. I shake my head and say, "Funny thing about that. I didn't buy a ticket. Some mysterious admirer sent it to me."

Ronan looks at me. "Well I guess I should be thankful that out of all that randomness in the universe, some mystery person sent you a ticket that sat you next to me."

The color drains from Declan's face and he mutters something.

"What was that, bro?" Ronan asks. Oh good, I'm not the only one who couldn't hear him.

"Frankie. That was supposed to be Mom's seat, but she couldn't make it into town. Frankie had the extra ticket," Declan tells Ronan

Furrowing my brow I ask, "Who's Frankie?"

Natalya responds, eager to show how much she knows about Declan's life. "Frankie is Declan's manager."

"Oh, right."

"Katie, is it?" She continues. God I hate her even more. "How do you know Frankie?"

"I don't," I respond. "I must have some other admirer." I lock eyes with Declan, but he just shrugs.

I look around the bar so I can avoid making eye contact with Declan again. You know, it figures. Just when I'm getting my life back together and on track, and even venturing out enough to meet people, this has to happen.

The others are talking but I'm not paying attention. I'm not feeling so great and I just want to get out of here. I can't believe what a colossal mess I've made of my life. Yet again.

Ronan hip checks me out of my pity party. "You okay?" he says, bending down to whisper into my ear.

"Yeah, I think I'm ready to go home now."

"Okay, baby. Let's get out of here."

I look up and the look on Declan's face says it all. He hates me.

******

11:35 p.m.: Declan

I cannot believe Frankie sent her the ticket. Son of a bitch. I know she was trying to help, but it totally backfired. Plus, I haven't filled her in on the Natalya situation yet.

Jeez, Kaitlin looks good. Her face is relaxed and she looks happy. I thought she was beautiful when she was pissed off. Happy elevates her to a whole new level. She looks up at Ronan as he says something to her.

Ronan.

How do I get her away from my brother? He was with me that week in New York. He heard me talk about her. Do I tell him that Kaitlin is the girl? Surely he would step aside for me. But what if he doesn't? I can see him trying to land Kaitlin just to prove he could do it. He would do that to another guy, but not to his brother. I hope. I don't want Kaitlin getting hurt by him. Then I hear her say she's ready to go. Crap.

Ronan answers, "Okay, baby. Let's get out of here."

The words are like a knife through my gut. Natalya is winding herself around me and I just want to shove her away. Kaitlin goes to take a step and she stumbles a bit. She's drunk. Oh, this is not good. Or this could be my chance to get her away from Ronan.

"Um, how are you getting home?"

She looks confused for a moment. It is obviously the first time this thought has crossed her mind. "Um, I guess I can take a cab?"

"How did you get downtown to begin with?"

"I drove. My car is in the parking garage over by the arena."

She can't leave her car there overnight. There will be nothing but a frame left in the morning.

"Ronan, how did you get here?"

"I drove too."

"You probably shouldn't be driving either."

He tries to shrug it off, but then says, "Probably not."

I think for a minute. "Tell you what. I'll drive Kaitlin's car to her house. Nat, you drive Ronan's car and follow us. Then we'll drop Ronan off at home and take his car back to the hotel. Ronan, get Frankie to bring you down in the morning to get your car."

No one can think of a better plan so we start walking toward the parking garage. Ronan and I room together when I'm here for training. I wanted to stay in my own bed tonight. If we head back to the apartment, I'll have to invite Natalya to stay with me, and I don't want to. We have separate hotel rooms, so I'm safe at the hotel. Ronan and Kaitlin are walking together ahead of us. Natalya keeps speeding up and then has to slow down because Kaitlin walks slower. I watch Kaitlin walk. I know that her limp is exaggerated because she's drunk. I also know that she looks good.

It is only a ten-minute walk until we get to her car, but it feels like forever, counting the moments until I can be with her.

Natalya has the full-on pout going. "Why do I have to drive Ronan?"

"Because it is the only way it works out. And at least you know Ronan. I'm afraid to leave you with this poor girl. You're likely to claw her eyes out."

She storms off, following Ronan to his car. Kaitlin gives me her keys and gets in the passenger side.

I walk around the driver's side and attempt to get in. I have to move the seat back all the way. It's a good thing no one's sitting behind me. The silence in the car is stifling. Finally, I can't take it anymore.

"You never called."

"You're not gay," she says in a huff.

"I never said I was."

"You're a figure skater!"

"Yeah, so?"

"You need to say that you're not gay. Otherwise it's implied. And you talked about your partner. What was I supposed to think?"

"I talked about my partner as in my pairs partner. Natalya."

"With whom you're in a relationship?" Her accusatory tone hangs heavily between us.

"I don't know."

"You don't know? What kind of crap answer is that?"

I can't help but smile. "Still off swearing?"

"Trying to be, although Natalya makes me want to unleash a few choice words. But you need to answer my question. Are you in a relationship with Natalya?"

"I don't know. We were involved for a couple of years, but that was over five years ago. We've been apart personally since. However, today she asked me to get back together. So I don't know."

"I saw you skate together. It was like watching the two of you have sex. You'll go back to her."

"What do you mean?"

"That number you did. It was like watching you in bed with her. Speaking of which, you spent the night in bed with me and never made a move."

She's jealous but has no right to be. She never called me. She was making out with my brother tonight. I focus on that.

"You were sucking face with my brother."

Chapter Nineteen
12:45 a.m.: Kaitlin

He's going to bring up that I kissed his brother? Damn him. Of course he's going to bring it up.

"Yeah, what's it to you?"

He looks at me, incredulous. "Did you tell Ronan that you're married?"

"No. It's none of his business."

"I think he'd think it was his business. We have very strong beliefs about marriage."

"I just met him for cryin' out loud!" My voice is loud in my small car.

"Yeah, but you felt you knew him enough to plan on having sex with him tonight, didn't you?"

"What's it to you Declan?"

"What do you mean, what's it to you?"

"I mean, why does it matter to you, Declan? You had your shot. I spent the night in bed with you and you never made a move."

"You never called me."

"I was dealing with a lot of stuff."

"Like what?"

"Like Tyler."

"So, what about Tyler?"

"Tyler is history."

"So you're free to do what you want, then."

"Yes, I am. I'm a big girl and I'm free to date who I want and have sex with who I want."

"Does that include my brother?"

Quietly, I say, "It's not like I knew he was your brother."

"And now that you know, is it going to change anything?"

"You mean, am I going to ask him to stay?"

His silence betrays his thought. I don't know what I'm going to do. I'm sure Ronan sort of expects an invitation. Before Declan got to the bar, I had totally planned on sleeping with Ronan tonight. I haven't been with anyone since Tyler and I wanted to do something so I would stop having sex dreams about Declan.

I doubt screwing his brother would actually help.

"Take a left here. I'm halfway down the block on the right."

He takes in my neighborhood with its Tudor-style condos. Looking out the window, I say, "I love my new place. Tyler and I were renting, so I bought this place. My dad helped me a little, but the job is going well, so I'll be able to pay him back within the next year or so."

"See, I would know this if you had ever called me." He pauses. "Why didn't you call me?"

I can't admit to him the truth, especially now, knowing that he is not really gay. Oh God, this is so embarrassing. I am such a moron.

"You can pull over here."

Declan parks the car on the side of the road and we both get out. He locks the doors and then hands me the keys. "This is a nice neighborhood."

I smile. "I do like it. I guess if I'm staying here in Michigan, this is pretty good."

Ronan has lumbered up and I notice how his movements are so much less graceful than Declan's. He's about an inch shorter and his brown hair is shorter. The family look is unmistakable, I imagine that if Declan ever cut his hair, the resemblance would be much stronger. How did I miss it?

"I'll walk you to your door, babe."

I see Declan stiffen when Ronan says this but don't react when Ronan puts his arm around me.

"Thanks for driving me back, Declan." Natalya didn't even bother to get out of the car. I nod toward Declan and head toward my door. I fumble with my keys in the lock. Ronan is standing behind me and reaches around me to help. The door swings open and I step into my foyer. Ronan steps in behind me and closes the door behind him.

"Sorry you had to drive back with my brother. He's kind of boring, but Natalya would have eaten you alive."

"It was tolerable."

"So you live in Grosse Pointe then."

"Yeah, pretty much here."

"I'm in—"

"Pontiac."

"Did I tell you that already?"

"Um, no. Your brother did. About him ..."

"Yes?"

"You two seem pretty close."

"I don't want to talk about Declan right now." He leans in and kisses me. My back is pressed up against the door and I have nowhere to go. While kissing Ronan was fun, though sloppy, earlier in the night, now it was churning my stomach.

I gently push Ronan away. "Sorry, Ronan. It's not going to happen."

He looks at me surprised and is then suspicious. "What changed?"

I look down at my feet. Should I be honest with him or just feed him a line of bull? Then I remember Declan saying that he is always honest, and I decide to go with that. "Declan."

"What did he tell you? That bastard. I'm gonna kill him."

"Ronan, calm down. He didn't tell me anything. I met him a while back and the timing just wasn't right. I know it's not right now, but if anything happens with you, then it will never happen with Declan."

"You know he's back with Natalya, right?"

"I know she wants to be back with him, but he's not so sure. I also know that the ink is barely dry on my divorce papers so I don't know that I'm ready for anything either. But I do know that I'm not willing to throw everything away for a quick tumble with you."

Ronan steps back and smiles. "All right Kaitlin. You win. I hope my brother knows he owes me."

******

1:07 a.m.: Declan

What the hell are they doing in there? I can't believe Ronan went in with her and shut the door. I can only imagine what is going on. They can't be having sex. Or could they? Kaitlin doesn't seem like the wham, bam, thank you ma'am type, but I've known Ronan to score in less ideal situations.

Natalya is sitting in the front seat, steaming. "I can't believe we're sitting out here. What is that ass doing in there? He can get laid some other time. Doesn't he realize we have to drive all the way out to Pontiac and then back into the city? I need my sleep. We're traveling tomorrow."

"Natalya, we're only going to Toronto. It's not like we're driving to California. Plus you can sleep on the bus. We don't even have to perform."

"But still, he's inconsiderate. I mean, he won't even remember her name or face in the morning, and she'll be just another nameless, faceless piece of ass that Ronan screwed."

I've had about all I can take of Natalya. If I didn't value my paycheck, I would walk off the tour right now just so my dealing with her would be done. Finally, the door opens, and Ronan comes out. The bastard is adjusting himself. Dammit. I don't know how he could do this to his own brother.

Wait—he doesn't know who Kaitlin is to me. But Kaitlin knows who Ronan is. He's just guilty of being too sexually active. But Kaitlin—how could she do this to me?

Ronan plops in the backseat. "Home, Jeeves."

"You know, as much as I want to sleep in my bed tonight, why don't we just go to the hotel. Ronan, you can stay with me and drive home in the morning."

No one objects, so we head back into Detroit. Ronan's a chatty drunk while Natalya is just pissed off. "This is so not how I had planned on this night going," she mutters under her breath.

Ronan and Natalya then start in on each other slinging insults like water balloons. When I can no longer stand it, I erupt at both of them. "ENOUGH!! Will you please just shut the hell up?"

The silence in the car that follows is thick. I'm mad at Ronan, although I know I have no right to be. I'm mad at Frankie for sending Kaitlin that ticket that landed her in my brother's arms in the first place. I'm so pissed at Kaitlin for never calling me. Gah! I sound like a whiny little girl.

After we've parked in the hotel garage, our footsteps are the only sound in the dark night as we head toward the elevator. Natalya is ten paces ahead, not bothering to wait for me in her irritation. Good. Then there will be no question about where I spend the night. She takes the elevator up, making me and Ronan wait for the next one.

Finally, Ronan breaks the silence. "So ... what happened back there? You lost your shit. And you never lose your shit."

"Sorry about that. You two were driving me crazy. I know you don't like her. I don't either, most of the time."

"Then why the hell does she think you're getting back together?"

"Because that's what she thinks she wants at this point. And you know Natalya. No one tells her no."

"Don't you think that's a big part of her personality problem?"

The elevator opens and we walk through the lobby to the other bank of elevators. "I think that's most of her problem."

"How can you even consider getting back with her?"

I think about it for a minute. We've exited to our floor and I walk ahead of Ronan to the room. "I dunno. It's easy."

"Nothing about that woman is easy. And what should be easy, she makes hard."

I think about what Ronan just said. He's right, of course. "It would be easy because she's here. I wouldn't have to try to land her."

"No, but you will always have to try to please her. And trust me, she will never be happy. No matter what you do, it will not be enough."

"I know. We just have this chemistry on the ice."

"You've tried it off the ice. It doesn't last. Especially once you're in school. You know she'll try to get you to keep doing tours or go out on cruise ships."

"Cruise ships?"

"Yeah, that's the big thing. Ice shows that perform on ships."

"Huh." I mull it over for a minute. "She'd totally try to get me on a ship, wouldn't she?"

"I would bet on it."

I get changed and give Ronan a pair of shorts. I spend a lot of time in hotel rooms. Probably more time than in my own apartment, at least lately. And each night, I think about that night I spent with Kaitlin.

Kaitlin.

I've got to tell Ronan about her. Swallowing hard, I finally start. "Hey—you remember that trip to New York in March?"

"Yeah." Ronan yawns. I know I won't have his attention too much longer.

"You remember I told you I met a woman in the airport?"

"Yeah. I think. I guess." He lets out a huge yawn. "You tappin' her? Afraid Nat will find out?"

"No, I'm not 'tappin' her.'" His crude expression pisses me off. Especially when I think of how close he probably came to "tappin" Kaitlin tonight. "It's Kaitlin."

"Who?"

"Kaitlin. You know from tonight. Kaitlin."

"Kaitlin's the airport girl?"

"Yeah."

"She said she knew you but the timing wasn't right. I didn't know you were talking about the same thing."

So Kaitlin told him about me. Interesting. "What else did she say?"

He's quiet and I'm pretty sure he's asleep. I know I need the sleep too. I feel tired down to the marrow of my bones. There is too much left on the tour for me to be this tired already. I know it has nothing to do with the physicality of everything, but rather the emotional ride I just went on.

Chapter Twenty
Friday, July 25, 2014
7:50 a.m.: Kaitlin

The morning sun hits my face, waking me from my deep slumber. Wait—the morning sun? What time is it? I roll over, ignoring the wave of nausea that hits me, and look at my clock. Oh, this is not good. Not good at all. I hop up and stumble to the bathroom, my foot catching no less than three times. Turning the water on for the shower, I sit down on the toilet and put my head between my legs. I guess drinking myself into a stupor after I got home last night was probably not the smartest of ideas.

After my shower, I get dressed and put my brace on. I still feel like the room is spinning. Vomiting is a definite possibility this morning. In the kitchen, I look at the bottle of vodka on the counter. The empty bottle of vodka. My stomach rolls again, and I run to the sink where I stand, heaving. There is no way I can go into work like this. I pick up my phone and call Trina, telling her I have some sort of stomach bug. Dropping the phone on my coffee table, I head to the kitchen to get something to drink. With work now out of the way, I give myself permission to lounge around. Oh hell, who am I kidding? I couldn't do anything, even if I wanted to at this point.

Lying on the couch, I stare at the ceiling. What the hell happened last night? Why was I such an idiot? I try to think back to the events that led me to my blackout once I got home. Thinking hurts my brain, so I stop. With my eyes closed I lay immobile, the self-pity washing over me again. I had been doing so well. I had finally gotten myself together. Sort of.

Dammit. Declan's freakin' brother. Of all the people I had to pick to have a random fling with, why did it have to be his brother? Why did Declan have to see me kissing him? I had thought, oh so many times, that my reunion with Declan would be something right out of a romantic movie.

I should call and apologize. Call Declan. The thought sends shivers down my spine and I get a bad feeling. A very bad feeling. The phone. Declan. The phone. Declan.

I sit up quickly, spilling my soda as I go. I grab my iPhone and slide the screen on. iMessenger is open. Oh. My. God.

I apparently drunk texted Declan throughout the night. About ten times. The messages becoming progressively more incoherent. I slam my eyes shut and clutch my phone to my chest, wishing it away. The only thing I have ever wished away this hard is my leg injury. I open my eyes and look at the phone. The messages are still there, mocking me with their absurdity.

Oh. My. God. I want to die. Right here, right now. Staring at them, I'm not only ashamed of my messages but of my grammar and spelling. Dear Lord, what was I thinking? I obviously wasn't thinking. Then I notice something. All of the messages have been delivered, but there is not a time stamp indicating that the messages have been read. He hasn't read them. But he will. And then he will think I am some weird stalker chick.

What do I do? Is it possible for the earth to open up and swallow me whole? That seems like the only viable solution right now. I lay there for a minute, and when that doesn't happen, I realize I'm going to have to figure out a plan B. Part of me wants to call Trina, but then she'd know I'm not sick but hung over, and I don't need that.

Sandy. I'll call Sandy. I look at the clock. It's a little after nine here, so it is just after seven in Utah. She'll be getting ready for work. She doesn't start seeing patients until nine on Fridays. She can tell me what to do. Relieved to have a plan, I'm glad I have a friend to call. I had reached out to Sandy just after my trip to New York, and now we messaged or texted several times a week. Once my physical therapist, now Sandy was probably my best friend.

"Kaitlin, are you okay? You sound terrible."

"Oh my God, Sandy. I need your help."

Sandy's voice is panicked. "What's wrong?"

"I got drunk and sent a lot of texts last night."

"Kaitlin!" she admonishes. "I thought you were off the sauce."

"I was. Until last night. Apparently, I went on quite the bender."

"Apparently?"

So I go on to recap for Sandy the random, mysterious appearance of the ticket to the ice show, the cute guy next to me, the multitude of drinks, and the less than six degrees of separation between Ronan and Declan. I also tell her about the world's biggest bitch, otherwise known as Declan's opposite-sex partner, Natalya.

"So he's not gay?"

"I know, right! No, not gay. Not at all. Straight as an arrow. Except, apparently when I'm in bed with him. But that's neither here nor there. Declan ends up driving me home in my car, with Natalya driving Ronan in his car. They followed us out here so they could go home together. Ronan and Declan are roommates for Pete's sake!"

"Okay, so nothing happened with Ronan then."

"He walked me in. After he assaulted me with his tongue, I told him I was interested in Declan."

"Yikes. So where does the drunken texting come in?"

"Me, a bottle of vodka, alone in my apartment with my phone. I texted Declan about ten times. It is so bad."

There's silence on the phone. Then I realize Sandy's laughing.

"Are you laughing at me?"

Her laughter is full on now. "Maybe a little."

"Nice. What a friend you are. But here's where I need you. I sent them, but he hasn't read them yet. What do I do? Can I save this somehow?"

She is quiet, thinking. "I think the only damage control you can do is to preemptively call him and tell him what you did."

"But then he's going to want to look at them and see what I did."

"There's nothing else you can do. What's the worst that can happen?"

******

9:38 a.m.: Declan

The banging on the door brings a sense of déjà vu. I'm just stuffing the last of my things into my bag. The bus is leaving at ten, and I still need to grab something to eat. Ronan left around seven and we did breakfast then, but I need to have some nourishment while on the bus. It's a good four and a half hours. Although the bus rides usually go by quickly with the camaraderie of the other skaters, I'm dreading being in a confined space with Natalya.

I open the door and it's her, impatiently tapping her foot. Give me a freakin' break.

"Are you almost ready?"

"Yeah, calm down." I do one last look around the hotel room, scanning for chargers and leftover items. I've learned from past mistakes. My phone is still sitting on the nightstand. Can't believe I almost left that! I walk over and slide it in my back pocket. I pick up my bags and walk behind Natalya to the elevator.

"Ronan get out okay this morning?"

I can't believe Natalya is actually being social and friendly, especially after last night. I essentially shut her out after seeing Kaitlin. Is she so dense as to think she still has a chance? We're together for several more weeks. I can't deal with that again.

"Yeah, he left around seven. He's gotta work this morning."

"Right, that whole nine-to-five thing. No thanks."

"What do you mean, no thanks? The nine-to-five thing is sort of a necessary evil."

"No, not really. Not for me." Her words hang in the air as the elevator doors close and shut us in.

"Why not for you?"

"Once I get married, I don't plan on working."

The elevator doors open and she marches out, shaking her hair with her head held high. I'm stunned into silence for a minute and then hurry after her. "Wait, what? You don't plan on working after you're married?"

"Nope."

Not that I had any doubt, but it becomes crystal clear that our lives—that we—are not compatible. Still, I feel the stubborn need to push. "You know I'll be in school for about four more years, right?"

"So you say. I'm not sure you'll even stick with it."

I want to hit her. Seriously. This is the real Natalya, the one that even the unbelievable on-ice chemistry can't hide. "I'm going to ignore that comment for the moment. What are we supposed to do for money while I'm in school?"

"Don't play dumb Declan. I know Frankie's gotten you all sorts of endorsement deals. Plus the *People* thing. That's got to put a pretty chunk of change in your pocket."

"That's how I'm paying for school. There won't be anything left."

"Then the obvious answer is that you are not the person I'm going to marry. I had already decided that anyway, but at least now I won't second guess myself."

She saunters out to the bus while my feet are rooted to the ground. I can't believe her. Her nerve. Mostly, I can't believe I ever entertained getting back together with her for even a nanosecond.

Running into the deli next door to the hotel, I order a turkey sandwich to go. I grab a bag of chips, a container of fruit, and a few bottles of water. This should last until we hit Toronto.

As we board the bus, I'm not in the mood to deal with the other cast members. Generally, the bus is a great time, but I'm not feelin' it today. I dig my headphones out of my bag and slip my phone out of my back pocket. Turning it on, I see I have a few voicemails and several texts. I silenced the phone before I went to sleep last night, afraid Nat would be harassing me to come to her room.

The first voicemail message is from Frankie, telling me how much she enjoyed the show. I certainly owe Frankie a call. I need to yell at her about the whole Kaitlin thing. I'm sure she had the best of intentions, but she really had no business sending Kaitlin that ticket.

The next voicemail message is from Kaitlin. She sounds terrible. "Um, hi Declan. It's Kaitlin ... I, um, I ahhh, need to ask a huge favor. Um, I sort of had a few nightcaps too many last night after you brought me home and *may* have accidentally texted you a few times. Um, I have no excuse for it. Please, I beg of you, please just delete them without reading them. I know it is a lot to ask, but they're awful drunk texts and I don't want you associating them with me, so can you please delete them? Okay, I'm sorry. 'Bye."

Obviously, I have to read them.

"It's Kaitlin. Are you ok?"

"Kaitlin here. I didn't know he was your brother. Sorry."

"Don't be mad."

"1 didn't sleep w/him even tho I wuz gonna."

"jut so u no, even when i was kissing ryan, 1 wanted it 2 b u."

"im gladdddddd ur not gay."

"urs sexxxxy when i dream u."

"why wont u ritw bkc?"

No wonder she didn't want me to read them. I can only imagine her level of mortification. These are hysterical. The smile grows on my face, just thinking about her. And as funny as these are, the best part is knowing she wants me. Like I want her. Natalya has taken herself out of the running and Kaitlin is now divorced. More important, she knows that I'm straight. Now we can finally be together.

The bus hitting a bump in the road knocks me out of my reverie. I'm on the road for almost two more months. Dammit.

Chapter Twenty-One
1:00 p.m.: Kaitlin

The phone silence is killing me. That's it. Declan thinks—no, knows—what a freak I am. It really is time to move on. Any chance I had with Declan is gone. As if making out with his brother wasn't bad enough, then I send him text after text after text, like some idiot teenager. If I didn't have a massive hangover, I'd consider drowning my sorrows at the bottom of a bottle.

See, that was my problem. I'd stopped drinking in March when I met Declan. I'd gone on a clean-living binge, getting rid of all things toxic, including my good-for-nothing husband. Tyler didn't contest the divorce. I'm not sure why he didn't initiate one in the first place; I'm guessing because he was too lazy.

Tyler. That was a mess. I can't believe I stood for that. It was like all of the resolve and determination and fight in my personality left when my career ended. I don't know exactly when he started being unfaithful to me. I think it was after the injury. Honestly, I'm not even sure though. God, I've made such a disaster out of my life. I wish I had a do-over for the past two years.

Well, three years actually, because I would have listened to my body and not him and my athletic trainer urging me to continue jumping, even when I knew I should have stopped. Because then I wouldn't be disabled. Then my jumping career wouldn't be over. Then I wouldn't have met Declan and wouldn't have lost him. Twice.

This is a downward spiral I can't let myself get sucked into. I was finally in a good place, even before I ran into Declan again. Certainly I can get back there. This is a momentary set back.

My phone rings and I nearly fall off the couch in my scramble to reach it. I try to rein in my disappointment when I see that it's Trina, not Declan. "Hey."

"Kaitlin, I'm so sorry to bother you, but is there any way you can come in right now? Are you still puking? Is it coming out the other end? Can you come in?"

"I guess. I'm not feeling stellar, but the last thing I ate seems to be staying down. I wonder if I had a touch of food poisoning or something."

"I hope so. I mean, I don't hope you had food poisoning, just that it's over and not contagious."

I like Trina. I really do. She's this tiny dynamo and she cracks me up. She brings a levity that I need to my life. "What's so important that I have to come in for?"

"There's a rep from the home office here. Apparently, we're going to be carrying a new product. It's a little band that you strap on your leg and it corrects foot drop. It totally replaces the need for your brace! I want them to try it out on you!"

No more brace. Kirby, gone forever. The mere thought of it makes my heart race. I know it wouldn't bring jumping back, at least not initially. But the freedom of no brace. Better shoe selection. Not tripping on my toes when I go to the bathroom during the middle of the night. No more blisters and hot spots when my foot swells during the humid summer. No more staring people when I wear shorts.

Short of a return to jumping, this would be the one thing in life that I really and truly want. Life without Kirby would mean a freedom that I thought was gone forever.

I head up the stairs as quickly as I dare with my bare feet and start tossing clothes around my room. Good thing I already showered. At least I won't head into work smelling like a distillery. I put on a pair of khaki Bermuda shorts, since my legs will need to be accessible and a flowing coral sleeveless top. I pull my hair back into a short, stumpy ponytail and put enough makeup on so that I don't look like a corpse. Donning Kirby and sliding it into my orthopedic sandals, the dreams of being brace free start racing through my mind again.

Stumping back down the stairs, I grab my phone, purse and keys and head out to my car, which is still parked in front of the condo where Declan left it. Upon getting in the car, I pull the seat up and start the engine. I notice a parking ticket on the window. Crap. Street cleaning this morning. Normally I park in my garage so I never even considered this. Oh well. Even a parking ticket can't dampen my spirits right now. The possibility of being brace free forever seems too good to be true.

However, once again, my delusions of grandeur are smacked in the face with the frying pan of reality as soon as I get to the office. Trina had the best of intentions. She really did. But she handles our billing and paperwork. She doesn't know the ins and outs of the products like I do. Like I should. I should have known better. The new product will mean ditching of some braces, but not for me. My injury is a peripheral nerve injury, which means the nerve in my leg was damaged. Plus my muscle died off as a result of the injury. This product works for people whose foot drop is caused by brain or spinal cord damage. Revolutionary for some; useless for me.

******

4:58 p.m.: Declan

My luggage has been deposited in my room. I grabbed a quick snack from the convenience store near the hotel, and now Natalya and I are headed to the rink for rehearsal. Sometimes the down days are a good chance to work out some details of the program that we're having difficulty with. We'll just skate a little bit, and then I think I'm meeting up with my mom for dinner. Sometimes my mom joins me and the cast. Natalya usually comes with me, since she's not too friendly with many other people. I would say she's not too friendly with other people in the cast, but it's really with people in general.

After a few warm-ups, practice lifts and jumps, we're ready to run through our routines. The full cast is going over the opening and closing production numbers, and then we'll get a chance to skate our individual ones. Since we were late add-ons to the tour—due to our surprise Olympic placing—we're low on the totem pole, and we rehearse last. Kind of sucks but I'm just happy to be on the tour. A month ago, I wanted to be done skating. Now that I'm back in it, I don't mind this last hurrah.

During the down time, Natalya is nowhere to be found. While I'm chatting with my buddy Bentley, I don't even notice that she's not here. Bentley and I are watching the other skaters perform, discussing and critiquing elements of their programs. Bentley's been doing this longer than I have and is no longer competing. We approach things differently and I think again today that we'd make a good coaching/choreography team. If only I wasn't quitting the sport for good.

When we only have two more numbers to go before ours, I head under the arena to warm up and stretch again. Natalya finally joins me. "Where have you been?"

"Why does it matter to you?"

"Just making friendly conversation. Relax."

"While you and Bentley were busy with your armchair quarterbacking, I was doing something proactive to solidify my future."

"Something or someone?"

She glares at me and then shrugs. "Same difference."

We take our turn on the ice and then we're done for the night. Our off-ice tension does not seem to affect our performance. Once we're sitting down to take our skates off, I ask Natalya about her dinner plans. I would like to go without her tonight, but I feel obligated to ask her.

"No, I have plans."

"Am I included?"

"No, of course not."

Just like Natalya. For the whole tour, our whole careers, I've included her in everything, even when I wanted nothing more than to get away from her. Now, she's working some poor sap and she drops me faster than a hot coal.

"I'm meeting up with my mom tonight so it's good you're all taken care of."

"Me too. I wouldn't want to sit through another dinner with your mother."

I drop my skates into my bag and stand up. "Jesus, Natalya. What the hell is your problem? Twenty-four hours ago, you were asking me to commit to you. Now you've got your super-bitch on and are insulting my mother. No wonder you're alone. You want to be taken care of? Why don't you think about someone else besides yourself for once? No one is ever going to want you the way you are. You make it too hard. You're too hard to like. Think about that."

I storm away and head back to the hotel. They provide us with a shuttle but I need the time to cool off so the walk helps with that. I can't believe I even considered getting back together with her. Part of me wants to think that she can't really be that bad, that she's lashing out at me because she's hurting on the inside. While I know it is most likely the reason, that doesn't make it any less infuriating.

Seeing my mom will make me feel better. I was sort of bummed that she didn't come down to Detroit but I understand. My dad always did the driving like that. While she will drive that far, she doesn't like to. She's done a lot that I never expected her to be able to do since Dad died. I know she's hoping that after I finish school, I'll move back to Toronto. I'm not so sure. I've been in Michigan for fifteen years now. By the time I finish school, it will be almost twenty. I'm sort of hoping that with me and Ronan down there, we'll be able to convince her to move down.

I'm showered and dressed and on my way back down to the hotel lobby when I think to check my phone to make sure the plans haven't changed. No new messages. That's good. But then that gets me thinking about Kaitlin. I smile, just thinking about her text messages.

"You look happy."

I look up to see my mom standing before me. "Mom!" I give her a big hug, picking her up off the ground.

"Ugh, Declan, put me down. You know I hate that."

"Just happy to see you."

"I'm happy to see you too. Where are we going for dinner?" Her voice still has that melodious brogue that instantly makes me feel like a kid again.

"You know where—Fran's."

"Of course. I don't know why I expected anything else."

"You know me, Mom. I like what I like."

She hands me her keys and we walk down the block to her car. I open the door for her and she slides in. My dad never let my mom open her own doors.

"So did you get to see that brother of yours?"

"Yeah, Ronan came to the show last night and I met up with him after. I guess Frankie was there too, but I didn't get to see her."

"Yeah, she told me."

"Yeah, I bet she doesn't want to talk to me right now."

"Oh?" Mom says it in a way that is a question, but part of me bets she knows all about it.

"Yeah. She did something behind my back, and I'm not very pleased with her."

"Frankie treats you like her own son. I'm sure whatever she did was in your best interest." She looks at me expectantly, waiting for details.

"A few months ago, I met a woman that I was really interested in. Nothing happened because she was married."

"If she's married, nothing better have happened."

"I know, Mom. Her marriage was just about over, but still, I didn't make a move. Anyway, I thought we really hit it off. I gave her my number and thought she would contact me. Apparently, she thought I was gay."

"Why do people always think male figure skaters are gay?" Mom says in a huff.

"Because most of them are. Anyway, she never called. But apparently, Frankie tracked her down and sent her your ticket. She was at the show last night. Sitting next to Ronan. With whom she really hit it off."

"Leave it to Ronan to woo the woman you couldn't."

"When we met up with Ronan later on, he was with Kaitlin. It was a bit awkward, to say the least."

"I don't know if I like this girl. A married woman should not be chasing after my sons."

"She's divorced now. I thought, all this time, she wasn't interested in me. But last night, after she got home, she apparently drank a bit too much and sent me several texts. This morning, she left me a voicemail begging me not to read the texts."

"So you read them, didn't you?"

"Yes, of course. They're hysterical."

"Are you still interested in her?"

I've parked the car and turned off the ignition. Quietly I say, "Yes. But I'm traveling for the next two months."

"Did you call her?"

"No." I get out of the car and walk around to open Mom's door. As I open the door, Mom says, "Why not?"

"Trying to figure out what to do."

"So what are you going to do now, other than send Frankie flowers for reuniting you with this woman?"

Chapter Twenty-Two
9:02 p.m.: Kaitlin

What a long and crappy day. Thank goodness this one is over. First the hangover and missing work, then the realization of the drunk text messages. Top it off with the parking ticket and the dashed hopes of ditching Kirby and I just want to crawl into bed for a year. But since I pretty much already did that once, I can't afford to do it again.

I call Sandy and give her the rundown on the day. Declan still has not indicated that he got my messages. "Maybe he lost his phone and will never know what a moron I am?" I say hopefully.

"That would be an amazing and wonderful coincidence, but it is highly unlikely."

I then tell Sandy about my crushing experience this afternoon with work. "Have you heard about this yet?"

"No, tell me about it."

I launch into what is essentially a sales pitch. I find myself choking on emotion as I go through and explain it, but I need to get over that. This will be one of my products. "It makes a functional e-stim unit portable. The unit, which is about the size of a half-deck of cards, straps on to the upper calf, right below the knee. There is a motion sensor in it that, based upon the position of the leg, sends an impulse at the right time. This causes a muscular contraction and the foot lifts up, essentially eliminating foot drop."

"That sounds so cool. Think you can swing a trip out here to show us?"

"It's not my territory, but I'll see what I can do."

"You should see about getting transferred back here. Now that Tyler is history, what do you have to keep you in Michigan?"

"Other than real estate, which is going to be a bear to sell?"

Sandy laughs. "Yeah, other than that."

I think about it for a minute. "I don't know that I can go back to Park City. Not yet."

"I thought you were doing better?"

"I am, but it's still hard. I think it would be difficult to see everyone and everything."

"I get it. I ran into Amanda today." Amanda Harris was one of my ski jumping teammates and we'd been fairly close before my injury.

"Oh? Where did you see her?"

There's a silence on the line. "I just saw her," Sandy finally says.

"Is she in the clinic?"

"You know I can't answer that."

"I know, privacy and HIPAA and all that crap. Okay, so how is Amanda doing?"

"She's good. She asked about you. I told her you were doing well." There's something in Sandy's voice that makes me think she's holding back. It's pretty clear that Amanda is being treated by Sandy for some sort of injury. I wonder if it has to do with that.

"Sandy, I know your physical therapist ethics prevent you from telling me any details, but is Amanda all right? You sound like something is bothering you."

The silence on the line is deafening. Finally Sandy starts. "I don't know how to say this, so I'm just gonna blurt it out. So, Amanda was asking how you were doing and I said good. I told her that you had finally kicked Tyler to the curb and were so much better for it."

Since Tyler had worked doing P.R. and marketing for the team, everyone knew him. I wasn't the first team member to sleep with him either. I'm not so sure how I became the unfortunate one to actually marry him.

She continues. "Amanda said she was glad and especially after everything that had happened."

"What does that mean?"

"That's what I asked her." Sandy pauses again and then lets out a deep breath. "This is so hard to say but here goes. Okay, um, apparently Tyler and Michele were having a thing."

"Michele? You mean Michele the athletic trainer who missed my symptoms and kept telling me I was fine to ski and train? That Michele?" My voice is all shrieky and weird.

"Yeah. This is the bad part. She's a bitch twice over."

"Like finding out that my husband screwed the woman responsible for ruining my life isn't bad enough?" I'm trying not to get hysterical. It's not working.

"Tyler and Michele were screwing around when you were injured. Tyler told Michele that you weren't hurt that badly and that you had lost your edge with the knee injury. He encouraged Michele to keep pushing you."

I mull this over, thinking about that horrible time. Recovering from an ACL tear and repair, the pain in my leg. Oh God, how bad it hurt. And when I went to Michele, repeatedly, she kept saying that I had to work through it and it was because my knee wasn't strong enough yet. For two weeks I kept trying, every day pushing through the pain. Training harder and longer until I couldn't walk, let alone jump. The pins and needles started and never went away. All because Michele was too busy boning my husband and listening to his cockamamie theories.

"Tyler told Michele to keep pushing me?"

"That's what Amanda said. That Michele was too busy doing the nasty with your husband, and that's why she missed what was happening to your leg."

"I know that. I've done some research. I had the classic signs and symptoms."

"I know. She should have caught it. I always wondered why she didn't. I guess now we know."

"You know, I've been trying not to blame her for what happened to me. But this kind of indicates that it really was her fault."

"Well, hers and Tyler's. He was as guilty. Actually, no, he was more guilty. He was your husband for Pete's sake!"

"No wonder he couldn't stand to look at me after."

"He wanted you to push through because he saw you as his meal ticket. We all knew that. Even you had to know that. I didn't know he could do something so underhanded though."

"Tyler told Michele to keep pushing me, and she did." Saying it again doesn't make it any more palatable.

"I'm sorry, but I thought you had a right to know."

I can't talk anymore. I say good-bye to Sandy and just sit on the couch, staring off into space. What else could possibly go wrong today?

******

9:58 p.m.: Declan

I'm gonna do this. I can do this. Why am I being such a jerk about doing this?

It is a simple phone call. That's all. I don't even have to dial her number these days. No chance of typing in the wrong digits. Why am I so nervous?

I'm pretty sure she's not going to reject me. Of course, the fact that I'm now in a different country could complicate the matter. And complications are not what I want right now. I just want to keep my head down, finish the tour without killing Natalya and then move on to something different. And never look back. Figure skating will be in my past and that's where it will stay.

Except even when I say this to myself, it sounds like an empty promise. Shallow. Fake. I think back to when Kaitlin asked me how men can just move on, forgetting everything they once had. I wonder if I'll struggle with that. It's not like I won't ever be able to skate again. I could do it for fun, or maybe even do a little choreography on the side. Bentley and I could collaborate, if we wanted. That would be a nice balance.

Wait—that's not what I need to be thinking about right now. I need to be thinking about calling Kaitlin. Before I lose my nerve, I hit the call button. One ring. What if she doesn't answer? Two rings. Will I leave a message? Three rings. What if Ronan is—

"Hello?"

"Kaitlin?"

"Yeah."

"It's Declan."

The line is silent for a minute and I look at my iPhone to make sure the call has not disconnected.

"I know." Her voice sounds weird. Bad weird. Like someone just died weird.

"Still there?"

"I am." Then nothing. Something's definitely wrong. I just talked to her yesterday. She's the one who texted me. She called me and left the voicemail. I'm just being polite and returning her call.

"What's up?" My voice is falsely cheerful, trying to draw her out.

She sighs. "Declan, I don't know if I can do this right now."

"Oh, is it a bad time? Do you want me to call you later?"

"My whole life is a bad time."

Her negativity irks me. I thought she was done with the pity party. She didn't seem this way last night. She was pissed at me for being not gay, but not dejected. "Why do you say that?"

"I just found out ... that ... God, I can't even articulate it."

"Start at the beginning."

Taking a deep breath in, she starts. "Okay. I can do this. I can tell you this." It's like she's giving herself a pep talk. "My athletic trainer missed my condition—the anterior compartment syndrome—that has caused my leg to be what it is."

"Kaitlin, that's not the beginning. Start at the beginning. You know, the *Before*." I use her term, weighing the word like she did that night in the hotel room. "Why did you have an athletic trainer?"

She pauses for a moment. I wish I could see her. "Wait—before you start, do you want to FaceTime? I want to see your face."

She's quiet again. Damn, I wish I was looking at her so I could have a better idea of what she's thinking. Finally, she speaks. "I, um, don't know how to use FaceTime."

"Seriously?"

"Yeah. I don't really have anyone to talk to that much."

"Okay, hang on a second. When it beeps, hit 'accept.'" I pull my iPhone away from my ear and tap the

FaceTime icon. The picture pops up and I can't really see anything. It takes me a minute to realize what it is. "Kaitlin, take the phone away from your ear."

Her face comes into focus. She looks terrible. Her eyes are all puffy and red. She's obviously been crying. I remember her saying she didn't really cry, so this must be bad. Or she was right, and it is just me. I smile at her and she gives me a tentative one back. "See, I brought you right into the twenty-first century with this new-fangled technology."

"Next thing you're gonna tell me is that there's this device where you can look up anything at any time and connect with people all over the world in the blink of an eye."

Chuckling, I say, "And this brilliant man called Al Gore invented it."

That makes her laugh a little too. My work isn't done, but I'm feeling a bit better about making her feel better. I see her give me a tentative smile. "I bet I look terrible" she says as she tries to smooth down her hair. It's pulled back but is falling down all around her face. I can tell she's sitting on her couch. Maybe laying on it. I wish I could see what the whole place looks like.

"I think you've had better days." That gets me a weak smile. "So, you were telling me what happened?" I prompt. "You said something about your athletic trainer missing what was going on in your leg."

"Right."

"Take a few steps back. Why did you have an athletic trainer in the first place?"

"Remember when I ran away from you at the airport after our flight was cancelled?"

"Yeah." I have no idea where she is going with this and what it has to do with her athletic trainer.

"I ran because I saw your Sochi bag. I ran because you were there and I wasn't."

She still has me confused. It's almost as if she's talking in circles. "Lots of people weren't there. That's why there was TV coverage."

"You don't understand. I was supposed to be there. I'm, I mean I was a ski jumper. I was at the top of my game when I first injured my ACL. I had participated in the lawsuit with the IOC to get women's ski jumping in the Games. I probably wasn't going to medal, but I would have jumped. I should have been in Sochi."

Chapter Twenty-Three
10:24 p.m.: Kaitlin

There. I finally said it. I finally told Declan that I was supposed to be at the Olympics. I see the shock wash over his face, quickly replaced by understanding. "Your leg—it took you out of jumping."

I nod. I think I like this FaceTime thing because I don't even have to speak.

"That's why you asked about getting the medals and then started crying. That's why you never want to talk about my skating and all of that."

My tears have started up again and all the words are caught in my throat. I can't speak, so I nod again.

"So, ski jumping? The one where you look like a flying squirrel?" The smile spreads across his face and I can see his dimples. He's sitting on a bed in a hotel room. I wish I was there with him. I can't help but laugh. Declan always knows what to say to lighten up the situation. "That was me, the flying squirrel."

He's quiet for a minute. "Things are definitely starting to fall into place now. But you've been dealing with this for a long time. What's different about tonight?"

"Where are you?" If there is any chance he's still in the area, I'm driving to see him. Tonight. I just need him to hug me right now.

"Toronto."

"Oh, I was hoping you were still here. In Detroit."

"Why?"

"Because I think this story would be so much easier to tell if I was sitting right next to you."

He twists the phone so I can see the empty spot next to him on the bed. Patting the bed with his hand, he says, "Consider this spot saved for you."

I give him a weak grin, but it's the best I can do right now. "The first time I ever went off the jump, I was terrified. I stood at the top of the jump, looking down and couldn't move. My dad was there with me, encouraging me to go. I had gone off jumps while skiing before, of course. I loved that. It took me two years to get good at moguls and slope jumps, and then I decided to try the big jump."

"How old were you?"

"Eight, I think? Maybe seven. Once I let go, it was fantastic. It was the best thing ever. The in-run part is not scary, and neither is the jumping part. That part is just awesome. The hard part is being at the top and letting go. And knowing once you do, you have no way to stop."

"So, you were meant to jump and kept at it. Now the whole Lake Placid-Park City thing makes sense."

"It's where the team training facility is."

"Did you jump all year or only when there's snow?"

"All year. Well, most of the year. That's why we— they—train in Park City."

"How do you ski if there's no snow?"

"On the run, our skis are in tracks. In winter, they're covered in ice. In the summer, they're porcelain that gets sprayed with water to make it slick like ice. We land on this long Astroturf kind of surface."

"That must be so much better than being out in the snow. I wish I could train on ice in the summer."

"I think that's called swimming."

He laughs, the phone shaking in his hand. I can't help but join him. "Actually, jumping in the summer can sort of suck. We still wear the suits and they're pretty hot. I've gotten heat stroke more than I care to admit. Once I get going, I don't want to stop. Annnnd then things start to go a little black."

"Didn't your coach or trainer stop you before you passed out?"

I shrug. "Sometimes. I was pretty stubborn and refused to stop. I used to hide how I was feeling so they wouldn't make me quit for the day. I just kept pushing though, even when I shouldn't have." Those words, hanging in the air, hit me hard. "God, I was so stupid."

I see Declan frown at my statement.

"I blew out my right ACL. I had surgery and was rehabbing that when my lower leg, like the shin area, started bothering me. I didn't say anything at first, figuring it was like shin splints because my mechanics were off. That's what Michele told me."

"Who's Michele?"

I get up and go into the kitchen. It's hard to remember to hold the phone in front of me so Declan can still see me and more than once I try to put the phone to my ear while I'm getting a get a glass of water. "Michele was the athletic trainer." I trudge up the stairs into my bedroom. After I set my water down, I flop on my bed.

"Where are you now?"

"My room."

"Show me."

"That would require me getting up. I don't feel like it right now. Can I show you later?"

He smiles. "I'm gonna hold you to that."

"So, Michele kept telling me my mechanics were off. My lower leg was killing me every time I walked, ran, did any training or jumped. She would massage it out after, which hurt even more. The only thing that helped was ice and ibuprofen. If I took a day off, it would help, but you can only take so many days off, especially since I had been out with the ACL for a while. We were ramping back up into competition season. Michele kept telling me that I had to work through it, push through it. The last few days, I could barely stand the pain. It was the worst thing I had ever been through. My foot was going numb, but Michele told me that it was part of the healing process."

"Didn't she know what it was?" He's angry. I can tell.

"That's the thing. All this time, I thought she just missed it. She didn't just miss it though. That's what makes this so hard today. That's why I'm so upset."

"What do you mean by that?" He's leaning forward, his body alert and engaged.

"I found out today that Michele was sleeping with Tyler when all this happened. He kept telling Michele that I needed to be pushed and that I was losing my edge."

"He was what? He did what?"

Tears start falling again, now that I've said the words aloud. They were hard enough to hear but even harder to say. "Tyler knew how important it was that I was at the top of my form by the beginning of the season. My performance was crap at that point. I mean, now it's obvious why I was sucking. Tyler kept telling Michele I needed to work harder. And she was so distracted by the bull Tyler was feeding her that she totally missed what was really happening."

******

10:58 p.m.: Declan

I can see her face, tears streaming down it. I hear her saying what she's saying but I'm having trouble understanding what she means.

"So you mean to tell me that your athletic trainer—your ATC—was too busy listening to the crap your husband was spouting to actually look at you and do her job?"

"Pretty much. He told her what to do and she did it."

"Do you think she wanted to get you out of the way? You know, eliminate the competition?"

"I don't know. I hadn't even thought of that, up until now. Thanks."

I can see her wheels turning, thinking about it. "How did you meet Tyler anyway?"

"I met him on the slopes at Whiteface. He worked there, running the ski lift. He was a player. I guess not much has changed. I was determined to not be interested in him. The more I was uninterested, the more interested he became. In the beginning, our relationship was kind of dumb. Neither one of us was faithful to the other. I mean, I was nineteen or twenty. He was twenty-five. He was still finishing up a program to be a mechanic. I should have realized that work was not his priority when it took him so long to get through school."

"Hey! I resemble that remark!"

She smiles at me. I love that I can make her smile. "You have an excuse. I'm guessing you were not out every weekend, nailing some chick instead of studying and working."

"I'll let you believe what you want to believe."

"Anyway, Tyler was hot stuff. Every little snow bunny was determined to be the one to snag him. He and I had hooked up several times, but neither one of us was committed to each other. One day, I overheard two girls talking, saying that he would never settle down. Never one to step down from a challenge, I decided I would be the one to snag him, for good. What an idiot I was!"

"So you got what you wanted then."

"Yeah, I guess. It was a whole be-careful-what-you-wish-for scenario. When we decided that I needed to move to Park City in 2009, we had to get married, since I couldn't stay on my dad's insurance anymore and there wasn't professional sponsorship. I thought it was all great, but I'm guessing that I actually had no idea what was really going on. I was so wrapped up in training, working on the lawsuit, lobbying to get women's jumping in the Vancouver Games, and trying to take classes that I didn't have much time for Tyler."

"Did he start cheating then?" If he were here, I'd kill him with my bare hands.

She shrugs. "Who knows? I thought he started cheating after my accident but now I'm guessing that he was never faithful. I was in Europe competing several months every year, and he didn't come with me most of the time. I don't know what he was up to when I was gone. He got a job that gave us both insurance, which is really all I needed from him. But after 2011, we had enough sponsors that the organization started providing us with insurance. I guess I should have walked away then, since I didn't really need him. He must have seen that coming. He said he didn't like being apart from me so much, so he started volunteering, doing some maintenance stuff and some P.R. stuff for the organization. Pretty soon, he was at the jump almost as much as I was. Even when I was travelling for competitions, which was pretty much constantly between September and February. I didn't think much about it." She drifts off, obviously lost in thought. She's lying on her bed, on her side. From the night spent with her in the hotel room, I know just what she looks like. FaceTime is great, but I wish I were there with her.

"So you found out that he was hooking up with the ATC?"

"Sadly, I'm so used to his cheating that that's not even what bothers me."

"It doesn't bother you?"

"Well, of course it bothers me, but he's been blatant about his cheating for two years now. Obviously. You remember the airport."

I remember seeing him with some terrible looking silicone tart. I remember him saying horrible things to Kaitlin, calling her awful names. And I remember her believing it. "How can I forget? I made twenty bucks off of it."

She laughs again. Earlier in the call, I didn't think I'd ever hear her laugh again. "You owe that money to the swear jar. You shouldn't have pocketed it."

"I'll take you someplace real nice the next time I see you. On you, of course."

She's quiet after I say that, biting her lip. I want to ask her what she's thinking about, but I know she needs to take her time. Finally she says, "When can I see you again?"

I go through the tour schedule. Forty-four more days.

"That's a long time. I wish you were here now." Her voice is so low I can barely hear her.

"I do too."

"Even after last night? Even after Ronan?"

"It's not like you knew he was my brother. Or did you?"

"It's funny. When I was talking to him during the show, I kept thinking he reminded me of you. I convinced myself it was just because I had you on the brain."

I can't resist. I wasn't going to tell her that I'd read her texts but I can't help myself. "Because you dream about me?"

Her free hand covers her face and the phone changes angles so that I can't really see her. Her voice muffled, I hear her say, "You read them! I asked you not to!"

I start laughing, thinking about her drunken rant. I can't stop and the more I try to stop laughing, the harder I laugh.

"Declan, it is not funny!"

I manage to choke out, "But it is funny. So. Very. Funny." I spit out in staccato words.

She's laughing too. "It's mortifying."

"But in a funny way."

I can see her again and she's wiping her eyes. This time, I think they're tears of laughter. A definite improvement.

Chapter Twenty-Four
Tuesday, July 29, 2014
12:32 p.m.: Kaitlin

"Hello?"

"Hey, Katie!"

"What's up, Deacon?"

He laughs, that deep throaty laugh of his. "Not much. We're on the road again. Headed toward Des Moines."

"Me too. On the road, I mean. Headed toward South Bend. I've already been through Lansing."

"Will you drive back tonight?"

"Probably not. I've got to be in Grand Rapids tomorrow so I might just stay in a hotel tonight."

"Is it okay to talk while you drive? I just wanted to hear your voice."

"I've got my Bluetooth on, so it's perfect. Keep me awake at least. Well, maybe it will keep me awake. Sometimes you bore me."

"I do not! You need to take that back!" He's indignant. It's fun to get him riled up.

"Okay, you don't always bore me. But I'm visiting the land of the fighting Irish. Maybe I can find myself an Irishman who never bores me."

"Well, after we do Des Moines, we're headed to Kansas City so I could find myself a nice farm girl who respects me for the sex symbol I am."

"Don't you mean a nice farm boy?"

"Oh shut it. You know I'm not gay. What do I need to do to prove it to you?"

"I saw the salmon sequins and spandex. I'm not sure there's anything you can do to prove it to me."

"I can think of some ways." His voice is suddenly serious and sultry. It's all I can do not to melt into the seat while I'm driving. I squirm a little.

"How much longer are you on tour?"

"Too long. Way too long."

I sigh. How is it that the most promising thing in my life is moving in a different direction than I am? I say as much to him.

"I know, Kaitlin. Trust me, I know."

******

Saturday, August 2, 2014
11:05 p.m.: Declan

"What's up?"

"Nothing much." She sounds tentative. "Is it okay that I called?"

"Yeah. I just got back to my room. Went out for a bite after the show."

"Am I interrupting anything? Do you have company?"

"Kaitlin Reynolds, are you fishing to see if I have someone in my room with me?"

"I refuse to answer that on the grounds that I may incriminate myself."

"Are you suddenly a lawyer?"

"No, but I watch a lot of *Law and Order*. Does that count?"

"Close enough. What' sup?"

"I ... um, I ... ah ..."

"Oh for the love of God, just spit it out."

"I just wanted to talk to you. Not about anything really. I just wanted to hear your voice. When I hear your voice, I remember how to be happy again."

"Has it been that hard, moving on with life?"

"So hard. Harder than I ever imagined. And I certainly never imagined I'd suck so badly at moving on. You know, I never thought about life after jumping. It was the end-all, be-all. It never occurred to me to look beyond. And even if I had competed in Sochi and hung around for Pyeong Chang in 2018, I would have still needed to have a plan for after."

"Okay, so I've gotta ask. The flying squirrel thing— what does it feel like to fly?"

"Oh my God, it's the most awesome feeling ever. Better than sex."

"You haven't been with the right man yet then."

"No, seriously. Flying is just the most liberating, exhilarating, peaceful feeling ever. You know when you are driving fast on a bright and sunny day and you roll down the window and let your hand surf the air?"

"Yeah."

"It's like that for your whole body."

"Doesn't that landing hurt?"

"No, not at all. Not when you do it right. You land on an incline, so there's really little impact."

"Crap."

"Crap what?"

"Now I can't focus on what you're saying. You said 'do it right' and 'impact' in the same sentence. Now I can only think of one thing."

"Great. Now that's all I'm thinking about too."

******

Tuesday, August 12, 2014
9:11 a.m.: Kaitlin

"Is it too early to call?"

"Never for you, darlin'." When he talks like that, I can detect just a trace of his brogue. "You need something?"

You. I want to scream 'YOU!' into the phone. "Was just missing you. That's all."

"That's good to hear. I'm missing you too. I'll be back to Michigan after Labor Day."

"That's good. That's just a few weeks away. Where are you now?"

"I don't even know. Somewhere in the western part of the country. They're all blending together. I'll hit your old stomping grounds soon."

"Where?"

"Salt Lake. We're there on ... August eighteenth. Anything I should hit specifically while I'm there?

"Oh, yeah. You've got to go to The Copper Onion and get a burger. They're amazeballs."

"Amazeballs? Is that even a word?"

"One taste of their burgers and you'll understand."

"Well, I'll see if I can make that happen then. I wish

you were going to be here to show me around. I want to see all the amazeballs things."

"That would be great." I hear a knock in the background.

"Kaitlin, hold on a sec." Muffled voices, a discussion going on. Then he's back. "I've got to run. We're having rehearsal early today. Sorry. I wanted to hear more about Salt Lake City and where I should go."

He disconnects. I think about Utah. So many hanging threads. So many unanswered questions. I've had no desire to return to Utah since I left. Until now, that is.

Chapter Twenty-Five
Monday, August 18, 2014
10:04 a.m.: Kaitlin

Retrieving my bag from the overhead storage compartment, I wish for the billionth time that Declan were with me. Of course, he can't be. I know that. I've come to terms with the way things are. Sort of. Not really. I pretend to be, but I hate it. He's away on tour, finishing his last tour. Then he's going to grad school. He's going to miss the first few weeks of school, so he'll be doing classes online. That means he's going to have even less time to talk to me. It's part of the reason I'm here.

This is pretty out of character for me at this point in my life, taking a risk like this. I'm pretending that I'm calm, cool, and collected but in reality, I'm freaking out inside. What if Declan doesn't want to see me? He's friendly and flirty on the phone, so I think he's going to be happy to see me. Our conversations have just left me wanting so much more. I just ... need to see him now. And when he started asking me about Salt Lake City, I knew I had unfinished business to take care of.

And as much as I want to see Declan, he's only a small part of the reason I've decided to make this trip. The real reason is that I need closure. I've stewed and ruminated for the past few weeks. I need to confront Michele. I need to talk to her about what happened and what she did to me. I've got to do this if I want to be able to move on with Declan.

Returning to Park City is going to be difficult. More than difficult, near impossible. Seeing the jump, seeing my friends jump—I get chest pains even thinking about it. I try some deep breathing to calm my nerves as I deplane.

Sandy is picking me up. It will be good to see her. I know it tore her apart to tell me about Tyler and Michele, but I'm glad she did. I had been in the dark for long enough. I wondered how many other people knew. How many people who I had thought were my friends were laughing behind my back at my louse of a husband cheating on me? A dark thought passes as I wonder if any of the other girls—girls who I had thought of as my sisters—were secretly glad when my career ended. In all honesty, I know at least a small part of me would have been relieved to have one of my biggest competitors taken out of the game. We were all close, but we were all rivals too. We fought together and against each other. We were Team USA; we were the world united to get our sport admitted, but we each jumped alone and wanted to come out on top.

Kind of messed up, really. Just like me. I guess I know why I used to fit in here. I feel like I've changed a lot over the last two years. For a while, it was not for the better, that's for sure.

Since I met Declan, I've started to get myself back together. It's taken me a while, but I'm finding out who I am. My whole identity had been tied up in jumping and competing for so long that I didn't know who I was without it. When it all ended, so abruptly and without my control, I was like a ship adrift at sea. Who could have ever imagined that some guy who ran into me at the airport would be my anchor?

I text Sandy that I've arrived so she can pull the car around and pick me up. It'll be good to see her. I'm so glad that we've rekindled our friendship. Another positive effect meeting Declan has had on me.

The sliding doors open and the heat assaults me. Whose bright idea was it to return to Utah in August anyway? Oh wait, it was mine. One benefit of Michigan is the cooler weather. Of course, winter there sucks. Am I too young to be a snow bird?

Sandy pulls up in her SUV and I slide in. She's got the AC blasting and I'm almost cold. Her dark blond hair is slicked back in a pony tail and she's wearing her khakis and short-sleeve T-shirt. She must be going to work after she drops me off. Her smile is warm, and I see her eyes dart down to my leg. I'm wearing shorts, something I never would have even dreamed of doing two years ago.

Lifting my braced leg up a bit I say, "They need to make these light sensitive so they get tan along with your skin."

"Who are you kidding? You don't get tan. You're the only person I know who lived here and still never got any color."

"I'm afraid of skin cancer."

"No, you lack pigment. Admit it."

"I admit I am of a certain pastiness. Some people find it attractive."

"Some people, as in a certain figure skater who happens to be in town tonight?"

"He may have commented that he may have liked the creamy smoothness of my skin."

"That's because it was winter and he thought you were just winter pale. I don't think he realizes you are one step ahead of an albino."

If there's one thing I've learned through this journey, it is that true friends are few and far between. Sandy is a true friend and I'm lucky that she accepted my apologies and took me back. I tell her as much, which causes her to blush under her tanned skin. "Back at ya, kid."

In my head, the drive from Salt Lake City to Park City is forever, but in reality it is only about twenty-five minutes. Since I'm dreading what comes next, it seems like twenty-five seconds before we're pulling up at Sandy's clinic. I know the facility well, having been a patient here several times. I go in and say hi to everyone. Donna at the front desk remembers me well. I chat with her while Sandy disappears in the back to get ready for her patients.

Walking back in here makes me feel in some ways like the past two years haven't happened and that I've never left. And then there is a part of me that feels like an alien visitor who has no part in this world. I've changed—grown—since I left Park City. Admittedly, the first part was pretty rough. I guess I could consider it a learning curve and that it has made me a better woman. Hopefully.

It's the middle of the day. The sun is hot and there doesn't appear to be a cloud in the sky. The sky is different down here. Everything is different. Or maybe it's just me.

I'm different now. I know I'm not complete. Not yet. That's why I'm here. I need to wrap this up before I can move on.

I don't want to confront Michele at work, but I don't know where else to find her. I head to Olympic Park, knowing where to turn without even having to think about it. As I pull into the parking lot, my heart feels like it's splitting in half, just as the artificial green of the slope bisects the rust and sepia of the surrounding mountains. Parking Sandy's car, I need to take a few deep breaths before I have the strength to get out. I spent years of my life here. This was my life. And now I'm going to confront the reason that life no longer exists.

******

12:58 p.m.: Declan

As the bus pulls into Salt Lake City, I can't help but think about Kaitlin. Like I need an excuse to think about her. I think about her way too much. It's getting to be a distraction. I need to focus right now. The tour only has a few more weeks. And we have a big decision to make.

Natalya and I had been last minute add-ons to the tour based on our performance at the Olympics. We hadn't been on anyone's radar before that. I personally was happy to be asked. Sort of like icing on the cake. Sure, the schedule was grueling, but I knew I could do it for the short term. Except now, it might not be the short term. The tour organizers like us. Well, they like me, and they tolerate Natalya. I'm sure my friendship with Bentley has something to do with it, but on occasion, the choreographers have even asked my opinion on things.

And now they've asked us to go on tour with them. A two-year contract. It would mean three months of rehearsals and six months of shows. The remaining three months are used for planning for the next tour. It would be good money.

It would mean I'd have to stay with Natalya and delay PT school. Hell, who am I kidding? It would mean not going to PT school. I know that. I'm already questioning my decision to go back.

It would also mean that Kaitlin and I would have no chance at a relationship. I can't ask her to commit to me if I'm gone half the year. More than that, depending on where rehearsals take place. Most years, they're in Denver, but that could change.

Natalya wants in, of course. A big part of me wants to do it too. I thought I was all done with skating. It was logical to quit. But now, it doesn't seem so logical. I know if I had never met Kaitlin, this decision would be a whole lot easier.

We check into the hotel and head right over to Energy Solutions Arena for a quick warm-up. Walking behind Natalya, I notice that she's limping. Not her normal "my knees are shot" limp either. She's really limping on her right leg. Of course, she's still trying to walk at super fast speed.

"Nat, slow down. Nat—wait up!" I double time my steps and easily catch up to her. "Are you okay?"

"Fine."

"Nat, I can see you're limping. What's wrong?"

"I'm fine."

"No, you're not. Did you do something?"

Hissing through her teeth, she pulls me off to the side. "I'm fine. Now stop asking. I don't want anyone to hear you and think that I can't skate."

"Can you skate? How bad is it?"

I see the break in her hard facade for just a fleeting moment before her chin sticks out. "I'm fine."

"No, Natalya you're not. Tell me. You have to tell me."

"I can finish the tour. I'll be fine."

"You need to get the trainer to look at that. Or better yet, Dr. Weston. I don't trust the trainer."

"Why don't you trust Scott? He's great."

"I, um, I have a friend who got misdiagnosed by her ATC and it caused permanent damage. I don't want that to happen to you."

"Who did that happen to?"

"No one you know."

"I know everyone you know. Who was it?"

"Nobody. It's not important. But I want you to see Dr. Weston."

We continue walking in to the rink. After a few warm ups, we sit down to lace up our boots. I see Natalya wince as she ties her right skate. "What hurts?"

Glaring at me, she says, "It's my shin. I think I have a stress fracture."

"Another one?" A side effect of Natalya's years of anorexia is osteoporosis. Her self-starvation has caused her body to go into what is essentially menopause, which causes hormonal changes and the associated decreased bone density. I learned about it during an undergrad nutrition class. The whole thing is known as the Female Athlete Triad. Natalya could be the poster child for it. "Jesus, Natalya, do you know what this could mean? We could lose the offer!"

"Does that mean you want to accept it?"

"I don't know. Sort of. I've had more fun on this tour than I expected. And it's not like we'd be competing, so we could do more fun stuff and not push ourselves as hard."

"No more side-by-side triples?"

"No more side-by-side triples. But that's assuming you can still skate. What if you can't? You have got to start taking better care of yourself!"

Her dark hair falls in a curtain around her downturned head as she says in a small voice, "I know. I'll call Ben tomorrow." She sits up, shaking her hair. With expert hands, she pulls it back tightly into a ponytail. Her face shows no sign of emotion. Her armor is on.

"Will you do what he says?"

"If it means we get to keep skating, then yes."

Oh shit. Now I'm locked in. If I say yes to the tour, then Natalya will get the help she needs. But that means saying no to PT school and to any possibility of a relationship with Kaitlin. Shit.

"Let's bag out of the run-through. I think I know what the issue is with our program." I look pointedly down at her leg. "We'll just head back, and you can ice your leg and rest until tonight."

"I can make it through the next two weeks and then I'll rest and heal. I don't need to baby it. It'll get better."

I get up and go find Marina, who is essentially our on-ice organizer and coach. There are more people higher up, but we really only deal with her. For all intents and purposes, she's our boss. Reporting to her that Nat is resting due to an injury makes me nervous. It's not like it doesn't happen. It happens all the time. I am uneasy that it will make the powers that be rethink their offer to us. Not that I'm certain I want to take it. Crap. I need someone to tell me what to do.

Chapter Twenty-Six
1:15 p.m.: Kaitlin

Walking through the doors, I'm so nervous about this. What am I going to say to Michele? I mean, she totally ruined my life. All because she was boinking my husband. Who is an idiot. But I married him first, so what does that say about me?

I want to scream at her about the hell I've been through. I mean, the pain alone of the injury. The surgery that followed was grotesque and still makes me want to vomit when I think about it. The loss of my career, my dream. She did this to me. I trusted her. We all trusted her. Her job was to fix us and make us better. She didn't do that.

I wonder who else there slept with my husband. Honestly, I wanted him because everyone did. The consummate competitor, I wanted to win in everything. Yeah, some winner I ended up to be. I have nothing to show for all my years of hard work. The skill is gone. The muscles are gone. The dream is gone. The husband is gone. Well, at least good riddance on that one.

"Kaitlin?"

To my left, exiting his office in a hurry is the head coach, Philip. The man I thought of as my Park City father. Seeing him is hard. I've missed him. I've missed all these people here. I cut myself off from them to spare my own shattered ego, never considering the void it would leave in my life. A void that I filled for so very long with anger. A smile spreads across my face, and I move to give Philip a hug. He stops and stands there, his hands held behind his back. The body language is unmistakably cold.

"How's it going?" I stutter, trying to recover from the awkwardness of his cold shoulder.

"I wish you had called. Can you have a seat in the lobby? I'll be right back."

I sit down while he disappears into his office. Sure, I wanted to confront Michele, but I was hoping to see some of my old teammates—my old friends—and possibly reconnect. I'm uneasy sitting here. There is no one walking around and here in this place where I used to spend all my days, I feel more alone than I have in a very long time.

After what feels like an eternity, Philip ushers me into the conference room. There is a phone in the middle of the long polished table, sitting there like a sentry. The cord snakes down and across to the wall. I have to be careful to step over it. Philip watches me walk with a close eye.

"Sit down, please." His voice is formal. Distant. Foreign. "Sharon is on her way over and Deirdre is on the phone." He points to the middle of the table, as if I can't see what phone he's talking about.

A small, tinny voice emerges from the phone. "Hello, Kaitlin." Deirdre is the director of the program. I can't imagine why she's been called to talk to me. She wasn't the world's friendliest person to begin with, and I never got the impression that she was a huge fan of mine.

"Hey, Deirdre. How's it going?"

"Fine." Her tone is clipped. Okay, I see she's no more fond of me than she was when I was still here in training. "Philip, is Sharon there yet?"

He's pacing around the room. "Not yet. She should be here any minute."

The name Sharon sounds familiar, but I don't know why. "Who's Sharon?"

"Sharon Brusczynski, our legal counsel."

Seriously? This cannot be happening. I'm sitting in what should be a cozy leather chair, and I'm more uncomfortable than the time I had to be in the exam room during my grandmother's pap smear. Philip sits down across from me and says, "Deirdre and I feel that it is best if you do not come on the property."

I stare at Philip's face and all of my old anger comes flooding back. As he shifts uncomfortably in his chair, I swallow hard, trying not to yell.

"So, Phil, what you're telling me is that, after all I've been through, I'm not allowed on the premises?"

"The facility is not open to the public at the moment."

"The public, Phil?" I know he doesn't like to be called Phil. He prefers Philip. "So, now I'm the public? I can't even go in and see my old friends and colleagues?"

Clearing his throat, he shifts nervously in his chair. "That's why Sharon is coming out. She has advised us that it would be in our best interest if no one was in contact with you."

Oh, this is rich.

"Seriously?"

"We cannot open ourselves up to more liability."

"Phil, how long have you known me?"

He's uneasy, running his hands through his thinning gray hair. "For a while now."

"Deirdre, you haven't known me quite as long as Phil has. I mean, he came to Lake Placid and sat in my dad's kitchen and told my dad how he would take care of me if I moved to Park City."

"You were an adult when you were injured." She's trying to defend her position.

"Right, I was. And for the past two years, in case you hadn't noticed, I've moved on from ski jumping. I've left it behind me. It's not what I wanted to do, but what I had to do. I really had no choice in the matter, now did I?"

Deirdre's voice floats through the room. "You were cut from the team Kaitlin. You are no longer part of this organization."

"And how many times in these two years have you heard me disparage the team or the sport?"

There is silence.

"How many news programs or magazine articles have you seen my story in?"

Again, no response.

"That's because the answer is zero. To all of it. I left Park City three months after my surgery, and I didn't look back. I couldn't even watch the games on TV. My life had been destroyed, but still I said nothing. Now, all I want to do is get a bit of closure, and you treat me like I'm a money-grubbing ambulance chaser?"

Deirdre speaks again. Philip is just sitting there, the pained look still plastered on his face.

"I had no choice when my dream was ripped from me. Stolen by someone else's greed and negligence. But you know that, don't you? You know the full story. How long have you known?"

Deirdre's voice has grown even brisker. "Isn't Sharon there yet?"

The door burst open and Sharon bustles through. Now I remember her. She's about four-foot-ten and causes grown men to quake in their boots. "Don't answer her questions, Philip."

Philip's mouth, which had been opened in preparation to answer slams shut.

"Did you bring your own representation? If not, we need you to sign this agreement."

She's got this package of papers that she has magically produced out of thin air. Not really, I saw her open her brief case, but she was really fast with producing this paperwork which will apparently silence me for life.

******

5:46 p.m.: Declan

I want to pull out of the show tonight. Natalya is adamant about skating. I can't understand why. It's just another show. There will be more. That is, if Natalya can get her shit together and start taking care of herself. I need to call the doctor and have him come and look at Natalya's leg. I'm pretty sure she's right and has a stress fracture. She had one in her spine a while back. I know it was absolute agony for her. It had to be. But she kept going. Sure, she bitched and moaned and was miserable. Even more so than normal.

She insists we're skating tonight. She even ate our pre-game meal to show me how committed she is to staying on the tour. One of the many things that bothers me about Natalya is her constant hot and cold. Like the crap she pulled in Detroit. Telling me in the morning that she wanted to be with me and then screwing one of the tech crew the next day to prove she didn't care about me. She's one hot mess, that's for sure. I know she's not going to change. I don't know why I keep expecting her to. What's the definition of insanity? Doing the same thing over and over and expecting a different result.

I need to talk this out with someone. This decision. My first instinct is to call Kaitlin. We've been talking a few times a week. It's the highlight of my week, talking to her. I can't tell her this though, because part of my dilemma is about her. Ronan will just tell me to "ditch the bitch" and come home to Michigan. I'm not sure what Frankie will say. I'd like to think she'd give me her honest opinion, but I also know that she stands to gain financially if we stay on tour. Because of that, I can't trust the answer she gives me.

I wish I could hash it out with my dad. I do the next best thing.

"Declan, to what do I owe this pleasure? Do you need money?"

"Very funny, Mom."

"So, what's the problem?"

"Who says there's a problem?"

"You're calling me. That's a huge red flag. You don't need money, so I'm guessing it's a problem with the ladies."

"Ladies being the operative word."

"I thought you were interested in this Kaitlin person?" I can hear the worry in her voice.

"I am. We've been talking. I can't see her until the tour is all done."

"Did you meet someone else?"

"No. I don't have time to meet anyone. I don't even have time for Kaitlin."

"Then who is the other lady?"

"When you put it that way, there is no other lady. The other person in the equation is Natalya."

"I will disown you if you go back to her, Declan Michael."

"Jeez, Mom. Tell me how you really feel."

"She makes you miserable. I will not sit here and watch you throw away your life on her."

"No, it's not that. It's not going back to her in that sense. We've been offered a contract to tour with the show for the next two years. We'd be strictly professionals on tour."

"Oh," she says quietly. It is not at all the reaction I expected her to have. I really thought she'd tell me to go for it. After all, she was the one who encouraged me to try figure skating in the first place. I was a pretty small kid and desperate to keep up with Ronan, who was a moose. I wanted to play hockey with him and his friends. My mom thought I was too delicate to hang with those brutes and signed me up for figure skating lessons. She told Dad it was to help with my control for hockey, but I think this was her plan all along.

"You don't sound thrilled with that."

"What about school?"

"I could defer it a few more years."

Her silence speaks volumes. I can picture her at home, sitting in her favorite rocking chair that was once my grandmother's.

"So I start in two years instead of now. No big deal."

"You won't start, Declan. We all know that. You'll get distracted by the next thing to come along and you won't become a PT."

Her words are brutal and honest. And the truth. Heck, the idea of becoming a PT was a distraction from skating. "You know me too well, Mom. But is it the worst thing in the world if I don't become a PT?"

"So, when the two years are up, what will you do for money then? You'll be in your mid-thirties, with no appreciable skills. At least not in a way that could support you."

"Thanks, Mom, for telling me I have no skills."

"You know what I mean. Your body won't hold out forever. You can't count on more endorsement deals because you're leaving the competition scene. Other than skating, you've never had a job. What will you do then?"

I can't answer her because I don't know. I've never thought that far ahead. I've never pictured myself old and gray. I try, and I just can't come up with that image. I certainly don't know if I see myself old, gray, and working as a PT, wearing khakis and a polo shirt.

The thought of being a PT came when I was in treatment for my back. I liked my therapist and thought the job seemed fun. I had taken physics and worked with the head of the department several times. To be a good figure skater, you really need to understand the physics of the human body. Natalya and I were in several demo videos for his classes—as well as for the networks and internet—to explain how physics makes skating happen. I thought it was so cool. Physical therapy, as the name implies, encompasses a lot of that. It is working out the movement patterns and the laws of nature within the body, restoring those patterns when they're out of whack. I'm interested in it, but now I'm questioning if this interest is enough to keep me content for the rest of my life.

"I don't know, Mom. That's why this is so hard. I thought I could just walk away and onto the next thing, but now I'm not so sure. I might not make it through PT school. I might fail and then I'd have even less, since I'll have spent my money on tuition."

"It seems you have a lot to think about."

I'm quiet for a minute. "What do you think Dad would say?"

She's silent again. I know bringing up Dad will make her sad, but I miss him too. I could sure use his advice, since I still haven't figured this all out.

"He'd probably say, 'Son, I can't believe you're still running around in all those fruity suits. Where did I go wrong?'"

I laugh, because I could hear him saying that. I know he was proud of me, but it boggled his mind sometimes that one son was a hockey player and the other was a figure skater. God, I remember him totally losing it because my costumes were too, well, you can imagine.

"That's exactly what he would say. But what would he tell me to do."

"He'd tell you what I'm going to tell you. Do what makes you happy. The rest will fall into place."

Chapter Twenty-Seven
7:22 p.m.: Kaitlin

I totally can't believe I'm doing this. I must be crazy. I might even be bordering on stalker crazy right now. I don't know what I expect to happen. Nothing has gone the way I planned thus far, so it's more than likely that this won't either. I mean, after I was escorted back to my car by security at Olympic Park, I didn't know what to do. The old anger started to seep back in. I mean, someone screwed up, and now I was disabled because of it.

All I wanted was to hear her own up to it. That's it. You would have thought that I was carrying a sawed-off shotgun the way Philip and Sharon treated me. Their behavior indicated that they know how much Michele is at fault for my injury. But they're too busy covering their own butts to think about what I've gone through.

The more I think about it, the more pissed off I get. Like super pissed off. Then I get tired of feeling this way. I thought that Kaitlin was gone for good, but it seems being here has brought it all back. It's not even being back and seeing my old stomping ground, or even the jump that has made me angry again. It is stupid people treating me like I will infect them with my disability by talking to them. As if my foot drop can be spread like Ebola.

I get that there are legal concerns. Their actions make me think that I could have grounds to sue. I just always figured that in a sport like ski jumping, being injured is a risk you take. You want to roll those dice, you need to expect some bad throws. Of course, that was before I found out that my husband's—make that ex-husband's—penis is the responsible party.

And what they don't get—what they can't understand—is that I would never sue. I'm sure people say that and then turn around and file a lawsuit. Even in my most bitter moments, I could never fathom operating that way. We fought so long and so hard to get our sport noticed. To get the U.S. team to compete and be taken seriously on the world stage. To get into the Olympics. To then get the corporate and private sponsorships to actually fund the dream.

I could never, ever do anything that would take that away from another girl. All the hard work of everyone involved. The whole organization is volunteer. All money goes into helping the girls train and compete. I couldn't take one dime away from the organization. From those girls and their dreams of flying.

That being said, I'm totally willing to accept their settlement offer, once I have a lawyer look at it. I'd been considering a civil suit against Michele and Tyler, just to cover future medical expenses, should they arise. The organization's offer might just do the trick though. A small offer, but an offer nonetheless. I'm not looking to get rich. I'm looking to be secure and to be able to move on.

All I wanted from this trip was closure.

Oh, and to see Declan too. That's the main reason why I chose to come back to Utah now. I don't care if I'm sitting in the audience and he doesn't even know I'm there. Talking to him on the phone isn't enough. I need to see him. In person. In 3-D, not a flat 2-D image on my phone or computer screen. Tonight, I'm going to see Declan skate.

I get to my seat just as the lights dim in Energy Solutions Arena. My seat is nowhere near as good as last time. I skip the beer too. There is a frumpy middle-aged woman sitting next to me and beside her is a girl about ten. I can tell from the look on her face that she wants to be a figure skater. I wish I knew Declan a little better, so I could introduce the two of them. But since I'm somewhat afraid he'll get a restraining order against me for showing up here, I don't think trying to have him meet this little girl would be a good idea. I mean, it's not stalker-like to fly all the way here just to watch him skate, right? I try to tell myself that he's going to be psyched to see me—I hope.

When I told Sandy I wanted to come down to see the show, she was full of encouragement. She tried to convince me that, seeing as how Declan and I talk regularly, this is not stalker-like behavior and is reasonable. She's stuck at work but will be here as soon as she can. The opening number has started, and I'm straining, looking for Declan and Natalya. They're not in it. That's odd. I know they usually are. Now I'm concerned. I pull out my phone, eager to text Declan, but restrain myself. About two minutes into the opening number, Sandy plops down in the empty chair next to me.

"What'd I miss?" She's out of breath and a bit disheveled from work.

"Declan's not out there. I don't know why. He was in this number in Detroit."

Just as the number is wrapping up, Declan and Natalya enter the ice. Declan picks her up and holds her over his head like she weighs nothing. Which she practically does. They glide around the ice, majestic and beautiful. Graceful. All the things I will never be. He puts her down like a delicate China doll and they strike their ending pose with the rest of the cast. I couldn't care less about any of the other skaters.

"Did you tell him you're here?" Sandy whispers during the next number.

"No. I don't want him to think I'm stalking him."

"Which you totally are."

"Which I totally am. Now shut up and watch the show."

I'm just as mesmerized by Declan this time as I was in Detroit. Maybe even a little more, now that we've been talking some. Watching him, I feel like I'm back in high school, desperate for the captain of the football team to notice me. Except in high school, I was the jock and the object of everyone's desire.

I know he's fond of me. I can say that with certainty. He calls me as much as I call him. We don't get to talk that much, but when we do, we can talk for hours. I'm totally selfish, but I can't wait until his skating is done so he can be back in Michigan. Sure, there will be some distance, but it's completely manageable.

I keep waiting for Declan to come out and skate again, but he never does. I'm starting to get concerned. Something is definitely going on. I know the show is winding down. I'm long past the antsy phase. I keep looking at my phone like it is going to magically provide the answers. Of course it won't, since Declan doesn't even know I'm here. I send him a text. "Are you ok?" Needless to say, there's no response.

Unable to stand it any longer I lean over to Sandy and whisper, "I'm going to go over by the tunnel where the skaters are coming in and out and see if I can find something out."

"I'll come with you. A lot of my Mormon friends from church work here. I might know someone or be able to get some intel for you ..."

We make our way up the stairs and down the corridor. Sandy is patient with me. It's been a long day; I'm tired and moving even more slowly than usual. My limp is more pronounced and my left hip is bothering me. I wore sandals all day and they put me out of alignment. Sandy had told me that this would probably happen and that eventually my left side would wear out from working overtime. I didn't expect it to start happening quite this soon, though.

As we start to walk down the stairs to get to the lowest level, I hear the opening bars of "Stay with Me." I try to hurry down the stairs. This causes me to slip and wrench my back trying to catch myself.

"Take your time. You wanna kill yourself?"

"This is Declan and Natalya. The super sexy one. You need to tell me what you think."

We make it down and watch their sensual number, the emotion so raw that I can practically feel my heart clench. God, I wish he would hold me like that. I wish I could move like that, instead of being this clumsy oaf I've turned into. I just so want to be the woman in Declan's arms, but watching the two of them together, I realize it will never happen for us. I can see how he is with her. That is not an act. It is not for show. Whether or not he realizes it, they have something together. They may fight like cats and dogs, but it is rooted in a deep-seated connection. One I will never have with him.

Even with this realization, I still stand here, watching him with her. I cannot take my eyes off of him. It takes me a minute to realize that there is an announcement being made. And then I realize the announcement is about Declan and Natalya.

"These are the newest permanent members of our cast, Declan McLoughlin and Natalya Koval. We're pleased to announce that McLoughlin-Koval will be with us for the next few years on tour. Please come out to see them again!"

Permanent. The next few years. On tour.

The words hit me like a punch to the gut. I need to get out of here. I look at the ice one last time and see Declan holding Natalya in his arms, cradling her like he's carrying her to bed. As they skate off the ice, I turn and walk away from him, one last time.

******

9:31 p.m.: Declan

This was a mistake, skating tonight. Even cutting out the other number, Natalya is barely holding on. This number is more show than skill, and there's a good portion of the number where I'm holding Natalya. She's in absolute and utter agony. We're going to the E.R. after this, whether she likes it or not. I'm pretty sure she's got a stress fracture. We're going to have to sit out the rest of the tour.

I think my decision just got easier because I'm positive the offer to join the tour will be rescinded. I can't think about that now. We've got to get through this number. We finally finish, and as we're taking our bows, Ken announces that Natalya and I are the newest permanent members of the cast.

What the hell?

I know if I look at Natalya, I'll want to strangle her and I can't do that in front of twenty-thousand witnesses. I can't believe she did this. Oh, actually I can. She accepted the offer, knowing that she has an injury that will sideline her for a while. I bet she's counting on lasting long enough to get the papers signed, so we're guaranteed something for next year. Damn, she is shrewd. I still want to kill her though. I look down and those feelings turn into concern as I see the sheer agony on her face. Her right leg is off the ice. Jesus, she can't even stand on it. I scoop her up and carry her off to the kiss and cry area. She may be in pain now, but she's going to have a lot more to cry about when I get done with her.

"We're done skating until you get this taken care of." Cradling her in my arms, I whisper this into her ear so no one else can hear me. I don't need this getting out until I know what the hell to do. I've got to call Frankie and get some help with damage control here. Natalya's end run makes me want to automatically pull back and quit. Again. I need time and distance until I can have a cooler head to think this thing through.

Setting her down on the bench, I'm much more gentle than I want to be. She's still clutching me. "Please don't leave me Declan. I need you. I'm scared there's something really wrong. It's never been this bad."

Her vulnerability unnerves me and I momentarily forget my anger. Kissing the top of her head, I sit down while we wait for the trainer to come over and check her out. We're not going back out for the finale. As gently as I can, I unlace Nat's boots, taking so much care on the right. I'm still a big clumsy oaf and tears start streaming down her face as I'm shimmying it off.

"I'm sorry, baby. I'm trying to be gentle."

"It just hurts so much."

"I know, honey. Hang in there. I'm here for you."

Todd, the trainer, appears with ice, and then Marina is standing there. I can't tell if she's mad or concerned. Her face has a one-emotion-fits-all look to it.

"Natalya needs X-rays. We're thinking it's a stress fracture."

Marina shakes her head at me. "You're probably right. She doesn't take care of herself. I'm making arrangements now. Go change. Todd and I have her."

Hustling out of the kiss and cry to the dressing room, I suddenly feel empty. I don't know what my future holds. I don't know what is going to happen tomorrow. For the first time, the thought of not being able to skate scares me. When I was burnt out and wanted to leave, I was fine with walking away. Now, knowing that it might be all over tonight—now—is sending me into a tailspin.

It makes me think of Kaitlin. For the first time, I start to understand why she was so angry and miserable.

She wasn't ready to walk away. She was in the prime of her career and then it was gone. I'm in the twilight of my career. I'm not even sure I want to keep going. But I want the choice to be mine. I don't want it taken away from me. I want control over my life.

I hang up my costumes and pack up my skates. Back in my own warm-ups, I grab Natalya's stuff, knowing she'll need to get out of her costume. I text Todd and tell him I'll be there in a minute. They're making arrangements for Natalya to go to the hospital. They've moved Natalya to a more private area under the rink. I bring her clothes to her and help her change. Although I've skated less today than we normally do, I'm exhausted. Just emotionally drained. It's gonna be a long night.

Chapter Twenty-Eight
9:45 p.m.: Kaitlin

God, he loves her. That's all I could think when they were on the ice. I watched him hold her, whisper into her ear, and I want to throw up. I want him to hold me like that. To caress me like that. To care for me like that. Feeling like a voyeur, I can't stop watching them. I need to stop. This is not good for me.

Funny. I was married to a man who was sleeping with anybody and everybody and it didn't really bother me. But I'm torn to pieces by seeing a friend with another girl. Sandy reaches over and touches my arm.

"You've seen enough. Let's go."

"I'm never going to see him again, am I?"

"Probably not like this. She doesn't look so good."

I look at Natalya, trying to see through my jealousy. She's so frail. I wonder how she can even skate. And she's holding her right shin, tears streaming down her normally stoic face. Looking at her, I can feel her pain. No, it's my pain. I can remember the pain in my leg, so terrible that I didn't think I could make it one more minute. I swear, I can feel my leg at this moment and it hurts. The burning and the feeling of knives stabbing me over and over. Pressure like my leg was in a vise grip. All of it is there again. Right now. I know it is my mind playing tricks on me, but God, it is so real.

Sandy is shaking my arm. I didn't even realize she was touching me. "Kaitlin, are you okay?"

Shaking my head to bring myself back to reality, I try to focus on my friend's face. "I think I just had a flashback. You know, like a war vet or something. I feel my leg again. Well, at least the pain in it. It was so real."

"It probably was a flashback. I don't doubt it."

"Like PTSD or something?"

"Exactly like PTSD. What you went through was very traumatic, and I'm guessing you never dealt with it properly, did you?"

"I was just pissed off and volatile for a few years. That's totally dealing with it properly, isn't it?"

Sandy smiles and it relaxes me. "Remind me not to go to you for counseling."

"I was actually a psych major, you know."

"That's one of the scariest things I've ever heard."

I smile at Sandy and we head out of the arena. I'm deflated and dejected. I came to Salt Lake for two reasons: to confront Michele and to see Declan again. I'm zero for two. We're quiet on the way back to Sandy's house. She had gotten a friend to drop her off at the show since I had her car. Finally, I say, "The only bright side to this whole thing is that I got to see you again. I'm glad that you're my friend. I don't have many and I don't know what I'd do without you."

"Awww, that's almost sweet and mushy. Not at all what I'd expect from you."

"I know. I'm going soft in my old age."

"What are you going to do now?"

"I have no idea. I mean, go back to Michigan and keep working. I'm actually pretty good at my job and I sort of like it."

"I think I'm the one who told you that in the first place."

"Shut up. I don't want it to go to your head."

"You should move back here."

"Even though I thought I hated the winters in Michigan, I kind of like the cooler temperatures. I can't deal with the heat."

"I thought you liked the warmer weather."

"Not anymore. The brace gets hot and sweaty and then I get breakdown. Plus the only sandals I can wear with it make my back and hip hurt if I'm on my feet a lot. And let's face it, people stare when I'm wearing shorts. The shorts season in Michigan is only about three weeks long."

"You do have a point there. Does it bother you when people stare?"

"Of course it does. I know what a freak I am. I don't need people staring at me."

"Has anyone ever asked you about it?"

I hadn't really thought about it. "You know, every so often a kid will ask. Their parents try to hush them up, but I usually just tell them that my leg doesn't work right, and if I didn't have the brace I would trip and fall a lot."

We're back at her house. "Thanks for putting up with me and letting me take your car today."

We're in the garage, and I have to hold onto the car as I navigate around in the dark. There's one step up and then we're into the brightly lit kitchen. Which is white, everywhere. And not white in a clean, neat way, but white because it is covered in flour. The cabinets, the counters, the floor. Everything. My foot skids on the slick surface and I nearly go down.

"What the—"

"VIOLET!!!" Sandy is screaming, in full-on-mommy mode. Of course, I know nothing about children, but it is after ten, so I would assume that a three-year-old would be sleeping.

Sandy's husband, Timothy, comes stumbling out from the living room. He's obviously been sleeping. He's wearing gym shorts and a white t-shirt that has seen better days. His hair, more white than normal, is standing on end and he looks like he's been through hell.

"You are never leaving me alone with that demon spawn again."

"Excuse me? Um, who used to use baby powder as cement in the back of his dump trucks? Where do you think she gets this from? And why the heck didn't you clean it up?"

"I just got her down. Like ten minutes ago. She screamed and cried for over an hour that she wanted you. And this was after the flour incident. I'm going to bed now. I can't deal with her. One of us isn't going to make it until she's four, and I'm pretty sure it's going to be me."

He storms off, and I can't help but laugh. Looking at the despair and despondency on Sandy's face, I know I shouldn't be laughing, but I am. For a person without kids, this is pretty damn funny. I'm pretty sure it would suck if it were me, but it's not, so I laugh. I would bet Sandy could use a stiff drink right now, but she's a Mormon, so the strongest stuff she has in the house is Robitussin. I pull myself together and tell Sandy to go to bed while I clean up. I get the distinct impression this is not the first time this has happened, nor will it be the last.

I've just about gotten the mess cleaned up when my phone rings. It's close to midnight. Who the heck could be calling me at this hour? I look, but don't recognize the number. "Hello?"

"Oh my God, Kaitlin, you answered! I'm sorry, did I wake you?"

"Declan?"

"Yeah, I know it's late. Were you sleeping?" He's rambling a bit.

"Are you all right?"

"No, things are really messed up right now. I saw your text and just took it as a sign that I needed to talk to you tonight. I kept getting signs that I should call you, and then my phone died. I need to remember to charge that stupid thing."

"What's going on?"

He sighs. "I don't even know which end is up right now. I just really need a friend, and I know you're the perfect person to talk to about this."

Crap. Did he just friend-zone me? I mean, I should know better, because I saw him with Natalya tonight. I know how much he cares about her. I can see the passion and the connection between them. I'm just one of his friends. Apparently it's only me who was hoping for more here. Originally, I thought he wasn't attracted to me because he was gay. Well, I was wrong there. Maybe it's just that I'm not that attractive to him. I understand, knowing how thin and dainty Natalya is. I'm the total opposite of her. I don't know why it hasn't occurred to me before now that if he's attracted to someone like her, there is no way he'd be attracted to someone like me.

"Well, I'm here, so talk away."

"You're sure it's not too late? Don't you have to work in the morning? I can't keep you up all night. I shouldn't have called you now."

He thinks I'm in Detroit. It is the middle of the night there. Yeah, I would not have been pleased to get this call then. I like my sleep once I'm sleeping. "I'm off tomorrow, so you got me."

There's a burst of noise that sounds like a loudspeaker in the background. He has to wait until that is done before he can start. "Crap, I don't even know where to begin."

"Why don't you tell me where you are?"

"I'm at the hospital."

"Hospital? Why are you at the hospital? Are you okay?"

"No, yeah. I mean, I'm fine. I'm here with Nat."

"What's wrong with her?" I can't keep the sarcasm out of my voice. It's one part sincere and two parts jealous that she is with Declan while I am not.

"You mean, besides the obvious?"

"You said it, not me."

"I could tell by the tone of your voice what you were thinking. She's back in with the doctor now, but I think she has a stress fracture in her tibia."

"Ouch." Damn, she has a stress fracture and was still skating—that has to be incredibly painful. But he doesn't know I was there tonight. I have to play dumb about it. "Is she still skating on it?"

"Sort of. We pulled out of one of our numbers and the finale. We did 'Stay with Me' but that was just too much for her."

"I hate that number." Thinking about how they look together, and their obvious passion, tears me apart inside. Not that I could ever skate, even before my injury, but when I see them skate to that song, I wish it were me with Declan out on the ice.

"Seriously? It's one of my favorites. I can't believe you don't like it." The indignation in his voice is apparent. "Why don't you like it?"

"It's not your skating or anything." I backpedal, not wanting him upset with me, but not wanting to reveal how I feel.

"What is it, then?"

"No, you skate beautifully. It's just—" Before I can continue, Declan cuts me off.

"Natalya's coming back. Can I call you when I get back to the hotel and can plug my phone in? It would be about a half hour or so."

"Tell me where you are, and I'll just call your room while your phone charges up."

"I'm at the Marriott. Room six-fifteen."

"Okay, talk to you in a little while. Give Natalya my best."

"You don't mean that." I can hear the smile in his voice.

"No, but I want you to think I'm a much nicer person than I really am."

"Kaitlin?"

"Yeah?"

"Thanks for being here for me."

He has no idea exactly how here for him I'm planning on being. I know driving down to his hotel is probably a bad idea. Being here in Salt Lake City is a bad idea. I'm full of bad ideas right now.

I finish cleaning Violet's mess and leave Sandy a note. She's given me carte blanche with her car, but I want her to know where I am. I don't even stop to change or freshen up. It's only as I'm driving west on I-80 through the mountains into Salt Lake that it occurs to me I probably should have at least brushed my teeth. Not that it's going to come to that. I'm his friend. He needs a friend right now. He's been there for me, and now it's my turn to be there for him.

******

12:16 a.m.: Declan

Natalya is good and doped up. She should sleep for about three days. It's not just a stress fracture. It's a fracture-fracture. She's got a cast on that leg and if it doesn't start to set, they're going to do surgery. We're off the tour. I don't know what this means about the offer, if it still stands. If I were the powers that be, I wouldn't keep the offer on the table. Who knows what Natalya will be like after this? I know that show skating isn't nearly as demanding as competition skating, but there's a real possibility that she won't be able to hack either after this.

Putting Natalya in her room with her phone next to her, I trudge down the hall to my room with barely enough energy to pick my feet up off the carpet. I wonder if Kaitlin is going to call me back. I want to talk to her about what is going on. I know that she can understand where I am right now. The thought of the career being over, just like that. I'm worried about Nat, too. At least I had been of a mind to give it up, and I had a plan for after. I can still carry out that plan. I have no idea what Natalya is going to do.

After I plug my phone in, I text Frankie and let her know what has happened. She's undoubtedly asleep, so I don't expect a reply before morning. I need a shower. I need to sleep for a hundred years. I could use a sandwich too.

Kaitlin's not going to call. She's probably asleep. It's after two where she is. I'll catch up with her in the morning. It was a lot to ask of her to sit up all night to talk me through this. Jeez, I hang out with too many girls. Most men would just shrug it off and move on. I need to be more like that.

My wallowing is interrupted by a knock on the door. My stomach drops, wondering who is on the other side. I'm worried that Natalya is up and about when she shouldn't be. Worse, it's Marina, to tell me we have to check out because we're off the tour. I head toward the door like a man heading to the guillotine.

Unlatching the chain, I pull the door open. The last person I expect to see is standing there. Kaitlin looks so good. I mean, she's a total mess. Her hair is falling out of a ponytail and looks gray. She doesn't look older, just tired. All over her face and glasses is a white ... powder? I don't know what the hell she's been doing or how she got here. I don't care. She's here.

Wait—why is she here?

It doesn't matter. She's here. I don't believe it. Am I so tired that I'm delusional and my eyes are playing tricks on me?

I can't even formulate a greeting. She's staring at me, just waiting for me to say something. Finally, she swallows hard and says, "Hey."

"I've been waiting for you to call ... but you're here?"

"You sounded so upset on the phone."

"I am upset." I'm also confused by her presence. Not in a bad way, just in a confused way. "How did you? When did you? But I thought ..."

"I think you need someone to hold you and tonight that's going to be me."

That's all the confirmation I need. I grab her face in my hands and crush my lips on hers. They're soft and full, just like I imagined they'd be. She parts them, allowing my tongue in. As our lips meet, I press her body close to mine, pulling her into the room. We stumble, me backward and her forward in our urgency. I move my hands down to her back and grasp the hem of her shirt. I want to yank it off. Jesus she feels good. She's got her arms locked around my torso and then I notice that she's trying to pull my shirt off. I let go of her for a moment so she can. I reciprocate and a puff of white powder fluffs into the air as her shirt comes over her head.

"What is that?"

"Flour."

"Were you baking at this hour?"

"No, Sandy's daughter got into the flour. I cleaned it up."

"You missed some."

"Where?"

I lean in and kiss her neck, right where it meets her collarbone. "Here," Her head tips back, giving me more access and she moans a little. "And here." I whisper, my voice strangely hoarse, as I kneel down and kiss down her breastbone. Her hands are in my hair, on either side of my head. I reach around and unhook her bra.

"Uhhh, Declan?"

Shit. Don't tell me to stop. I don't think I can stop. I know I don't want to stop. Leaning back, I look up at her. Her face is flushed and her mouth is open. She gently pulls on my head until I'm standing up. She rises up to kiss me on the mouth and falls into me a bit.

"On the bed. I can't stand up and do this."

"Wanna make a bet?" I reach around her luscious ass and pick her up. Her mouth is on mine and, God, she is so hot, her bare skin against mine. Her legs wrap around my waist. I want to just press her into the wall like this, but, feeling her brace against my bare back, I know I need to take things a little slowly. Well, not slowly, but more conservatively. At least this time.

Chapter Twenty-Nine
Tuesday, August 19, 2014
6:15 a.m.: Kaitlin

There's a phone ringing and it's not mine. I look over at Declan and he's still fast asleep. Naked but asleep. Oh my God, look at his body. He's sprawled on his back and the sheet is barely covering anything. It is the most beautiful thing I've ever seen. It could be a sculpture. And it's mine. Or at least it was last night.

Holy cow.

I nudge Declan, thinking he probably should be answering his phone. Most people don't get calls at this hour for a social visit. He lets out a "Hmmmm" and rolls over. Now I'm looking at his back and butt. It is all I can do not to lean over a take a bite out of it. Damn, he is one fine specimen. Every inch of that man is sculpted and hard. I pull the sheet up around me, self-conscious of my body which is no longer firm and fit. It's certainly better than it was in March when I first met him, though.

Looking around the hotel room, I see the remnants of our escapades. Clothes strewn about. My brace, discarded on the chair. Wet towels on the floor from our shower. The thought of the shower brings a smile to my face. It'll take a lot to wipe that off. Declan's phone is silent for a minute and then starts ringing again.

He starts moving and grumbling, still half-asleep. "Natalya, what can you possibly want this early?"

The sound of her name on his lips drenches me in despair. No matter what happened here last night, she's going to come first. He obviously thinks it's her on the phone. I wonder if he even realizes that I'm in bed with him. God, I'm such an idiot. What had I been thinking?

Declan finally rolls toward me and smiles through sleepy eyes. "Mornin'."

"You gonna answer your phone or what?"

"It's probably just Nat calling to bitch at me about something. Even when we don't have to train early, she gets her jollies by waking me up early. She knows I don't do mornings well."

He's looking at me now. His explanation makes sense, but I still can't shake the feeling that there will always be her in between us. "What's wrong?"

"When you said her name, I thought it was because you thought she was here with you, not me."

"Seriously?" He's propped up on his side, facing me. I'm sitting up against the headboard, my legs out in front. His hand wanders under the sheet and starts delicately grazing up and down my thigh. "You think I wouldn't remember that you were here? That last night happened? Kaitlin, what do you take me for?"

"It's not what I take you for; it's what I take me for."

"What's that supposed to mean?"

I can't think with his hand on my thigh like that. It's making me tingle in all the right places and turning my brain off. That was the problem last night. I let my lady parts do all the thinking. And where did it get me? Lying naked next to this Adonis with my flabby butt and my floppy foot.

"I can't form a coherent thought when you're doing that, you know."

He leans in and kisses me. "That's the plan."

Before things can get too far (not like they have that far to go since we're already naked), Declan's phone rings again, alerting us that something is going on and someone needs to talk to him. Apparently.

"Frankie, what is it? Do you know what time it is?"

He's quiet, listening to her. With the sheet wrapped around me, I get up and go to the bathroom. I need to think about what has happened and try to figure out what is going to happen. Declan may or may not be going on tour for two years. He may or may not still have a skating career. He may or may not be going to grad school in Michigan. There is no way that I can figure out the future until Declan does. We have no future until he knows where he's going and what he's doing. Me being in the picture is just going to make that more confusing for him. I shouldn't have come here last night. It's just muddied the waters. God, I hate that I have this self-doubt. When my body worked fine, I had all the confidence in the world. Now, with my bum leg and my even bigger bum ex-husband, I seem to have no self-esteem left.

I use my finger to brush my teeth and splash some water on my face. The flour that I was covered in was washed off when we were in the shower. At least I can walk away from this with some good memories. I'm going to have to leave and let Declan decide what is best for him. I had no choice in my future. I need to give him options without feeling beholden to anyone. I can still hear him on the phone. I'm trying to give him privacy so I stand by the door for a moment before I come out of the bathroom. I hear him say, "I don't know how I'm going to get out of this mess."

Hearing that is like a punch to the gut. Even worse than what happened with Philip earlier. The jumping stuff is in my past, but I thought Declan was my future. I guess not. I need to get out of here.

Coming out of the bathroom, I find Declan sitting on the edge of his bed, head in his hands. Oh crap. His body language indicates that he regrets last night as much as his words did. I try not to disturb him as I limp around the room, picking up my clothes. If I'm near furniture, I find myself leaning on it. I don't like anyone to see me like this. I know it doesn't bother Declan. I wish it didn't bother me though. I need to get dressed and leave as quickly as I can. Then I'll hightail it back to Michigan and drown my sorrows in some tubs of ice cream before I try to start over. Yet again.

Funny, my marriage ending didn't hurt as much as this is going to.

******

6:26 a.m.: Declan

"Frankie, that's the thing. I don't know what I want to do."

"What the hell, Declan? Either you want to skate or you don't. If Natalya can't skate, we'll find you someone else to skate with. I'm sure there's someone else out there looking for a partner."

"I never thought of that."

"That's why you pay me the big bucks, baby. Now what do you want me to tell them? I'm calling them at eight to negotiate this."

"I don't know."

"If you don't, then who does?"

"Good question. I don't know how I'm going to get out of this mess." I can hear Kaitlin coming out of the bathroom. "Lemme call you back in a bit." Dropping the phone on the nightstand, I rub the sides of my head, hoping the right answer will magically come to me. What am I going to do? I mean, and this is terrible, but there is part of me that's slightly relieved that Nat is hurt. With her being out of commission, I figured the offer would be off the table. Damn Frankie and her pit bull tenacity. I mean, it's totally what I pay her for, but still.

I turn around and Kaitlin's mostly dressed. Her clothes are fairly rumpled and still spattered with flour. She's hesitant with her walking and she picks up her brace. She sits down on the bed with her back to me, and I can tell she's upset. She can't be sorry about last night, can she? She's the one who told me she liked sex. I mean, she came to my hotel room in the middle of the night. What did she think was going to happen?

I'm still buck-naked. I get up and dig out a pair of boxer briefs from my suitcase and then pick my shorts up off the floor. Running my hands through my hair, I look at Kaitlin. I can tell she wants to say something, so I just wait.

"I'll be out of here as soon as I get my brace on."

Okay, that is not at all what I expected her to say. "What? You can't just leave."

"It's for the best. This is going to be hard enough on me as it is."

"Why?"

Her back is still to me. I wish I could see her face. "Because I'm no good at this anymore. I used to be, but I'm different than I was back then."

"Good at what? Kaitlin, what are you talking about?"

"Doing the casual thing. Walking away."

"Kaitlin, look at me." I kneel down in front of her. I expect her to be crying but she's not. She has always said that she doesn't cry easily. Of course, she was usually crying when she said this, so I didn't believe her. Tears or not, the look on her face indicates she's very upset. "What's going on? Tell me."

"I'll get out of your hair now. I'm sorry for showing up like that last night. I know it was wrong."

"Wait—what? You think last night was a mistake?"

She nods. "Don't you?"

"Um, no. Why would you think it was a mistake?"

She can't meet my eyes. She's looking all around the room. "I was trying to give you privacy while you were on the phone, but I heard you say you didn't know how you were going to get out of this mess."

God, she's so stoic but so weak at the same time. I lean in, grab her chin in my hand and bring her lips to mine. She's reticent at first, but yields quickly, opening her mouth to mine. Finally I pull back. "You are not the mess I was talking about. I was talking about my career. I don't know what I'm going to do."

"Me being here just isn't right, right now. Is it?"

I continue kissing her, speaking in between. "You make the decision interesting. To say the least. But you here, with me." I kiss her for longer this time. "Is just perfect."

She finally pulls back, breathless. "What do you want, Declan?"

"You." I lean in again.

She leans away. "For your career, what do you want?"

I sink down onto my heels and close my eyes. "I just don't know. I can't decide."

"You've never had to make these decisions before, have you?"

I'm uncomfortable on the floor, so I get up and sit on the bed next to her. "Not really. My mom decided I should start skating. My coach told me what to do. Then Frankie. Now I need to make this decision for myself and I don't know what to do."

"What do you want, Declan?"

I know the answer in my gut. "I want to keep skating. I thought I could give it up and walk away, but I don't want to."

"Good. You've made your decision. But now I have to do what I have to do, and that's let you be. Because if I don't leave now, I'll never be able to."

Chapter Thirty
5:30 p.m.: Kaitlin

I'm going through security again, and the old feelings of being angry at the world are coming back. Anger is a lot easier than the heartbreak I currently feel. I walked away from Declan, for his own good. He wants to skate. I'm not going to stand in his way. I wouldn't have let a stupid guy get in the way of my dream. Oh wait, I did. I just didn't know it. This whole trip was a waste of time and money. I didn't get to confront Michele. I gave my heart and body to Declan only to have him refuse it. Okay, he didn't really refuse it, but my wounded heart feels like his choice to keep skating is a rejection of a relationship with me.

I limp my way through security, slamming my bags down a little harder than I need to. At least I was able to change my flight to leave today. Sandy wanted me to stay a few more days, but what is the point? This city—this state—is just a symbol of my ultimate failure. In everything.

Bending over to put Kirby on, I lose my balance and fall. Right down on my ass. Not because anyone ran into me. And this time, there was no one to catch me. Declan was right when he said he wouldn't always be there to catch me. I sit on the floor for a moment, stunned and defeated. Why does my life have to be this hard? Why can't I ever catch a break?

Before the self-pity totally consumes me, I get my brace back on and stand up. I can do this. I can keep moving. I have to keep moving. Today is the first day of the rest of my life, right? No, today cannot be the first day. Today is just a continuation of yesterday which was a pretty crap-tastic day. I'll wallow for today and then let tomorrow be the first day. Tomorrow will be better.

I get the brace back on and stand up to get going. I don't have a lot of time to get to the flight back to my boring life without Declan. I can't believe I came all the way out here. I can't believe I slept with him. I can't believe he chose skating over me. If I were still jumping, he would want me.

What do I have to offer him? A lifetime of a career in which I'm on the road. A physical disability that will limit me more and more as the years go on. No college education.

But he's not done with school either. If he keeps skating, he'll be even worse off than I am. At least I have a full-time job that pays pretty well. I would be able to support him if he needed it. Not that he would, being one of *People's* sexiest bachelors and all. Oh my God, I had sex with one of *People*'s sexiest bachelors. Twice. That thought brings a smile to my face. Okay, that is a bright side. It had been a really long time since I had sex. At least it was good. Well, not good, but fantastic.

Thinking about the fantastic sex sort of makes me start to feel depressed again, so I think about what I need to do when I get home. First things first; after I throw things to get out my anger, I'm going to write a letter to Michele. They can't prevent me from sending her a letter. I can let her know what she did to me and get my closure that way. Okay, one thing off my list.

The trip back to Detroit is uneventful, which is always a good thing when you're flying. I get back to Grosse Pointe and enter my dark condo, fighting the feelings of loneliness sweeping over me. What I wouldn't give to have Declan here. At least some of the time. Some of the time would be better than none of the time, right? Oh God, what did I do, walking away from him? So what that he'd be gone six to nine months out of the year. I'm on the road a lot for my job as well. I have my territory, but it has me driving all over Michigan and even into Ohio. That doesn't include the trade shows that I go to.

We could have made it work. If only I wasn't such an incredible idiot. But I am. And it's probably too late.

I should call him and beg him to try to work it out with me. Why would he want to? I'm always running away from him. He called me on it the first day I met him, and yet I keep doing it. I wish I knew why. Maybe I'm just like my mother, who takes off when the going gets tough. When the real world interrupts the fantasy. Crap, I am just like her.

My phone rings and my dad's name flashes on the screen. "Hey."

"Hey, pumpkin. You got a minute?"

"Yeah, what's up?"

"Kev is getting married. He wants to know if you'll come to the wedding."

"Of course I will! Why didn't he call me to tell me himself?"

"He was afraid he'd say something to upset you, and then you wouldn't come."

"He's my only brother, Dad. Of course I'll be there. It's to that Becky girl, right?"

Dad laughs. "Yeah, who else?"

"I dunno. I didn't know if there was some hometown gossip I missed out on, or anything." Dad is quiet and doesn't say anything, so I keep talking. "I know I've been pretty unbearable for the past two years. I'm sorry about that, and I'm working to change."

"That's good to hear. You were quite the piece of work, you know."

"Dad, am I like Mom? Running away when things are hard."

"No, you pushed us away, but I don't see that you ran away. It was hard, watching you go through all that."

"Didn't Mom push us away too?"

"No, she didn't push; she just gave up. That's not what you did at all. But I felt like I had failed you again. First, I couldn't make your mom stay, and then I couldn't get through to you after your surgery. I knew Tyler wasn't taking good care of you, and you wouldn't let me take care of you."

"Tyler was only taking care of himself. That's how I got where I am."

"What do you mean by that?"

I tell Dad what I'd found out about Tyler and Michele. My dad is silent, and I know he's plotting how he's going to kill Tyler. "In fact, I just got back from Utah. I flew out there to confront Michele."

"What happened?"

"Philip wouldn't let me see her. Deirdre called in the lawyers and they wanted me to sign all this stuff saying that I won't sue them."

"You may have grounds you know."

"Dad, don't you know me better than that? Suing

would just hurt the organization. My career is done. There is nothing I can do to bring it back. Causing them financial hardship will only hurt the girls who still have hope."

"Kaitlin, that is the most selfless thing I've ever heard you say."

"Well, plus they offered me a small settlement to help with medical expenses. I'm having a lawyer look at it, but I plan to accept. I was considering a civil suit, but it won't bring my foot or my career back." I pause, the next statement so very hard to say, "I'm sorry for being so terrible these last two years."

"I'm sorry for letting you push me away."

"I wish you weren't in New York so I could give you a hug."

"Well, I'll see you soon for the wedding, so you can give me that hug then."

"Soon? Like how soon? When is the wedding?"

"Six weeks. And I'm supposed to ask, are you bringing a guest?"

******

6:38 p.m.: Declan

She's been gone for twelve hours now. I'm starting to think she's not coming back. I know she's not, but I can't believe she really walked away after last night. When I opened the hotel door and saw her standing there, she looked like an angel. Covered in flour, but an angel nonetheless. What we did after that was anything but angelic.

I know why she left. It's all my fault. I picked skating. In her mind, it was skating or her. Obviously, if I'm on tour, things would be difficult. Maybe she wants someone who comes home every night. That wouldn't be me, if I was on tour. Of course, if I was just training people in Bloomfield Hills, I could still skate and be in Michigan most of the time. Competition season would require some travel, but surely that would be acceptable. Kaitlin would understand. After all, she used to travel to Europe for a good part of the year.

Damn it, why didn't I think of this earlier?

Picking up my phone, I call Frankie.

"Declan, baby. What's shaking?"

"I don't want it. I don't want to tour."

"What? I got them to give you an offer, even if Nat is out. Still two years with the show. You can't pass that up."

"I need you to work a different deal."

"I don't think a better offer is going to come along."

"I'm not asking for a better offer, I'm asking for a different offer. I want to coach and train and choreograph. Out of Bloomfield Hills."

"What? You can't give up your career for someone else's."

"I still want to go to school, but not just yet. Physical therapy isn't the right fit for me. I like some aspects of it, but I can't see me really doing it for a job. I'm gonna coach and choreograph for a year or two until I can figure out what I want to be when I grow up."

"Are you sure?"

"For the first time, yes. Going to PT school wasn't sitting well. Neither was staying on tour. That's why I couldn't decide. Now I know why. Neither one was the right choice."

"Is this about that girl?"

"Partially. Mostly. I know I want to be with her. I think she's my future. I'm just sorry I wasted almost six months before we could figure it out."

"Okay, I'll let them know your decision. Once I tell them though, it's done. You'll have to come home."

"Good. That's where I want to be."

Chapter Thirty-One
Saturday, August 23, 2014
1:32 p.m.: Kaitlin

Hitting the send button emails my dad my itinerary for travel. I'm flying into Albany and then renting a car to drive up to Lake Placid. Dad offered to drive down and get me, but it's a three-hour drive each way. I'm excited to go home to see my dad and Kev. I'm sad that Kev and I had drifted apart to the point that I didn't even know he was getting married. I know I've been difficult, but I'm still the only sister he's got.

I called him after talking to my dad, and I think we're in a better place. I'm going to spend that whole week in New York. Somehow, my dad convinced me to enter into the world of public speaking. I'm going to be giving a motivational speech at Whiteface for jumpers just starting out. The national championships will be held there the week after the wedding. It will be the first time I've talked about jumping in public since I retired. I know I'm going to get questions about it. I think I'm prepared. Or I will be by the time it rolls around. It was not something I ever considered doing, but I need something positive to focus on. Maybe, if I can inspire someone else, I'll have my own inspiration again.

The wedding is the first weekend in October. If I'm lucky, the foliage will still be in full force. More likely, there will be snow. At that point in the year, it could go either way. I'm flying in on Thursday to beat the rush of people wanting to spend one last weekend hiking and camping in the Adirondacks. I used to love hiking. At one point in my life, I'd had hopes of hiking all forty-six peaks in the Adirondacks. I'll have to be happy with my thirty-two.

My doorbell rings. I look at the clock. I'm not expecting anyone. It's probably the mailman. I don't think I'm due to get a package, but who doesn't love surprises?

The answer is me. When I open the door and see Declan standing there.

Why is he doing this to me? Why does he have to make this so hard? Why can't he just let me be?

"Can I come in?" he finally says.

His hair is shorter. Much shorter. He does look a lot more like Ronan, just as I'd suspected he would. I think I miss the curls, but this is a very good look for him as well. Like anything could look bad on him. Well, that salmon spandex wasn't a good look, but I digress.

I step aside, and he brushes past. I try not to be too creepy, but I can't help inhaling his glorious scent as he moves by me. As he gets down the hall, he looks around and then walks into the living room. He plops down on my couch without saying a word.

"Make yourself at home." I can't keep the sarcasm out of my voice.

"Thank you, I will."

"What do you want, Declan?"

"You. I want you."

"You've had me. You can't have me again. I can't give myself to you again."

"Why not?"

"Don't you understand anything? I thought you of all people would get it. That you would understand what it is like to have the rug pulled out from underneath you. To have your world collapse and your dreams wrenched away. When that happened, I was lost. Adrift. It took me so long to find myself again. To find out who I was. I was no longer Kaitlin the ski jumper. Kaitlin the athlete. Kaitlin the wife. I had to find a new Kaitlin. Meeting you helped set me on the right course. You pointed me in the right direction. I was on a good course. And then I saw you again. And we started talking. And I realized I was in love with you. So in love with you that I flew to Utah to see you. And I went to you and we made love. And then you picked skating over me." I keep pacing around my coffee table while he watches me.

"But Kaitlin, that's the thing. I came to tell you—"

"No, Declan. I get why you chose skating over me. If I had the choice of jumping or Tyler, I would have picked jumping. I didn't love him. And you don't love me. I get it. It's just hard to face over and over."

"Would you shut up for a minute and let me speak, woman?"

I'm taken aback at his abrupt manner. My mouth hangs open and I'm frozen in place, standing across from him.

"Before you tear me a new one, you need to know that I love you too."

"What?"

"I love you too. That's what I came here to tell you. Please listen to me. When you left the hotel last week, I was in utter turmoil. You asked for my honest answer. Honestly, I'm not ready to give up skating. I don't want to be on tour for most of the year, though. I'm not ready to go to PT school either."

"Declan, you need to make up your mind."

"Kaitlin, will you stop yammering and listen to me? I have made up my mind. Frankie worked her magic and got me what I want. Well, most of what I want."

"And what is that?"

"I'm going to be coaching and choreographing in Bloomfield Hills. It will require some travel during competition season, but nothing like being on tour."

"What about school?" He just said he loves me. He's staying here in Michigan. I can't believe this is happening. This sort of thing doesn't happen to me. My head is spinning.

"I don't know. I don't think being a PT is the right fit for me, but I'm not sure what I want to do. I might take some business classes to learn how to market myself better. Nothing this semester though."

"So ..."

"So, I'm back. For good."

"And you love me?"

"Yes, of course I do. I think of you all the time. I have since the first moment I ran into your ass. God, that day, in the airport hotel, it was all I could do not to jump you. Sleeping with you in my arms that night was the best and worst thing that could have happened to me."

"And then I never called."

"No, you never did. Why didn't you?"

During these past few weeks of phone calls, I'd wondered when he'd ask me this. I'm glad it hasn't come up until now. I wouldn't have been able to tell him the truth before.

"The truth?"

"You know I only ever want honesty from you."

"Because, even though it was ridiculous after only a day, I felt like I was falling in love with you."

"Back then?"

"Yes, but that was when I thought you were gay. I knew I could never have you, and I was dealing with so much other crap that unrequited love wasn't something I wanted to put on my plate."

"I can't believe you thought I was gay." He picks up the pillow next to him and throws it at me.

"Dude, you're a male figure skater. You have—had—better hair than I do. Did. What was I supposed to think?"

"You don't like my hair? I've been waiting for years to be able to cut it."

"No, it looks good. Although you look a bit more like Ronan now."

"Okay, I'll let it grow out."

"Maybe just a little." I toss the pillow back to him. "Why didn't you do anything—make a move on me—when we were in the hotel?"

"You were married. I know you said it was almost over, but I couldn't ask you to break your marriage vows like that."

"You know I would have said yes."

"Now I do. If I had known how easy you were, I would have tried a little harder."

I toss the pillow at him again. "You know, for someone who comes over here to profess his love, you're awfully far away."

******

4:57 p.m.: Declan

"Oh my God, Declan. I think my legs are jelly. I mean both of them, not just the bum one." Kaitlin is still breathing heavily.

I'm panting a bit too. "That's okay. You can just lie there. I won't be long."

She whacks me in the stomach. "You can't have anything left in you, a man your age."

I smile and kiss her forehead. I'm propped up on my elbow, lying at her side. "I am an Olympic athlete you know."

"Not anymore, you old fart. Wait until you see how fast everything turns to mush. Trust me."

I stroke her thigh. "You're getting all firm again. What are you doing?"

"I've been going to the gym. I do the elliptical and bike. It's so different from before. That was all weight training and plyometrics. I was so lean that I didn't need to do much cardio. I need to get back to being that lean."

"Don't get too lean. I like a little booty to hold onto."

"Really? I thought men like women stick-thin like Natalya."

I shudder. The sound of her name makes me shrivel in all the wrong places. "Ugh. No. I hated touching her. She felt like a bag of bones. That's not what a woman should feel like."

"What should a woman feel like?" Kaitlin says coyly.

I lean in and give those luscious lips a kiss. "You."

She sighs into my mouth and if I weren't so tired, I would want to go again. She does have a point that I'm getting older, and the stamina is not what it used to be, at least in this department. Not that I'm going to tell her that though.

"I can't believe you're here. I can't believe this is real. I think I feel ... happy?" Kaitlin sounds confused.

"Why are you questioning that you feel happy? Shouldn't you be happy?"

"The last time I felt this happy was when I was mid-flight in a jump. It is so amazing and peaceful. I didn't think I'd ever be able to get that feeling again."

"Will you always miss it?"

She settles back into the pillow and has a far away dreamy look on her face. "I think so. I miss the girls on the team, and I miss the training, believe it or not. I miss that my body used to be a machine that worked so well. But mostly, I miss the feeling of flying through the air." She's quiet for a minute. "What do you think you'll miss?"

I hadn't thought about it, since I will still be skating. "I think the adrenaline rush that comes with competing."

She smiles and stretches out, her arms reaching overhead. They settle up near her face, and she is absent mindedly playing with her hair again. Her hair is longer than it was when I met her.

"You always play with your hair. Did you know you do that?"

Her fingers stop. "No, I guess I didn't. When I was competing, my hair was long so I always had to put it in braids to stay out of the way under the helmet. I cut it short in anger, and now I'm constantly trying to pull it back. I have to wait for it to get long so I can braid it again."

"I like it short. It frames your face and brings out your eyes."

"Are you sure you're not gay?" she teases.

Rolling on top of her, pressing my body into hers, I say, "Do I need to prove it again?"

She laughs and shoves me off. "No, please don't. I get it. You're a very manly man. Who wears orange spandex."

"It wasn't orange, it was salmon."

"You're not helping your cause here."

I roll to my back so we're lying shoulder to shoulder. "So what else is on the agenda for today?"

She groans and gets up. She totters off to the bathroom, her gait off kilter with her foot bare. I'm amazed at how she gets around with a leg that doesn't do what it's supposed to do. A few minutes later, she comes out of the bathroom, wrapped in a pink kimono-type robe. She sits down in the chair across the room and starts to put her brace on.

"I've got to go shopping today, I'm sorry."

"You *have* to go?"

She shrugs. "Yeah, my brother is getting married in October and I need a dress for the wedding. I have trouble finding stuff that looks decent, so I need to start looking. Shoot me now."

"About the wedding or the dress?"

"Yes. It will be my first time back in Lake Placid since my injury. I'm going to get a whole lot of pitying looks. Then there's the dress thing. I can't wear good shoes anymore because of Kirby." She lifts her leg, which is now encased in its brace. "People stare and I look stupid."

I get up and walk across the room. Kneeling down before her, I give her a sweet kiss on the lips. "You'll look beautiful in whatever you wear. Just please don't make me go shopping with you."

Laughing, Kaitlin says, "Okay, I guess you are straight. Will you be here when I get back?"

"I was thinking about going home."

"Oh."

"You're more than welcome to come out, or I can come back. I just didn't bring anything with me."

"You're in Pontiac? Or Bloomfield Hills? Where are you?"

"The apartment is in Pontiac, but I train in Bloomfield Hills."

"And that's, what? Forty-five minutes?"

"If you have a lead foot, it is."

Pointing down to her foot she says, "Well, I just happen to have a lead foot. I can make it in thirty."

"We'll figure this out. When I'm coaching, I'll have to be in Bloomfield a lot."

"I'm all over the state for my job anyway. We can do this, as long as you're not picking up any young hotties at the rink."

"The only young hotties vying for my attention have a package that I'm not interested in, so you're safe."

I stand and pull her up. After a long embrace she says, "So, we're good?"

"We're very good."

Chapter Thirty-Two
Wednesday, October 8, 2014
5:00 p.m.: Kaitlin

"My name is Kaitlin Reynolds. I was born here in Lake Placid and got my start on this very mountain. I started skiing when I was four years old. Ever trying to keep up with my big brother, Kevin, I first started jumping when I was seven. The thought of a seven-year-old ski jumping sounds scary, but it isn't. Kids have a natural fearlessness that propels them forward where adults are frozen. There is that moment of fear, though, when you let go of the bar, because once you let go, there is nothing to stop you. It is much like taking any risk in life. Once you let go, you're off and flying. Sometimes, when you're midair, a gust of wind comes along and sends you off course. You do your best to correct it, but you can't always salvage that jump. You can't see the wind coming. You can't prepare for it. You can't avoid it. But what you can do is get up and jump again. And again. And again.

"Like everything else in life, you will get out of ski jumping what you put into it. Things will be hard. Things will be great. You will make good friends. You will have teammates who are better than you. Not everyone will get to the Olympics. I didn't. I was injured and had to retire the year before the Sochi games.

"I'm not going to lie. This week, as the best of the best American ski jumpers take to the jump for Nationals, it will be hard for me to watch. I will always miss jumping—soaring—flying. But I would not be the person I am today if I had not been a jumper. I've learned so much from jumping, both on the mountain and off.

"Life is a lot like ski jumping. You only get to soar once you've taken the risk. Sometimes, you get knocked off course, and you can't correct it. But you can get back up and jump again. It took me a while to figure that out.

"Sometimes, no matter how hard you work, life doesn't go as planned. Not achieving that one goal you've decided is important doesn't mean you're a failure. Maybe you chose one goal, but you were meant for different things. We don't always know the great cosmic plan. Maybe our goal is really just a step along the way to our final destination. Sometimes, while on the journey, we get lost and need help finding our way. Asking for help doesn't mean you're weak. It means you're strong and smart enough to know you can't do it by yourself.

"My life, my career are completely different from what I imagined when I was a child. While I have medals and trophies, the one I wanted most of all is missing. And I can finally say that it is okay. It's been hard. It's been a struggle. There have been days that I wanted to give up and never get out of bed again.

"I never thought that I'd be a salesperson. But when I think about it, I'm so much more. I'm helping people every day to get out of bed, to function, to live. That's good stuff. And now, I am also blessed to have the chance to share my stories and the wisdom I've gained the hard way—the real hard way. I'm here, working with Team USA, to motivate and educate the next generation of female ski jumpers. We fought so hard to get to this point. I wasn't ready to stop jumping when I did. I've finally figured out a way to focus that energy into something positive.

"I've learned that the tenacity I once showed on the jump still is there. I've still got it in me. And you do too. Find your passion. Close your mouth, open your ears and take it all in. Ask for help. Don't shut down. Don't run away from your problems. They're still there and have a way of finding you. And never stop caring. Because when you close your heart off, none of the rest of it matters."

THE END

ACKNOWLEDGMENTS

None of my books would ever come to fruition without the support of my best friend, Michele Vagianelis. I can't say thank you enough. Maybe someday I'll be able to pay you for all your P.R. efforts. For now, Starbucks will have to do.

A huge thank you to Women's Ski Jumping USA, especially to Kathryn Zwack, for answering endless emails and giving me all sorts of useful information, and to Sarah Hendrickson for giving me some behind the scenes details all while competing (and winning!). I was inspired to write this story while watching the Olympics. I hope I did your sport justice.

Thank you Erin Nuzzi for being so open and allowing me to poke and prod and pry.

Thank you for Meghan Nicchi for not only putting up with our family, but also allowing me to pick your brains about Athletic Training. Since you knew the ATC was going to be the villain, I don't even have to say that you bear no resemblance.

Thank you to Carolyn Kruse for giving me some behind-the-scenes knowledge about figure skating.

My beta team is the best: Becky Monson, Jayne Denker, Celia Kennedy, Tracy Krimmer, Susan Rys, and Chrissy Wolfe. Thank you for all your insight, feedback, and suggestions.

I'm not sure if I would have made it this far without the support and brilliance of the Chick Lit Chat HQ group. The best group ever.

Thank you Aven Ellis for encouraging me to go through with this story. Without you, I probably would have forgotten all about it, and your writing motivates me to write better.

Becky Monson is my incredibly clever and talented cover designer. This cover was so challenging, yet she was incredibly patient. I love the final! In a word, amazeballs.

Thank you Karen Pirozzi and Cahren Morris for being my editors extraordinaire. I've learned so much from both of you. One day, I hope there aren't as many red marks.

As always, I wouldn't have the strength to continue without the love and encouragement of my family. Mom and Dad, thank you for all the support over the years. Patrick, thank you for your quiet encouragement. Jake and Sophia, as proud as I am about my books, the thing that makes me the most proud is being your mother.

ABOUT THE AUTHOR

Telling stories of resilient women, Kathryn Biel hails from upstate New York and is a spouse and mother of two wonderful and energetic kids. In between being Chief Home Officer and Director of Child Development of the Biel household, she works as a school-based physical therapist. She attended Boston University and received her Doctorate in Physical Therapy from The Sage Colleges. After years of writing countless letters of medical necessity for wheelchairs, finding increasingly creative ways to encourage the government and insurance companies to fund her clients' needs, and writing entertaining annual Christmas letters, she decided to take a shot at writing the kind of novel that she likes to read. Her musings and rants can be found on her personal blog, Biel Blather. She is the author of *Good Intentions* (2013), *Hold Her Down* (2014), *I'm Still Here* (2014), *Jump, Jive, and Wail* (2015), *Killing Me Softly* (2015), and *Live For This* (2016).

If you've enjoyed this book, please help the author out by leaving a review on Amazon and Goodreads. A few minutes of your time makes a huge difference to an indie author!

Connect with Kathryn:
Amazon Author Central:
http://www.booklinker.net/mylinks.php

Blog: http://kathrynbiel.blogspot.com

Facebook: https://www.facebook.com/kathrynrbiel

Twitter: https://twitter.com/KRBiel

Goodreads: http://bit.ly/KRBgoodreads

E-mail: kathrynbiel@outlook.com

Made in the USA
Middletown, DE
20 June 2023

32929594R00139